MR & MRS DONA
PO BOX 953
NORWOOD, CO

D1623804

THE RANSOM
OF RED CHIEF
and Other Stories

O. HENRY

THE RANSOM
OF RED CHIEF
and Other Stories

O. HENRY

GRAMERCY BOOKS
NEW YORK ~ AVENEL

Compilation and Introduction
copyright © 1996 by
Random House Value Publishing, Inc.
All rights reserved under International and Pan-American
Copyright Conventions.

This 1996 edition is published by Gramercy Books,
a division of Random House Value Publishing, Inc.,
40 Engelhard Avenue, Avenel, N.J. 07001.

Gramercy Books and colophon are trademarks of
Random House Value Publishing, Inc.

Random House
New York • Toronto • London • Sydney • Auckland

Printed and bound in the United States of America.

Library of Congress Cataloging-in-Publication Data

Henry , O., 1862-1910.
    The ransom of Red Chief and other stories by O. Henry / O. Henry.
      p. cm.
    ISBN 0-517-14692-4
    1. United States—Social life and customs—Fiction. I. Title.
PS2649.P5A6   1995
813'.52—dc20   95-24476
                                            CIP

8 7 6 5 4 3 2 1

CONTENTS

FOREWORD

"There are stories in everything"

—O. HENRY

IN AN INTERVIEW with a *New York Times* reporter, O. Henry gave the secrets to writing a great short story: "Rule 1. Write stories that please yourself. There is no Rule 2. . . . If you can't write a story that pleases yourself, you'll never please the public."

If this is indeed the case, then O. Henry was a very pleased man. He wrote hundreds and hundreds of short stories, sometimes one a week, and, in doing so, also pleased a public that today considers him one of the best American short story writers that ever lived.

O. Henry didn't start out as a writer. He grew up in the late 1800s in North Carolina, in a middle-class household, and his first job after school was working as a pharmacist in his uncle's drugstore.

But filling prescriptions was confining to the young O. Henry, whose real name was William Sidney Porter. He much preferred listening to the customers, watching their expressions, observing their dress. Still, he grew restless after a few years. When he got the chance to travel to the brand-new state of Texas in 1882 with a group of friends, he quickly jumped at it.

In Texas, O. Henry began working at a bank. He also mastered a Mexican dialect and learned the ways of the wild West. Unfortunately, he was indicted for stealing money from the bank. Whether he was guilty or innocent remains a mystery to this day, but the fact is that he ran away to Central America, where he lived for several years. He eventually came home to the States because his young wife was dying of tuberculosis.

Poor man. O. Henry's life was beginning to read like one of his short stories. In a tragic turn of fate, his wife died—and he was sent to jail for three years. But those years in jail proved fruitful. It was there that he learned to appreciate the underdog, the silent masses, and he went on to champion the downtrodden of the world. He also wrote his first short story, which was published in a major magazine.

It was about this time that William Sidney Porter became O. Henry. Some say he chose the name because it had once been the name of his cat. He'd call out, "Come here, oh Henry!" Some say he borrowed the pseudonym from a famous pharmacist, Etienne-Ossian Henry. Still others say his adopted name came from his prison warden, Orrin Henry. Whatever its roots, the name O. Henry stuck and, as his success grew, it became a legendary name, one synonymous with the short story.

The stories O. Henry first wrote depicted what he knew: the rural South, the wild West, and Central America. His famous story "The Ransom of Red Chief," published in *The Saturday Evening Post,* was the quintessential tale. It had all the O. Henry trademarks: two downtrodden men trying to get even with the rich in a story filled with adventure, authentic dialogue, and his trademark surprise twist at the end. Although this story was written after O. Henry had moved on to city life, it evoked the time he spent in the countryside—as it also brings turn-of-the-century small-town America magically alive.

In 1903, O. Henry came to New York and everything changed. The city dazzled him and he left rural America and the West, its heroes and villains, behind him. "I would like to live a lifetime on each street in New York. Every house has a drama in it," O. Henry said when he first laid eyes on the cobblestone streets. Here was life, teeming with energy, seething with adventure and love—from the couples in the horse-drawn cabs to the denizens of the brick tenements that lined the East Side, from the brand-new hurly-burly of the Coney Island amusement park to the dark oak pubs that dotted every corner of the city.

During the next four years, O. Henry wrote about his adopted city, recreating the sights and smells and dialects of turn-of-the-century Manhattan. And today, thanks to the genius of O. Henry, this world comes alive once again. You can see the tiny apartment in the famous love story "Gifts of the Magi." You can hear the old-fashioned cash registers ringing in the department store in "The Trimmed Lamp." You can almost touch the leaves of the lobby plant in "The Rubber Plant Story." And you can feel the beating rain and fierce gusts of autumn wind in "The Last Leaf."

O. Henry lived to be only forty-seven years old, but he left a legacy that has endured throughout a century and will continue to delight well into the next century. As each generation of readers discovers O. Henry, he will live again—and become as timeless as the sights and sounds, the joys and the sorrows, of a world long past.

KARLA DOUGHERTY

Montclair, New Jersey
1995

THE RANSOM
OF RED CHIEF
and Other Stories

O. HENRY

THE RANSOM OF RED CHIEF
The Tale of a Reformed Kidnapper

IT LOOKED LIKE a good thing: but wait till I tell you. We were down South, in Alabama—Bill Driscoll and myself—when this kidnapping idea struck us. It was, as Bill afterward expressed it, "during a moment of temporary mental apparition"; but we didn't find that out till later.

There was a town down there, as flat as a flannel-cake, and called Summit, of course. It contained inhabitants of as undeleterious and self-satisfied a class of peasantry as ever clustered around a Maypole.

Bill and me had a joint capital of about six hundred dollars, and we needed just two thousand dollars more to pull off a fraudulent town-lot scheme in Western Illinois with. We talked it over on the front steps of the hotel. Philoprogenitiveness, says we, is strong in semi-rural communities; therefore, and for other reasons, a kidnapping project ought to do better there than in the radius of newspapers that send reporters out in plain clothes to stir up talk about such things. We knew that Summit couldn't get after us with anything stronger than constables and, maybe, some lackadaisical bloodhounds and a diatribe or two in the Weekly Farmers' Budget. So, it looked good.

We selected for our victim the only child of a prominent citizen named Ebenezer Dorset. The father was respectable and tight, a mortgage fancier and a stern, upright collection-plate passer and forecloser. The kid was a boy of ten, with bas-relief freckles, and hair the color of the cover of the magazine you buy at the newsstand when you want to catch a train. Bill and me figured that Ebenezer would melt down for a ransom of two thousand dollars to a cent. But wait till I tell you.

About two miles from Summit was a little mountain, covered

with a dense cedar brake. On the rear elevation of this mountain was a cave. There we stored provisions.

One evening after sundown, we drove in a buggy past old Dorset's house. The kid was in the street, throwing rocks at a kitten on the opposite fence.

"Hey, little boy!" says Bill, "would you like to have a bag of candy and a nice ride?"

The boy catches Bill neatly in the eye with a piece of brick.

"That will cost the old man an extra five hundred dollars," says Bill, climbing over the wheel.

That boy put up a fight like a welter-weight cinnamon bear; but, at last, we got him down in the bottom of the buggy and drove away. We took him up to the cave, and I hitched the horse in the cedar brake. After dark I drove the buggy to the little village, three miles away, where we had hired it, and walked back to the mountain.

Bill was pasting court-plaster over the scratches and bruises on his features. There was a fire burning behind the big rock at the entrance of the cave, and the boy was watching a pot of boiling coffee, with two buzzard tail-feathers stuck in his red hair. He points a stick at me when I come up, and says, "Ha! cursed paleface, do you dare to enter the camp of Red Chief, the terror of the plains?"

"He's all right now," says Bill, rolling up his trousers and examining some bruises on his shins. "We're playing Indian. We're making Buffalo Bill's show look like magic-lantern views of Palestine in the town hall. I'm Old Hank, the Trapper, Red Chief's captive, and I'm to be scalped at daybreak. By Geronimo! that kid can kick hard."

Yes, sir, that boy seemed to be having the time of his life. The fun of camping out in a cave had made him forget that he was a captive himself. He immediately christened me Snake-eye, and Spy, and announced that, when his braves returned from the warpath, I was to be broiled at the stake at the rising of the sun.

Then we had supper; and he filled his mouth full of bacon and bread and gravy, and began to talk. He made a during-dinner speech something like this: "I like this fine. I never camped out before; but I had a pet 'possum once, and I was nine last birthday. I hate to go to school. Rats ate up sixteen of Jimmy Talbot's aunt's speckled hen's eggs. Are there any real Indians in these woods? I want some more gravy. Does the trees moving make the wind blow? We had five puppies. What makes your nose so red, Hank? My father has lots of money. Are the stars hot? I whipped Ed Walker twice, Saturday. I don't like girls. You dassent catch toads unless with a string. Do oxen make any noise? Why are oranges round? Have you got beds to sleep on in this cave? Amos Murray has got six toes. A parrot can talk, but a monkey or a fish can't. How many does it take to make twelve?"

Every few minutes he would remember that he was a pesky red-skin, and pick up his stick rifle and tiptoe to the mouth of the cave to rubber for the scouts of the hated paleface. Now and then he would let out a war-whoop that made Old Hank, the Trapper, shiver. That boy had Bill terrorized from the start.

"Red Chief," says I to the kid, "would you like to go home?"

"Aw, what for?" says he. "I don't have any fun at home. I hate to go to school. I like to camp out. You won't take me back home again, Snake-eye, will you?"

"Not right away," says I. "We'll stay here in the cave a while."

"All right!" says he. "That'll be fine. I never had such fun in all my life."

We went to bed about eleven o'clock. We spread down some wide blankets and quilts and put Red Chief between us. We weren't afraid he'd run away. He kept us awake for three hours, jumping up and reaching for his rifle and screeching: "Hist! pard," in mine and Bill's ears, as the fancied crackle of a twig or the rustle of a leaf revealed to his young imagination the stealthy approach of the outlaw band. At last, I fell into a troubled sleep, and dreamed that I had been kidnapped and chained to a tree by a ferocious pirate with red hair.

Just at daybreak, I was awakened by a series of awful screams from Bill. They weren't yells, or howls, or shouts, or whoops, or yawps, such as you'd expect from a manly set of vocal organs—they were simply indecent, terrifying, humiliating screams, such as women emit when they see ghosts or caterpillars. It's an awful thing to hear a strong, desperate, fat man scream incontinently in a cave at daybreak.

I jumped up to see what the matter was. Red Chief was sitting on Bill's chest, with one hand twined in Bill's hair. In the other he had the sharp case-knife we used for slicing bacon; and he was industriously and realistically trying to take Bill's scalp, according to the sentence that had been pronounced upon him the evening before.

I got the knife away from the kid and made him lie down again. But, from that moment, Bill's spirit was broken. He laid down on his side of the bed, but he never closed an eye again in sleep as long as that boy was with us. I dozed off for a while, but along toward sunup I remembered that Red Chief had said I was to be burned at the stake at the rising of the sun. I wasn't nervous or afraid; but I sat up and lit my pipe and leaned against a rock.

"What are you getting up so soon for, Sam?" asked Bill.

"Me?" says I. "Oh, I got a kind of a pain in my shoulder. I thought sitting up would rest it."

"You're a liar!" says Bill. "You're afraid. You was to be burned at sunrise, and you was afraid he'd do it. And he would, too, if he could find a match. Ain't it awful, Sam? Do you think anybody will pay out money to get a little imp like that back home?"

"Sure," said I. "A rowdy kid like that is just the kind that parents dote on. Now, you and the Chief get up and cook breakfast, while I go up on the top of this mountain and reconnoiter."

I went up on the peak of the little mountain and ran my eye over the contiguous vicinity. Over toward Summit I expected to see the sturdy yeomanry of the village armed with scythes and pitchforks beating the countryside for the dastardly kidnappers. But what I saw was a peaceful landscape dotted with one man plowing with a dun mule. Nobody was dragging the creek; no couriers dashed hither and yon, bringing tidings of no news to the distracted parents. There was a sylvan attitude of somnolent sleepiness pervading that section of the external outward surface of Alabama that lay exposed to my view. "Perhaps," says I to myself, "it has not yet been discovered that the wolves have borne away the tender lambkin from the fold. Heaven help the wolves!" says I, and I went down the mountain to breakfast.

When I got to the cave I found Bill backed up against the side of it, breathing hard, and the boy threatening to smash him with a rock half as big as a coconut.

"He put a red-hot boiled potato down my back," explained Bill, "and then mashed it with his foot; and I boxed his ears. Have you got a gun about you, Sam?"

I took the rock away from the boy and kind of patched up the argument. "I'll fix you," says the kid to Bill. "No man ever yet struck the Red Chief but what he got paid for it. You better beware!"

After breakfast the kid takes a piece of leather with strings wrapped around it out of his pocket and goes outside the cave unwinding it.

"What's he up to now?" says Bill anxiously. "You don't think he'll run away, do you, Sam?"

"No fear of it," says I. "He don't seem to be much of a home body. But we've got to fix up some plan about the ransom. There don't seem to be much excitement around Summit on account of his disappearance; but maybe they haven't realized yet that he's gone. His folks may think he's spending the night with Aunt Jane or one of the neighbors. Anyhow, he'll be missed today. Tonight we must get a message to his father demanding the two thousand dollars for his return."

Just then we heard a kind of war-whoop, such as David might have emitted when he knocked out the champion Goliath. It was a sling that Red Chief had pulled out of his pocket, and he was whirling it around his head.

I dodged, and heard a heavy thud and a kind of a sigh from Bill, like a horse gives out when you take his saddle off. A rock the size of an egg had caught Bill just behind his left ear. He loosened himself all over and fell in the fire across the frying pan of hot water for washing the dishes. I dragged him out and poured cold water on his head for half an hour.

By and by, Bill sits up and feels behind his ear and says: "Sam, do you know who my favorite Biblical character is?"

"Take it easy," says I. "You'll come to your senses presently."

"King Herod," says he. "You won't go away and leave me here alone, will you, Sam?"

I went out and caught that boy and shook him until his freckles rattled.

"If you don't behave," says I, "I'll take you straight home. Now, are you going to be good, or not?"

"I was only funning," says he sullenly. "I didn't mean to hurt Old Hank. But what did he hit me for? I'll behave, Snake-eye, if you won't send me home, and if you'll let me play the Black Scout today."

"I don't know the game," says I. "That's for you and Mr. Bill to decide. He's your playmate for the day. I'm going away for a while, on business. Now, you come in and make friends with him and say you are sorry for hurting him, or home you go, at once."

I made him and Bill shake hands, and then I took Bill aside and told him I was going to Poplar Cove, a little village three miles from the cave, and find out what I could about how the kidnapping had been regarded in Summit. Also, I thought it best to send a peremptory letter to old man Dorset that day, demanding the ransom and dictating how it should be paid.

"You know, Sam," says Bill, "I've stood by you without batting

an eye in earthquakes, fire and flood—in poker games, dynamite outrages, police raids, train robberies and cyclones. I never lost my nerve
yet till we kidnapped that two-legged skyrocket of a kid. He's got me
going. You won't leave me long with him, will you, Sam?"

"I'll be back sometime this afternoon," says I. "You must keep
the boy amused and quiet till I return. And now we'll write the letter
to old Dorset."

Bill and I got paper and pencil and worked on the letter while
Red Chief, with a blanket wrapped around him, strutted up and down,
guarding the mouth of the cave. Bill begged me tearfully to make the
ransome fifteen hundred dollars instead of two thousand. "I ain't at-
tempting," says he, "to decry the celebrated moral aspect of parental
affection, but we're dealing with humans, and it ain't human for anybody to give up two thousand dollars for that forty-pound chunk of
freckled wildcat. I'm willing to take a chance at fifteen hundred dollars. You can charge the difference up to me."

So, to relieve Bill, I acceded, and we collaborated a letter that ran
this way:

Ebenezer Dorset, Esq.:

*We have your boy concealed in a place far from Summit. It is useless
for you or the most skillful detectives to attempt to find him. Absolutely, the
only terms on which you can have him restored to you are these: We
demand fifteen hundred dollars in large bills for his return; the money to be
left at midnight tonight at the same spot and in the same box as your reply
—as hereinafter described. If you agree to these terms, send your answer in
writing by a solitary messenger tonight at half-past eight o'clock. After crossing Owl Creek, on the road to Poplar Cove, there are three large trees about
a hundred yards apart, close to the fence of the wheat field on the right-hand
side. At the bottom of the fence-post, opposite the third tree, will be found a
small pasteboard box.*

*The messenger will place the answer in this box and return it imme-
diately to Summit.*

*If you attempt any treachery or fail to comply with our demand as
stated, you will never see your boy again.*

*If you pay the money as demanded, he will be returned to you safe
and well within three hours. These terms are final, and if you do not accede
to them no further communication will be attempted.*

TWO DESPERATE MEN

I addressed this letter to Dorset, and put it in my pocket. As I was about to start, the kid comes up to me and says, "Aw, Snake-eye, you said I could play the Black Scout while you was gone."

"Play it, of course," says I. "Mr. Bill will play with you. What kind of a game is it?"

"I'm the Black Scout," says Red Chief, "and I have to ride to the stockade to warn the settlers that the Indians are coming. I'm tired of playing Indian myself. I want to be the Black Scout."

"All right," says I. "It sounds harmless to me. I guess Mr. Bill will help you foil the pesky savages."

"What am I to do?" asks Bill, looking at the kid, suspicious.

"You are the hoss," says Black Scout. "Get down on your hands and knees. How can I ride to the stockade without a hoss?"

"You'd better keep him interested," said I, "till we get the scheme going. Loosen up."

Bill gets down on his all fours, and a look comes in his eye like a rabbit's when you catch it in a trap.

"How far is it to the stockade, kid?" he asks in a husky manner of voice.

"Ninety miles," says the Black Scout. "And you have to hump yourself to get there on time. Whoa, now!"

The Black Scout jumps on Bill's back and digs his heels in his side.

"For Heaven's sake," says Bill, "hurry back, Sam, as soon as you can. I wish we hadn't made the ransom more than a thousand. Say, you quit kicking me or I'll get up and warm you good."

I walked over to Poplar Cove and sat around the post office and store, talking with the chawbacons that came in to trade. One whisker-ando says that he hears Summit is all upset on account of Elder Eben-ezer Dorset's boy having been lost or stolen. That was all I wanted to know. I bought some smoking tobacco, referred casually to the price of black-eyed peas, posted my letter surreptitiously, and came away. The postmaster said the mail carrier would come by in an hour to take the mail on to Summit.

When I got back to the cave Bill and the boy were not to be found. I explored the vicinity of the cave, and risked a yodel or two, but there was no response.

So I lighted my pipe and sat down on a mossy bank to await developments.

In about half an hour I heard the bushes rustle, and Bill wabbled out into the little glade in front of the cave. Behind him was the kid, stepping softly like a scout, with a broad grin on his face. Bill stopped, took off his hat and wiped his face with a red handkerchief. The kid stopped about eight feet behind him.

"Sam," says Bill, "I suppose you'll think I'm a renegade, but I couldn't help it. I'm a grown person with masculine proclivities and habits of self-defense, but there is a time when all systems of egotism and predominance fail. The boy is gone. I have sent him home. All is off. There was martyrs in old times," goes on Bill, "that suffered death rather than give up the particular graft they enjoyed. None of 'em ever was subjugated to such supernatural tortures as I have been. I tried to be faithful to our articles of depredation; but there came a limit."

"What's the trouble, Bill?" I asks him.

"I was rode," says Bill, "the ninety miles to the stockade, not barring an inch. Then, when the settlers was rescued, I was given oats. Sand ain't a palatable substitute. And then, for an hour I had to try to explain to him why there was nothin' in holes, how a road can run both ways, and what makes the grass green. I tell you, Sam, a human can only stand so much. I takes him by the neck of his clothes and drags him down the mountain. On the way he kicks my legs black-and-blue from the knees down; and I've got to have two or three bites on my thumb and hand cauterized.

"But he's gone"—continues Bill—"gone home. I showed him the road to Summit and kicked him about eight feet nearer there at one kick. I'm sorry we lose the ransom; but it was either that or Bill Driscoll to the madhouse."

Bill is puffing and blowing, but there is a look of ineffable peace and growing content on his rose-pink features.

"Bill," says I, "there isn't any heart disease in your family, is there?"

"No," says Bill, "nothing chronic except malaria and accidents. Why?"

"Then you might turn around," says I, "and have a look behind you."

Bill turns and sees the boy, and loses his complexion and sits down plump on the ground and begins to pluck aimlessly at grass and little sticks. For an hour I was afraid for his mind. And then I told him that my scheme was to put the whole job through immediately and that we would get the ransom and be off with it by midnight if old Dorset fell in with our proposition. So Bill braced up enough to give the kid a weak sort of a smile and a promise to play the Russian in a Japanese war with him as soon as he felt a little better.

I had a scheme for collecting that ransom without danger of being caught by counterplots that ought to commend itself to professional kidnappers. The tree under which the answer was to be left—and the money later on—was close to the road fence with big, bare fields on all sides. If a gang of constables should be watching for any one to come for the note they could see him a long way off crossing the fields or in the road. But, no, sirree! At half-past eight I was up in that tree, as well hidden as a tree toad, waiting for the messenger to arrive.

Exactly on time, a half-grown boy rides up the road on a bicycle, locates the pasteboard box at the foot of the fence-post, slips a folded piece of paper into it, and pedals away again back toward Summit.

I waited an hour and then concluded the thing was square. I slid down the tree, got the note, slipped along the fence till I struck the woods, and was back at the cave in another half an hour. I opened the note, got near the lantern and read it to Bill. It was written with a pen in a crabbed hand, and the sum and substance of it was this:

Two Desperate Men.

Gentlemen: I received your letter today by post, in regard to the ransom you ask for the return of my son. I think you are a little high in your demands, and I hereby make you a counter-proposition, which I am inclined to believe you will accept. You bring Johnny home and pay me two hundred and fifty dollars in cash, and I agree to take him off your hands. You had better come at night, for the neighbors believe he is lost, and I couldn't be responsible for what they would do to anybody they saw bringing him back.

VERY RESPECTFULLY,
EBENEZER DORSET

"Great pirates of Penzance!" says I; "of all the impudent——"

But I glanced at Bill, and hesitated. He had the most appealing look in his eyes I ever saw on the face of a dumb or a talking brute.

"Sam," says he, "what's two hundred and fifty dollars, after all? We've got the money. One more night of this kid will send me to a bed in Bedlam. Besides being a thorough gentleman, I think Mr. Dorset is a spendthrift for making us such a liberal offer. You ain't going to let the chance go, are you?"

"Tell you the truth, Bill," says I, "this little he ewe lamb has somewhat got on my nerves, too. We'll take him home, pay the ransom and make our getaway."

We took him home that night. We got him to go by telling him that his father had bought a silver-mounted rifle and a pair of moccasins for him, and we were going to hunt bears the next day.

It was just twelve o'clock when we knocked at Ebenezer's front door. Just at the moment when I should have been abstracting the fifteen hundred dollars from the box under the tree, according to the original proposition, Bill was counting out two hundred and fifty dollars into Dorset's hand.

When the kid found out we were going to leave him at home he started up a howl like a calliope and fastened himself as tight as a leech to Bill's leg. His father peeled him away gradually, like a porous plaster.

"How long can you hold him?" asks Bill.

"I am not as strong as I used to be," says old Dorset, "but I think I can promise you ten minutes."

"Enough," says Bill. "In ten minutes I shall cross the Central, Southern and Middle Western States, and be legging it trippingly for the Canadian border."

And, as dark as it was, and as fat as Bill was, and as good a runner as I am, he was a good mile and a half out of Summit before I could catch up with him.

THE DISSIPATED JEWELER

You will not find the name of Thomas Keeling in the Houston city directory. It might have been there by this time, if Mr. Keeling had not discontinued his business a month or so ago and moved to other parts. Mr. Keeling came to Houston about that time and opened up a small detective bureau. He offered his services to the public as a detective in rather a modest way. He did not aspire to be a rival of the Pinkerton agency, but preferred to work along less risky lines.

If an employer wanted the habits of a clerk looked into, or a lady wanted an eye kept upon a somewhat too gay husband, Mr. Keeling was the man to take the job. He was a quiet, studious man with theories. He read Gaboriau and Conan Doyle and hoped some day to take a higher place in his profession. He had held a subordinate place in a large detective bureau in the East, but as promotion was slow, he decided to come West, where the field was not so well covered.

Mr. Keeling had saved during several years the sum of $900, which he deposited in the safe of a businessman in Houston to whom he had letters of introduction from a common friend. He rented a small upstairs office on an obscure street, hung out a sign stating his business, and burying himself in one of Doyle's Sherlock Holmes stories, waited for customers.

Three days after he opened his bureau, which consisted of himself, a client called to see him.

It was a young lady, apparently about 26 years of age. She was slender and rather tall and neatly dressed. She wore a thin veil which she threw back upon her black straw hat after she had taken the chair

Mr. Keeling offered her. She had a delicate, refined face, with rather quick gray eyes, and a slightly nervous manner.

❧

"I CAME TO see you, sir," she said in a sweet, but somewhat sad, contralto voice, "because you are comparatively a stranger, and I could not bear to discuss my private affairs with any of my friends. I desire to employ you to watch the movements of my husband. Humiliating as the confession is to me, I fear that his affections are no longer mine. Before I married him he was infatuated with a young woman connected with a family with whom he boarded. We have been married five years, and very happily, but this young woman has recently moved to Houston, and I have reasons to suspect that he is paying her attentions. I want you to watch his movements as closely as possible and report to me. I will call here at your office every other day at a given time to learn what you have discovered. My name is Mrs. R——, and my husband is well known. He keeps a small jewelry store on —— Street. I will pay you well for your services and here is twenty dollars to begin with."

The lady handed Mr. Keeling the bill and he took it carelessly as if such things were very, very common in his business.

He assured her that he would carry out her wishes faithfully, and asked her to call again the afternoon after the next at four o'clock, for the first report.

The next day Mr. Keeling made the necessary inquiries toward beginning operations. He found the jewelry store, and went inside ostensibly to have the crystal of his watch tightened. The jeweler, Mr. R., was a man apparently 35 years of age, of very quiet manners and industrious ways. His store was small, but contained a nice selection of goods and quite a large assortment of diamonds, jewelry, and watches. Further inquiry elicited the information that Mr. R. was a man of excellent habits, never drank, and was always at work at his jeweler's bench.

Mr. Keeling loafed around near the door of the jewelry store for several hours that day and was finally rewarded by seeing a flashily dressed young woman with black hair and eyes enter the store. Mr. Keeling sauntered nearer the door, where he could see what took place inside. The young woman walked confidently to the rear of the store, leaned over the counter and spoke familiarly to Mr. R. He rose from his bench and they talked in low tones for a few minutes. Finally, the jeweler handed her some coins, which Mr. Keeling heard clinking as they passed into her hands. The woman then came out and walked rapidly down the street.

❧

MR. KEELING'S CLIENT was at his office promptly at the time agreed upon. She was anxious to know if he had seen anything to corroborate her suspicions. The detective told her what he had seen.

"That is she," said the lady, when he had described the young woman who had entered the store. "The brazen, bold thing! And so Charles is giving her money. To think that things should come to this pass."

The lady pressed her handkerchief to her eyes in an agitated way.

"Mrs. R.," said the detective, "what is your desire in this matter? To what point do you wish me to prosecute inquiries?"

"I want to see with my own eyes enough to convince me of what I suspect. I also want witnesses, so I can instigate suit for divorce. I will not lead the life I am now living any longer."

She then handed the detective a ten-dollar bill.

On the day following the next, when she came to Mr. Keeling's office to hear his report, he said: "I dropped into the store this afternoon on some trifling pretext. This young woman was already there, but she did not remain long. Before she left, she said: 'Charlie, we will have a jolly little supper tonight as you suggest; then we will come around to the store and have a nice chat while you finish that setting for the diamond broach with no one to interrupt us.' Tonight, Mrs. R., I think, will be a good time for you to witness the meeting between your husband and the object of his infatuation, and satisfy your mind how matters stand."

"The wretch," cried the lady with flashing eyes. "He told me at dinner that he would be detained late tonight with some important work. And this is the way he spends his time away from me!"

"I suggest," said the detective, "that you conceal yourself in the store, so you can hear what they say, and when you have heard enough you can summon witnesses and confront your husband before them."

"The very thing," said the lady. "I believe there is a policeman whose beat is along the street the store is on who is acquainted with our family. His duties will lead him to be in the vicinity of the store after dark. Why not see him, explain the whole matter to him and when I have heard enough, let you and him appear as witnesses?"

"I will speak with him," said the detective, "and persuade him to assist us, and you will please come to my office a little before dark tonight, so we can arrange to trap them."

∽

THE DETECTIVE HUNTED up the policeman and explained the situation.

"That's funny," said the guardian of the peace. "I didn't know R. was a gay boy at all. But, then, you can never tell about anybody. So his wife wants to catch him tonight. Let's see, she wants to hide herself inside the store and hear what they say. There's a little room in the back of the store where R. keeps his coal and old boxes. The door between is locked, of course, but if you can get her through that into the store she can hide somewhere. I don't like to mix up in these affairs, but I sympathize with the lady. I've known her ever since we were children and don't mind helping her to do what she wants."

About dusk that evening the detective's client came hurriedly to his office. She was dressed plainly in black and wore a dark round hat and her face was covered with a veil.

"If Charlie should see me he will not recognize me," she said.

Mr. Keeling and the lady strolled down the street opposite the jewelry store, and about eight o'clock the young woman they were watching for entered the store. Immediately afterwards she came out with Mr. R., took his arm, and they hurried away, presumably to their supper.

The detective felt the arm of the lady tremble.

"The wretch," she said bitterly. "He thinks me at home innocently waiting for him while he is out carousing with that artful, designing minx. Oh, the perfidy of man."

Mr. Keeling took the lady through an open hallway that led into the backyard of the store. The outer door of the back room was unlocked, and they entered.

"In the store," said Mrs. R., "near the bench where my husband works is a large table, the cover of which hangs to the floor. If I could get under that I could hear every word that was said."

Mr. Keeling took a big bunch of skeleton keys from his pocket and in a few minutes found one that opened the door into the jewelry store. The gas was burning from one jet turned very low.

The lady stepped into the store and said: "I will bolt this door from the inside, and I want you to follow my husband and that woman. See if they are at supper, and if they are, when they start back, you must come back to this room and let me know by tapping thrice on the door. After I listen to their conversation long enough I will unbolt the door, and we will confront the guilty pair together. I may need you to protect me, for I do not know what they might attempt to do to me."

THE DETECTIVE MADE his way softly out and followed the jeweler and the woman. He soon discovered that they had taken a private room in a little out of the way restaurant and had ordered supper. He lingered about until they came out and then hurried back to the store, and entering the back room, tapped three times on the door.

In a few minutes the jeweler entered with the woman and the detective saw the light shine more brightly through a crack in the door. He could hear the man and woman conversing familiarly and constantly, but could not distinguish their words. He slipped around again to the street, and looking through the window, could see Mr. R. working away at his jeweler's bench, while the black-haired woman sat close to his side and talked.

"I'll give them a little time," thought Mr. Keeling, and he strolled down the street.

The policeman was standing on the corner.

The detective told him that Mrs. R. was concealed in the store, and that the scheme was working nicely.

"I'll drop back behind now," said Mr. Keeling, "so as to be ready when the lady springs her trap."

The policeman walked back with him, and took a look through the window.

"They seem to have made up all right," said he. "Where's the other woman gotten to?"

"Why, there she is sitting by him," said the detective.

"I'm talking about the girl R. had out to supper."

"So am I," said the detective.

"You seem to be mixed up," said the policeman. "Do you know that lady with R.?"

"That's the woman he was out with."

"That's R.'s wife," said the policeman. "I've known her for fifteen years."

"Then, who—?" gasped the detective. "Lord A'mighty, then who's under the table?"

Mr. Keeling began to kick at the door of the store.

Mr. R. came forward and opened it. The policeman and the detective entered.

"Look under that table, quick," yelled the detective. The policeman raised the cover and dragged out a black dress, a black veil, and a woman's wig of black hair.

"Is this lady your w-w-wife?" asked Mr. Keeling excitedly, pointing out the dark-eyed young woman, who was regarding them in great surprise.

"Certainly," said the jeweler. "Now what the thunder are you looking under my tables and kicking down my door for, if you please?"

"Look in your show cases," said the policeman, who began to size up the situation.

❧

THE DIAMOND RINGS and watches that were missing amounted to $800, and the next day the detective settled the bill.

Explanations were made to the jeweler that night, and an hour later Mr. Keeling sat in his office busily engaged in looking over his albums of crook's photos.

At last he found one, and he stopped turning over the leaves and tore his hair. Under the picture of a smooth-faced young man, with delicate features was the following description:

"JAMES H. MIGGLES, alias Slick Simon, alias The Weeping Widow, alias Bunco Kate, alias Jimmy the Sneak, General confidence man and burglar. Works generally in female disguises. Very plausible and dangerous. Wanted in Kansas City, Oshkosh, New Orleans, and Milwaukee."

This is why Mr. Thomas Keeling did not continue his detective business in Houston.

THE RUBBER PLANT'S STORY

WE RUBBER PLANTS form the connecting link between the vegetable kingdom and the decorations of a Waldorf-Astoria scene in a Third Avenue theater. I haven't looked up our family tree, but I believe we were raised by grafting a gum overshoe onto a 30-cent table d'hôte stalk of asparagus. You take a white bulldog with a Bourke Cockran air of independence about him and a rubber plant and there you have the fauna and flora of a flat. What the shamrock is to Ireland the rubber plant is to the dweller in flats and furnished rooms. We get moved from one place to another so quickly that the only way we can get our picture taken is with a kinetoscope. We are the vagrant vine and the flitting fig tree. You know the proverb: "Where the rubber plant sits in the window the moving van draws up to the door."

We are the city equivalent to the woodbine and the honeysuckle. No other vegetable except the Pittsburg stogie can withstand as much handling as we can. When the family to which we belong moves into a flat they set us in the front window and we become lares and penates, flypaper and the peripatetic emblem of "Home Sweet Home." We aren't as green as we look. I guess we are about what you would call the soubrettes of the conservatory. You try sitting in the front window of a $40 flat in Manhattan and looking out into the street all day, and back into the flat at night, and see whether you get wise or not—hey? Talk about the tree of knowledge of good and evil in the garden of Eden—say! suppose there had been a rubber plant there when Eve—but I was going to tell you a story.

The first thing I can remember I had only three leaves and belonged to a member of the pony ballet. I was kept in a sunny window, and was generally watered with seltzer and lemon. I had plenty of fun in those days. I got cross-eyed trying to watch the numbers of the automobiles in the street and the dates on the labels inside at the same time.

Well, then the angel that was molting for the musical comedy lost his last feather and the company broke up. The ponies trotted away and I was left in the window ownerless. The janitor gave me to a refined comedy team on the eighth floor, and in six weeks I had been set in the window of five different flats. I took on experience and put out two more leaves.

Miss Carruthers, of the refined comedy team—did you ever see her cross both feet back of her neck?—gave me to a friend of hers who had made an unfortunate marriage with a man in a store. Consequently I was placed in the window of a furnished room, rent in advance, water two flights up, gas extra after ten o'clock at night. Two of my leaves withered off here. Also, I was moved from one room to another so many times that I got to liking the odor of the pipes the expressmen smoked.

I don't think I ever had so dull a time as I did with this lady. There was never anything amusing going on inside—she was devoted to her husband, and, besides leaning out the window and flirting with the iceman, she never did a thing toward breaking the monotony.

When the couple broke up they left me with the rest of their goods at a secondhand store. I was put out in front for sale along with the jobbiest lot you ever heard of being lumped into one bargain. Think of this little cornucopia of wonders, all for $1.89: Henry James's works, six talking machine records, one pair of tennis shoes, two bottles of horseradish, and a rubber plant—that was me!

One afternoon a girl came along and stopped to look at me. She had dark hair and eyes, and she looked slim, and sad around the mouth.

"Oh, oh!" she says to herself. "I never thought to see one up here."

She pulls out a little purse about as thick as one of my leaves and fingers over some small silver in it. Old Koen, always on the lookout, is ready, rubbing his hands. This girl proceeds to turn down Mr. James and the other commodities. Rubber plants or nothing is the burden of her song. And at last Koen and she come together at 39 cents, and away she goes with me in her arms.

She was a nice girl, but not my style. Too quiet and sober

looking. Thinks I to myself: "I'll just about land on the fire escape of a tenement, six stories up. And I'll spend the next six months looking at clothes on the line."

But she carried me to a nice little room only three flights up in quite a decent street. And she put me in the window, of course. And then she went to work and cooked dinner for herself. And what do you suppose she had? Bread and tea and a little dab of jam! Nothing else. Not a single lobster, nor so much as one bottle of champagne. The Carruthers comedy team had both every evening, except now and then when they took a notion for pig's knuckle and kraut.

After she had finished her dinner my new owner came to the window and leaned down close to my leaves and cried softly to herself for a while. It made me feel funny. I never knew anybody to cry that way over a rubber plant before. Of course, I've seen a few of 'em turn on the tears for what they could get out of it, but she seemed to be crying just for the pure enjoyment of it. She touched my leaves like she loved 'em, and she bent down her head and kissed each one of 'em. I guess I'm about the toughest specimen of a peripatetic orchid on earth, but I tell you it made me feel sort of queer. Home never was like that to me before. Generally I used to get chewed by poodles and have shirtwaists hung on me to dry, and get watered with coffee grounds and peroxide of hydrogen.

This girl had a piano in the room, and she used to disturb it with both hands while she made noises with her mouth for hours at a time. I suppose she was practicing vocal music.

One day she seemed very much excited and kept looking at the clock. At eleven somebody knocked and she let in a stout, dark man with towsled black hair. He sat down at once at the piano and played while she sang for him. When she finished she laid one hand on her bosom and looked at him. He shook his head, and she leaned against the piano.

"Two years already," she said, speaking slowly—"do you think in two more—or even longer?"

The man shook his head again. "You waste your time," he said, roughly I thought. "The voice is not there." And then he looked at her in a peculiar way. "But the voice is not everything," he went on. "You have looks. I can place you, as I told you if——"

The girl pointed to the door without saying anything, and the dark man left the room. And then she came over and cried around me again. It's a good thing I had enough rubber in me to be waterproof.

About that time somebody else knocked at the door. "Thank goodness," I said to myself. "Here's a chance to get the waterworks turned off. I hope it's somebody that's game enough to stand a bird and a bottle to liven things up a little." Tell you the truth, this little girl made me tired. A rubber plant likes to see a little sport now and then. I don't suppose there's another green thing in New York that sees as much of gay life unless it's the chartreuse or the sprigs of parsley around the dish.

When the girl opens the door in steps a young chap in a traveling cap and picks her up in his arms, and she sings out "Oh, Dick!" and stays there long enough to—well, you've been a rubber plant too, sometimes, I suppose.

"Good thing!" says I to myself. "This is livelier than scales and weeping. Now there'll be something doing."

"You've got to go back with me," says the young man. "I've come two thousand miles for you. Aren't you tired of it yet, Bess? You've kept all of us waiting so long. Haven't you found out yet what is best?"

"The bubble burst only today," says the girl. "Come here, Dick, and see what I found the other day on the sidewalk for sale." She brings him by the hand and exhibits yours truly. "How one ever got away up here who can tell? I bought it with almost the last money I had."

He looked at me, but he couldn't keep his eyes off her for more than a second.

"Do you remember the night, Bess," he said, "when we stood under one of those on the bank of the bayou and what you told me then?"

"Geewillikins!" I said to myself. "Both of them stand under a rubber plant! Seems to me they are stretching matters somewhat!"

"Do I not," says she, looking up at him and sneaking close to his vest, "and now I say it again, and it is to last forever. Look, Dick, at its leaves, how wet they are. Those are my tears, and it was thinking of you that made them fall."

"The dear old magnolias!" says the young man, pinching one of my leaves, "I love them all."

Magnolia! Well, wouldn't that—say! those innocents thought I was a magnolia! What the—well, wasn't that tough on a genuine little old New York rubber plant?

AN UNKNOWN ROMANCE

THE FIRST PALE star peeped down the gorge. Above, to illimitable heights reached the Alps, snow-white above, shadowy around, and black in the depths of the gorge.

A young and stalwart man, clad in the garb of a chamois hunter, passed up the path. His face was bronzed with sun and wind, his eye was frank and clear, his step agile and firm. He was singing fragments of a Bavarian hunting song, and in his hand he held a white blossom of the edelweiss he had plucked from the cliff. Suddenly he paused, and the song broke, and dropped from his lips. A girl, costumed as the Swiss peasants are, crossed the path along one that bisected his, carrying a small stone pitcher full of water. Her hair was of the lightest gold and hung far below her trim waist in a heavy braid. Her eyes shone through the gathering twilight, and her lips, slightly parted, showed a faint gleam of the whitest teeth.

As if impelled by a common impulse, the hunter and the maiden paused, each with their eyes fixed upon the other. Then the man advanced, and doffing his feathered hat, bowed low and spake some words in the German language. The maiden answered, speaking haltingly and low.

Then a door opened in a cottage almost hidden among the trees, and a babble of voices was heard. The maiden's cheeks turned crimson, and she started to go, but as she went, she turned her eyes and looked at the hunter still. He took a step after her, and stretched out his hand as if to stay her. She tore a bunch of blue gentians from her bosom and threw them toward him. He caught them as they fell, then ran lightly and gave into her hand the edelweiss bloom that he carried.

She thrust it into her bosom, then ran like a mountain sprite into the cottage, where the voices were.

The hunter stopped for a while, then went his way more slowly up the mountain path, and he sang no more. As he went he pressed the flowers frequently to his lips.

∽

The wedding was to be one of the showiest, and the society of the metropolis was almost begging for invitations.

The groom-elect brought the ancient lineage of the Van Winklers and a position at the topnotch of society for his portion. The bride brought a beauty that was flawless, and five million dollars. The arrangement had been made in a businesslike manner. There had been no question of love. He had been courteous, and politely attentive, and she had acquiesced listlessly. They had first met at a fashionable summer resort. The family of the Van Winklers and the money of the Vances were about to unite.

The wedding was to be at high noon.

Pelham Van Winkler had had a fire built in the ancient tiled fireplace of one of his rooms, although the weather was warm. He sat on the edge of a writing table, and tossed handfuls of square-shaped letters, some tied with ribbons, into the fire. He smiled a little ironically as they flamed up, or as here and there among them he would find a withered flower, a scented glove, or a lock of beribboned hair.

The last sacrifice to the flames was a dried and pressed cluster of blue gentians.

Van Winkler sighed, and the smile left his face. He recalled the twilight scene among the Alps mountains, where he was wandering with three or four companions on a summer tour, gay and careless, and dressed in the picturesque garb of chamois hunters. He recalled the picture of a lovely peasant girl with eyes that held him with a charm of power, crossing the mountain road, and pausing for a moment to toss him the bunch of gentian flowers. Had he not been a Van Winkler and owed a duty to the name, he would have sought her out and married her, for her image had never left his eyes or his heart since that twilight eve. But society and the family name claimed him, and today, at high noon, he was to marry Miss Vance, the daughter of the millionaire iron founder.

Pelham Van Winkler tossed the bunch of blue gentians into the fire and rang for his valet.

∾

Miss Augusta Vance had flown from the irritating presence of fussy female friends and hysterical relatives to her boudoir for a few moments' quiet. She had no letters to burn; no past to bury. Her mother was in an ecstasy of delight, for the family millions had brought them places in the front row of Vanity Fair.

Her marriage to Pelham Van Winkler was to be at high noon. Miss Vance fell suddenly into a dreamy reverie. She recalled a trip she had taken with her family a year before, to Europe, and her mind dwelt lingeringly upon a week they had spent among the foothills of the Alps in the cottage of a Swiss mountaineer. One evening at twilight she had gone with a pitcher across the road and filled it from a spring. She had fancied to put on that day the peasant costume of Babette, the daughter of their host. It had become her well, with her long braid of light-gold hair and blue eyes. A hunter had crossed the road as she was returning—an Alpine chamois hunter, strong, stalwart, bronzed and free. She had looked up and caught his eyes, and his held hers. She went on, and still those magnetic eyes claimed her own. The door of the cottage had opened and voices called. She started and obeyed the impulse to tear a bunch of gentians from her bosom and throw them to him. He had caught them, and springing forward gave her an edelweiss flower. Not since that evening had the image of that chamois hunter left her. Surely fate had led him to her, and he seemed a man among men. But Miss Augusta Vance, with a dowry of five millions, could not commit the folly of thinking of a common hunter of the Alps mountains.

Miss Vance arose and opened a gold locket that lay upon her dressing case. She took from it a faded edelweiss flower and slowly crumpled it to dust between her fingers. Then she rang for her maid, and the church bells began to chime outside for the marriage.

A DOUBLE-DYED DECEIVER

I

THE TROUBLE BEGAN in Laredo. It was the Llano Kid's fault, for he should have confined his habit of manslaughter to Mexicans. But the Kid was past twenty; and to have only Mexicans to one's credit at twenty is to blush unseen on the Rio Grande border.

It happened in old Justo Valdos's gambling house. There was a poker game at which sat players who were not all friends, as happens often where men ride in from afar to shoot Folly as she gallops. There was a row over so small a matter as a pair of queens; and when the smoke had cleared away it was found that the Kid had committed an indiscretion, and his adversary had been guilty of a blunder. For, the unfortunate combatant, instead of being a Greaser, was a high-blooded youth from the cow ranches, of about the Kid's own age and possessed of friends and champions. His blunder in missing the Kid's right ear only a sixteenth of an inch when he pulled his gun did not lessen the indiscretion of the better marksman.

The Kid, not being equipped with a retinue, nor bountifully supplied with personal admirers and supporters—on account of a rather umbrageous reputation even for the border—considered it not incompatible with his indisputable gameness to perform that judicious tractional act known as "pulling his freight."

Quickly the avengers gathered and sought him. Three of them overtook him within a rod of the station. The Kid turned and showed his teeth in that brilliant but mirthless smile that usually preceded his deeds of insolence and violence, and his pursuers fell back without making it necessary for him even to reach for his weapon.

But in this affair the Kid had not felt the grim thirst for encoun-

ter that usually urged him on to battle. It had been a purely chance
row, born of the cards and certain epithets impossible for a gentleman
to break that had passed between the two. The Kid had rather liked
the slim, haughty, brown-faced young chap whom his bullet had cut
off in the first pride of manhood. And now he wanted no more blood.
He wanted to get away and have a good long sleep somewhere in the
sun on the mesquite grass with his handkerchief over his face. Even a
Mexican might have crossed his path in safety while he was in this
mood.

The Kid openly boarded the northbound passenger train that
departed five minutes later. But at Webb, a few miles out, where it was
flagged to take on a traveler, he abandoned that manner of escape.
There were telegraph stations ahead; and the Kid looked askance at
electricity and steam. Saddle and spur were his rocks of safety.

The man whom he had shot was a stranger to him. But the Kid
knew that he was of the Corralitos outfit from Hidalgo; and that the
poachers from that ranch were more relentless and vengeful than Kentucky feudists when wrong or harm was done to one of them. So, with
the wisdom that has characterized many great fighters, the Kid decided to pile up as many leagues as possible of chaparral and pear
between himself and the retaliation of the Corralitos bunch.

Near the station was a store; and near the store, scattered among
the mesquites and elms, stood the saddled horses of the customers.
Most of them waited, half asleep, with sagging limbs and drooping
heads. But one, a long-legged roan with a curved neck, snorted and
pawed the turf. Him the Kid mounted, gripped with his knees, and
slapped gently with the owner's own quirt.

If the slaying of the temerarious cardplayer had cast a cloud over
the Kid's standing as a good and true citizen, this last act of his veiled
his figure in the darkest shadows of disrepute. On the Rio Grande
border if you take a man's life you sometimes take trash; but if you
take his horse, you take a thing the loss of which renders him poor,
indeed, and which enriches you not—if you are caught. For the Kid
there was no turning back now.

With the springing roan under him he felt little care or uneasi-
ness. After a five-mile gallop he drew in to the plainsman's jogging
trot, and rode northeastward toward the Nueces River bottoms. He
knew the country well—its most tortuous and obscure trails through
the great wilderness of brush and pear, and its camps and lonesome
ranches where one might find safe entertainment. Always he bore to

the east; for the Kid had never seen the ocean, and he had a fancy to lay his hand upon the mane of the great Gulf, the gamesome colt of the greater waters.

So after three days he stood on the shore at Corpus Christi, and looked out across the gentle ripples of a quiet sea.

Captain Boone, of the schooner Flyaway, stood near his skiff, which one of his crew was guarding in the surf. When ready to sail he had discovered that one of the necessaries of life, in the parallelogram-matic shape of plug tobacco, had been forgotten. A sailor had been despatched for the missing cargo. Meanwhile the captain paced the sands, chewing profanely at his pocket store. ·

A slim, wiry youth in high-heeled boots came down to the water's edge. His face was boyish but with a premature severity that hinted at a man's experience. His complexion was naturally dark; and the sun and wind of an outdoor life had burned it to a coffee brown. His hair was as black and straight as an Indian's; his face had not yet been upturned to the humiliation of a razor; his eyes were a cold and steady blue. He carried his left arm somewhat away from his body, for pearl-handled .45s are frowned upon by town marshals, and are a little bulky when packed in the left armhole of one's vest. He looked beyond Captain Boone at the gulf with the impersonal and expression-less dignity of a Chinese emperor.

"Thinkin' of buyin' that 'ar gulf, buddy?" asked the captain, made sarcastic by his narrow escape from a tobaccoless voyage.

"Why, no," said the Kid gently, "I reckon not. I never saw it before. I was just looking at it. Not thinking of selling it, are you?"

"Not this trip," said the captain. "I'll send it to you C.O.D. when I get back to Buenas Tierras. Here comes that capstanfooted lubber with the chewin'. I ought to've weighed anchor an hour ago."

"Is that your ship out there?" asked the Kid.

"Why, yes," answered the captain, "if you want to call a schooner a ship, and I don't mind lyin'. But you better say Miller and Gonzales, owners, and ordinary, plain, Billy-be-damned old Samuel K. Boone, skipper."

"Where are you going to?" asked the refugee.

"Buenas Tierras, coast of South America—I forget what they called the country the last time I was there. Cargo—lumber, corru-gated iron, and machetes."

"What kind of a country is it?" asked the Kid—"hot or cold?"

"Warmish, buddy," said the captain. "But a regular Paradise

Lost for elegance of scenery and be-yooty of geography. Ye're wakened every morning by the sweet singin' of red birds with seven purple tails, and the sighin' of breezes in the posies and roses. And the inhabitants never work, for they can reach out and pick steamer baskets of the choicest hothouse fruit without gettin' out of bed. And there's no Sunday and no ice and no rent and no troubles and no use and no nothin'. It's a great country for a man to go to sleep with, and wait for somethin' to turn up. The bananys and oranges and hurricanes and pineapples that ye eat comes from there."

"That sounds to me!" said the Kid, at last betraying interest. "What'll the expressage be to take me out there with you?"

"Twenty-four dollars," said Captain Boone: "grub and transportation. Second cabin. I haven't got a first cabin."

"You've got my company," said the Kid, pulling out a buckskin bag.

With three hundred dollars he had gone to Laredo for his regular "blowout." The duel in Valdo's had cut short his season of hilarity, but it had left him with nearly $200 for aid in the flight that it had made necessary.

"All right, buddy," said the captain. "I hope your ma won't blame me for this little childish escapade of yours." He beckoned to one of the boat's crew. "Let Sanchez lift you out to the skiff so you won't get your feet wet."

II

THACKER, THE UNITED States consul at Buenas Tierras, was not yet drunk. It was only eleven o'clock; and he never arrived at his desired state of beatitude—a state wherein he sang ancient maudlin vaudeville songs and pelted his screaming parrot with banana peels—until the middle of the afternoon. So, when he looked up from his hammock at the sound of a slight cough, and saw the Kid standing in the door of the consulate, he was still in a condition to extend the hospitality and courtesy due from the representative of a great nation.

"Don't disturb yourself," said the Kid easily. "I just dropped in. They told me it was customary to light at your camp before starting in to round up the town. I just came in on a ship from Texas."

"Glad to see you, Mr. ——," said the consul.

The Kid laughed.

"Sprague Dalton," he said. "It sounds funny to me to hear it. I'm called the Llano Kid in the Rio Grande country."

"I'm Thacker," said the consul. "Take that cane-bottom chair. Now if you've come to invest, you want somebody to advise you. These dingies will cheat you out of the gold in your teeth if you don't understand their ways. Try a cigar?"

"Much obliged," said the Kid, "but if it wasn't for my corn shucks and the little bag in my back pocket, I couldn't live a minute." He took out his "makings," and rolled a cigarette.

"They speak Spanish here," said the consul. "You'll need an interpreter. If there's anything I can do, why, I'd be delighted. If you're buying fruit lands or looking for a concession of any sort, you'll want somebody who knows the ropes to look out for you."

"I speak Spanish," said the Kid, "about nine times better than I do English. Everybody speaks it on the range where I come from. And I'm not in the market for anything."

"You speak Spanish?" said Thacker thoughtfully. He regarded the Kid absorbedly.

"You look like a Spaniard, too," he continued. "And you're from Texas. And you can't be more than twenty or twenty-one. I wonder if you've got any nerve."

"You got a deal of some kind to put through?" asked the Texan with unexpected shrewdness.

"Are you open to a proposition?" said Thacker.

"What's the use to deny it?" said the Kid. "I got into a little gun frolic down in Laredo and plugged a white man. There wasn't any Mexican handy. And I come down to your parrot-and-monkey range just for to smell the morning glories and marigolds. Now, do you *sabe?*"

Thacker got up and closed the door.

"Let me see your hand," he said.

He took the Kid's left hand, and examined the back of it closely.

"I can do it," he said excitedly. "Your flesh is as hard as wood and as healthy as a baby's. It will heal in a week."

"If it's a fist fight you want to back me for," said the Kid, "don't put your money up yet. Make it gun work, and I'll keep you company. But no barehanded scrapping, like ladies at a tea party, for me."

"It's easier than that," said Thacker. "Just step here, will you?"

Through the window he pointed to a two-story white-stuccoed house with wide galleries rising amid the deep green tropical foliage on a wooded hill that sloped gently from the sea.

"In that house," said Thacker, "a fine old Castilian gentleman and his wife are yearning to gather you into their arms and fill your pockets with money. Old Santos Urique lives there. He owns half the gold mines in the country."

"You haven't been eating loco weed, have you?" asked the Kid.

"Sit down again," said Thacker, "and I'll tell you. Twelve years ago they lost a kid. No, he didn't die—although most of 'em here do from drinking the surface water. He was a wild little devil, even if he wasn't but eight years old. Everybody knows about it. Some Americans who were through here prospecting for gold had letters to Señor Urique, and the boy was a favorite with them. They filled his head with big stories about the States; and about a month after they left, the kid disappeared, too. He was supposed to have stowed himself away among the banana bunches on a fruit steamer, and gone to New Orleans. He was seen once afterward in Texas, it was thought, but they never heard anything more of him. Old Urique has spent thousands of dollars having him looked for. The madam was broken up worst of all. The kid was her life. She wears mourning yet. But they say she believes he'll come back to her someday, and never gives up hope. On the back of the boy's left hand was tattooed a flying eagle carrying a spear in his claws. That's old Urique's coat of arms or something that he inherited in Spain."

The Kid raised his left hand slowly and gazed at it curiously.

"That's it," said Thacker, reaching behind the official desk for his bottle of smuggled brandy. "You're not so slow. I can do it. What was I consul at Sandakan for? I never knew till now. In a week I'll have the eagle bird with the frog-sticker blended in so you'd think you were born with it. I brought a set of the needles and ink just because I was sure you'd drop in some day, Mr. Dalton."

"Oh, hell," said the Kid. "I thought I told you."

"All right, 'Kid,' then. It won't be that long. How does Señorito Urique sound, for a change?"

"I never played son any that I remember of," said the Kid. "If I had any parents to mention they went over the divide about the time I gave my first bleat. What is the plan of your roundup?"

Thacker leaned back against the wall and held his glass up to the light.

"We've come now," said he, "to the question of how far you're willing to go in a little matter of the sort."

"I told you why I came down here," said the Kid simply.

"A good answer," said the consul. "But you won't have to go that far. Here's the scheme. After I get the trademark tattooed on your hand I'll notify old Urique. In the meantime I'll furnish you with all of the family history I can find out, so you can be studying up points to talk about. You've got the looks, you speak the Spanish, you know the facts, you can tell about Texas, you've got the tattoo mark. When I notify them that the rightful heir has returned and is waiting to know whether he will be received and pardoned, what will happen? They'll simply rush down here and fall on your neck, and the curtain goes down for refreshments and a stroll in the lobby."

"I'm waiting," said the Kid. "I haven't had my saddle off in your camp long, pardner, and I never met you before; but if you intend to let it go at a parental blessing, why, I'm mistaken in my man, that's all."

"Thanks," said the consul. "I haven't met anybody in a long time that keeps up with an argument as well as you do. The rest of it is simple. If they take you in only for a while it's long enough. Don't give 'em time to hunt up the strawberry mark on your left shoulder. Old Urique keeps anywhere from $50,000 to $100,000 in his house all the time in a little safe that you could open with a shoe buttoner. Get it. My skill as a tattooer is worth half the boodle. We go halves and catch a tramp steamer for Rio Janeiro. Let the United States go to pieces if it can't get along without my services. *Que dice, señor?*"

"It sounds to me!" said the Kid, nodding his head. "I'm out for the dust."

"All right, then," said Thacker. "You'll have to keep close until we get the bird on you. You can live in the back room here. I do my own cooking, and I'll make you as comfortable as a parsimonious Government will allow me."

Thacker had set the time at a week, but it was two weeks before the design that he patiently tattooed upon the Kid's hand was to his notion. And then Thacker called a *muchacho,* and despatched this note to the intended victim:

El Senor Don Santos Urique,
La Casa Blanca.

My Dear Sir: I beg permission to inform you that there is in my house as a temporary guest a young man who arrived in Buenas Tierras from the

United States some days ago. Without wishing to excite any hopes that may not be realized, I think there is a possibility of his being your long-absent son. It might be well for you to call and see him. If he is, it is my opinion that his intention was to return to his home, but upon arriving here, his courage failed him from doubts as to how he would be received.

YOUR TRUE SERVANT,
THOMPSON THACKER.

Half an hour afterward—quick time for Buenas Tierras—Señor Urique's ancient landau drove to the consul's door, with the bare-footed coachman beating and shouting at the team of fat, awkward horses.

A tall man with a white mustache alighted, and assisted to the ground a lady who was dressed and veiled in unrelieved black.

The two hastened inside, and were met by Thacker with his best diplomatic bow. By his desk stood a slender young man with clear-cut, sun-browned features and smoothly brushed black hair.

Señora Urique threw back her heavy veil with a quick gesture. She was past middle age, and her hair was beginning to silver, but her full, proud figure and clear olive skin retained traces of the beauty peculiar to the Basque province. But, once you had seen her eyes, and comprehended the great sadness that was revealed in their deep shadows and hopeless expression, you saw that the woman lived only in some memory.

She bent upon the young man a long look of the most agonized questioning. Then her great black eyes turned, and her gaze rested upon his left hand. And then with a sob, not loud, but seeming to shake the room, she cried *"Hijo mio!"* and caught the Llano Kid to her heart.

III

A MONTH AFTERWARD the Kid came to the consulate in response to a message sent by Thacker.

He looked the young Spanish *caballero.* His clothes were imported, and the wiles of the jewelers had not been spent upon him in vain. A more than respectable diamond shone on his finger as he rolled a shuck cigarette.

"What's doing?" asked Thacker.

"Nothing much," said the Kid calmly. "I eat my first iguana steak today. They're them big lizards, you *sabe?* I reckon, though, that frijoles and side bacon would do me about as well. Do you care for iguanas, Thacker?"

"No, nor for some other kinds of reptiles," said Thacker.

It was three in the afternoon, and in another hour he would be in his state of beatitude.

"It's time you were making good, sonny," he went on, with an ugly look on his reddened face. "You're not playing up to me square. You've been the prodigal son for four weeks now, and you could have had veal for every meal on a gold dish if you'd wanted it. Now, Mr. Kid, do you think it's right to leave me out so long on a husk diet? What's the trouble? Don't you get your filial eyes on anything that looks like cash in the Casa Blanca? Don't tell me you don't. Everybody knows where old Urique keeps his stuff. It's U. S. currency, too; he don't accept anything else. What's doing? Don't say 'nothing' this time."

"Why, sure," said the Kid, admiring his diamond, "there's plenty of money up there. I'm no judge of collateral in bunches, but I will undertake for to say that I've seen the rise of $50,000 at a time in that tin grub box that my adopted father calls his safe. And he lets me carry the key sometimes just to show me that he knows I'm the real little Francisco that strayed from the herd a long time ago."

"Well, what are you waiting for?" asked Thacker angrily. "Don't you forget that I can upset your applecart any day I want to. If old Urique knew you were an impostor, what sort of things would happen to you? Oh, you don't know this country, Mr. Texas Kid. The laws here have got mustard spread between 'em. These people here'd stretch you out like a frog that had been stepped on, and give you about fifty sticks at every corner of the plaza. And they'd wear every stick out, too. What was left of you they'd feed to alligators."

"I might as well tell you now, pardner," said the Kid, sliding down low on his steamer chair, "that things are going to stay just as they are. They're about right now."

"What do you mean?" asked Thacker, rattling the bottom of his glass on his desk.

"The scheme's off," said the Kid. "And whenever you have the pleasure of speaking to me address me as Don Francisco Urique. I'll guarantee I'll answer to it. We'll let Colonel Urique keep his money. His little tin safe is as good as the time-locker in the First National Bank of Laredo as far as you and me are concerned."

"You're going to throw me down, then, are you?" said the consul.

"Sure," said the Kid cheerfully. "Throw you down. That's it. And now I'll tell you why. The first night I was up at the colonel's house they introduced me to a bedroom. No blankets on the floor—a real room, with a bed and things in it. And before I was asleep, in comes this artificial mother of mine and tucks in the covers. 'Panchito,' she says, 'my little lost one, God has brought you back to me. I bless his name forever.' It was that, or some truck like that, she said. And down comes a drop of rain and hits me on the nose. And all that stuck by me, Mr. Thacker. And it's been that way ever since. And it's got to stay that way. Don't you think that it's for what's in it for me, either, that I say so. If you have any such ideas, keep 'em to yourself. I haven't had much truck with women in my life, and no mothers to speak of, but here's a lady that we've got to keep fooled. Once she stood it; twice she won't. I'm a lowdown wolf, and the devil may have sent me on this trail instead of God, but I'll travel it to the end. And now, don't forget that I'm Don Francisco Urique whenever you happen to mention my name."

"I'll expose you today, you—you double-dyed traitor," stammered Thacker.

The Kid arose and, without violence, took Thacker by the throat with a hand of steel, and shoved him slowly into a corner. Then he drew from under his left arm his pearl-handled .45 and poked the cold muzzle of it against the consul's mouth.

"I told you why I come here," he said with his old freezing smile. "If I leave here, you'll be the reason. Never forget it, pardner. Now, what is my name?"

"Er—Don Francisco Urique," gasped Thacker.

From outside came a sound of wheels, and the shouting of someone, and the sharp thwacks of a wooden whipstock upon the backs of fat horses.

The Kid put up his gun, and walked toward the door. But he turned again and came back to the trembling Thacker, and held up his left hand with its back toward the consul.

"There's one more reason," he said slowly, "why things have got to stand as they are. The fellow I killed in Laredo had one of them same pictures on his left hand."

Outside, the ancient landau of Don Santos Urique rattled to the door. The coachman ceased his bellowing. Señora Urique, in a voluminous gay gown of white lace and flying ribbons, leaned forward with a happy look in her great soft eyes.

"Are you within, dear son?" she called in the rippling Castilian.

"Madre mio, yo vengo (Mother, I come)," answered the young Don Francisco Urique.

After Twenty Years

THE POLICEMAN ON the beat moved up the avenue impressively. The impressiveness was habitual and not for show, for spectators were few. The time was barely 10 o'clock at night, but chilly gusts of wind with a taste of rain in them had well nigh depeopled the streets.

Trying doors as he went, twirling his club with many intricate and artful movements, turning now and then to cast his watchful eye adown the pacific thoroughfare, the officer, with his stalwart form and slight swagger, made a fine picture of a guardian of the peace. The vicinity was one that kept early hours. Now and then you might see the lights of a cigar store or of an all-night lunch counter; but the majority of the doors belonged to business places that had long since been closed.

When about midway of a certain block the policeman suddenly slowed his walk. In the doorway of a darkened hardware store a man leaned, with an unlighted cigar in his mouth. As the policeman walked up to him the man spoke up quickly.

"It's all right, officer," he said, reassuringly. "I'm just waiting for a friend. It's an appointment made twenty years ago. Sounds a little funny to you, doesn't it? Well, I'll explain if you'd like to make certain it's all straight. About that long ago there used to be a restaurant where this store stands—'Big Joe' Brady's restaurant."

"Until five years ago," said the policeman. "It was torn down then."

The man in the doorway struck a match and lit his cigar. The light showed a pale, square-jawed face with keen eyes, and a little white scar near his right eyebrow. His scarfpin was a large diamond, oddly set.

"Twenty years ago tonight," said the man, "I dined here at 'Big Joe' Brady's with Jimmy Wells, my best chum, and the finest chap in the world. He and I were raised here in New York, just like two brothers, together. I was eighteen and Jimmy was twenty. The next morning I was to start for the West to make my fortune. You couldn't have dragged Jimmy out of New York; he thought it was the only place on earth. Well, we agreed that night that we would meet here again exactly twenty years from that date and time, no matter what our conditions might be or from what distance we might have to come. We figured that in twenty years each of us ought to have our destiny worked out and our fortunes made, whatever they were going to be."

"It sounds pretty interesting," said the policeman. "Rather a long time between meets, though, it seems to me. Haven't you heard from your friend since you left?"

"Well, yes, for a time we corresponded," said the other. "But after a year or two we lost track of each other. You see, the West is a pretty big proposition, and I kept hustling around over it pretty lively. But I know Jimmy will meet me here if he's alive, for he always was the truest, stanchest old chap in the world. He'll never forget. I came a thousand miles to stand in this door tonight, and it's worth it if my old partner turns up."

The waiting man pulled out a handsome watch, the lids of it set with small diamonds.

"Three minutes to ten," he announced. "It was exactly ten o'clock when we parted here at the restaurant door."

"Did pretty well out West, didn't you?" asked the policeman.

"You bet! I hope Jimmy has done half as well. He was a kind of plodder, though, good fellow as he was. I've had to compete with some of the sharpest wits going to get my pile. A man gets in a groove in New York. It takes the West to put a razor edge on him."

The policeman twirled his club and took a step or two.

"I'll be on my way. Hope your friend comes around all right. Going to call time on him sharp?"

"I should say not!" said the other. "I'll give him half an hour at least. If Jimmy is alive on earth he'll be here by that time. So long, officer."

"Good-night, sir," said the policeman, passing on along his beat, trying doors as he went.

There was now a fine, cold drizzle falling, and the wind had risen from its uncertain puffs into a steady blow. The few foot passengers astir in that quarter hurried dismally and silently along with coat collars turned high and pocketed hands. And in the door of the hardware store the man who had come a thousand miles to fill an appointment, uncertain almost to absurdity, with the friend of his youth, smoked his cigar and waited.

About twenty minutes he waited, and then a tall man in a long overcoat, with collar turned up to his ears, hurried across from the opposite side of the street. He went directly to the waiting man.

"Is that you, Bob?" he asked doubtfully.

"Is that you, Jimmy Wells?" cried the man in the door.

"Bless my heart!" exclaimed the new arrival, grasping both the other's hands with his own. "It's Bob, sure as fate. I was certain I'd find you here if you were still in existence. Well, well, well!—twenty years is a long time. The old restaurant's gone, Bob; I wish it had lasted, so we could have had another dinner there. How has the West treated you, old man?"

"Bully; it has given me everything I asked it for. You've changed lots, Jimmy. I never thought you were so tall by two or three inches."

"Oh, I grew a bit after I was twenty."

"Doing well in New York, Jimmy?"

"Moderately. I have a position in one of the city departments. Come on, Bob; we'll go around to a place I know of, and have a good long talk about old times."

The two men started up the street, arm in arm. The man from the West, his egotism enlarged by success, was beginning to outline the history of his career. The other, submerged in his overcoat, listened with interest.

At the corner stood a drugstore, brilliant with electric lights. When they came into this glare each of them turned simultaneously to gaze upon the other's face.

The man from the West stopped suddenly and released his arm.

"You're not Jimmy Wells," he snapped. "Twenty years is a long time, but not long enough to change a man's nose from a Roman to a pug."

"It sometimes changes a good man into a bad one," said the tall man. "You've been under arrest for ten minutes, 'Silky' Bob. Chicago thinks you may have dropped over our way and wires us she wants to have a chat with you. Going quietly, are you? That's sensible. Now, before we go to the station here's a note I was asked to hand you. You may read it here at the window. It's from Patrolman Wells."

The man from the West unfolded the little piece of paper handed him. His hand was steady when he began to read, but it trembled a little by the time he had finished. The note was rather short.

Bob: I was at the appointed place on time. When you struck the match to light your cigar I saw it was the face of the man wanted in Chicago. Somehow I couldn't do it myself, so I went around and got a plainclothes man to do the job.

Jimmy

A Retrieved Reform

A GUARD CAME to the prison shoe shop, where Jimmy Valentine was assiduously stitching uppers, and escorted him to the front office. There the warden handed Jimmy his pardon, which had been signed that morning by the governor. Jimmy took it in a tired kind of way. He had served nearly ten months of a four-year sentence. He had expected to stay only about three months, at the longest. When a man with as many friends on the outside as Jimmy Valentine had is received in the "stir" it is hardly worthwhile to cut his hair.

"Now, Valentine," said the warden, "you'll go out in the morning. Brace up, and make a man of yourself. You're not a bad fellow at heart. Stop cracking safes, and live straight."

"Me?" said Jimmy in surprise. "Why, I never cracked a safe in my life."

"Oh, no!" laughed the warden. "Of course not. Let's see, now. How was it you happened to get sent up on that Springfield job? Was it because you wouldn't prove an alibi for fear of compromising somebody in extremely high-toned society? Or was it simply a case of a mean, old jury that had it in for you? It's always one or the other with you innocent victims."

"Me?" said Jimmy, still blankly virtuous. "Why, warden, I never was in Springfield in my life!"

"Take him back, Cronin," smiled the warden, "and fix him up with outgoing clothes. Unlock him at seven in the morning, and let him come to the bull pen. Better think over my advice, Valentine."

At a quarter past seven on the next morning Jimmy stood in the warden's outer office. He had on a suit of the villainously fitting, ready-made clothes and a pair of the stiff, squeaky shoes that the state furnishes to its discharged, compulsory guests.

The clerk handed him a railroad ticket and the five-dollar bill with which the law expected him to rehabilitate himself into good citizenship and prosperity. The warden gave him a cigar, and shook hands. Valentine, 9762, was chronicled on the books "Pardoned by Governor," and Mr. James Valentine walked out into the sunshine.

Disregarding the song of the birds, the waving green trees, and the smell of the flowers, Jimmy headed straight for a restaurant. There he tasted the first sweet joys of liberty in the shape of a broiled chicken and a bottle of white wine—followed by a cigar a grade better than the one the warden had given him. From there he proceeded leisurely to the depot. He tossed a quarter into the hat of a blind man sitting by the door, and boarded his train. Three hours set him down in a little town near the state line. He went to the café of one Mike Dolan and shook hands with Mike, who was alone behind the bar.

"Sorry we couldn't make it sooner, Jimmy, me boy," said Mike. "But we had that protest from Springfield to buck against, and the governor nearly balked. Feeling all right?"

"Fine," said Jimmy. "Got my key?"

He got his key and went upstairs, unlocking the door of a room at the rear. Everything was just as he had left it. There on the floor was still Ben Price's collar button that had been torn from that eminent detective's shirtband when they had overpowered Jimmy to arrest him.

Pulling out from the wall a folding bed, Jimmy slid back a panel in the wall and dragged out a dust-covered suitcase. He opened this and gazed fondly at the finest set of burglar's tools in the East. It was a complete set, made of specially tempered steel, the latest designs in drills, punches, braces and bits, jimmies, clamps and augers, with two or three novelties, invented by Jimmy himself, in which he took pride. Over seven hundred dollars they had cost him to have made at—a place where they make such things for the profession.

In half an hour Jimmy went downstairs and through the café. He was now dressed in tasteful and well-fitting clothes, and carried his dusted and cleaned suitcase in his hand.

"Got anything on?" asked Mike Dolan genially.

"Me?" said Jimmy in a puzzled tone. "I don't understand. I'm representing the New York Amalgamated Short Snap Biscuit Cracker and Frazzled Wheat Company."

This statement delighted Mike to such an extent that Jimmy had to take a seltzer-and-milk on the spot. He never touched "hard" drinks.

A week after the release of Valentine, 9762, there was a neat job of safe-burglary done in Richmond, Indiana, with no clue to the author. A scant eight hundred dollars was all that was secured. Two weeks after that a patented, improved, burglarproof safe in Logansport was opened like a cheese to the tune of fifteen hundred dollars, currency; securities and silver untouched. That began to interest the rogue-catchers. Then an old-fashioned bank safe in Jefferson City became active and threw out of its crater an eruption of bank notes amounting to five thousand dollars. The losses were now high enough to bring the matter up into Ben Price's class of work. By comparing notes, a remarkable similarity in the methods of the burglaries was noticed. Ben Price investigated the scenes of the robberies, and was heard to remark, "That's Dandy Jim Valentine's autograph. He's resumed business. Look at that combination knob—jerked out as easy as pulling up a radish in wet weather. He's got the only clamps that can do it. And look how clean those tumblers were punched out! Jimmy never has to drill but one hole. Yes, I guess I want Mr. Valentine. He'll do his bit next time without any short-time or clemency foolishness."

Ben Price knew Jimmy's habits. He had learned them while working up the Springfield case. Long jumps, quick getaways, no confederates, and a taste for good society—these ways had helped Mr. Valentine to become noted as a successful dodger of retribution. It was given out that Ben Price had taken up the trail of the elusive cracksman, and other people with burglarproof safes felt more at ease.

One afternoon Jimmy Valentine and his suitcase climbed out of the mail hack in Elmore, a little town five miles off the railroad down in the blackjack country of Arkansas. Jimmy, looking like an athletic young senior just home from college, went down the board sidewalk toward the hotel.

A young lady crossed the street, passed him at the corner, and entered a door over which was the sign "The Elmore Bank." Jimmy Valentine looked into her eyes, forgot what he was, and became another man. She lowered her eyes and colored slightly. Young men of Jimmy's style and looks were scarce in Elmore.

Jimmy collared a boy that was loafing on the steps of the bank as if he were one of the stockholders, and began to ask him questions about the town, feeding him dimes at intervals. By and by the young lady came out, looking royally unconscious of the young man with the suitcase, and went her way.

"Isn't that young lady Miss Polly Simpson?" asked Jimmy, with specious guile.

"Naw," said the boy. "She's Annabel Adams. Her pa owns this bank. What'd you come to Elmore for? Is that a gold watch chain? I'm going to get a bulldog. Got any more dimes?"

Jimmy went to the Planters' Hotel, registered as Ralph D. Spencer, and engaged a room. He leaned on the desk and declared his platform to the clerk. He said he had come to Elmore to look for a location to go into business. How was the shoe business, now, in the town? He had thought of the shoe business. Was there an opening?

The clerk was impressed by the clothes and manner of Jimmy. He, himself, was something of a pattern of fashion to the thinly gilded youth of Elmore, but he now perceived his shortcomings. While trying to figure out Jimmy's manner of tying his four-in-hand he cordially gave information.

Yes, there ought to be a good opening in the shoe line. There wasn't an exclusive shoe store in the place. The dry-goods and general stores handled them. Business in all lines was fairly good. Hoped Mr. Spencer would decide to locate in Elmore. He would find it a pleasant town to live in, and the people very sociable.

Mr. Spencer thought he would stop over in the town a few days and look over the situation. No, the clerk needn't call the boy. He would carry up his suitcase himself; it was rather heavy.

Mr. Ralph Spencer, the phoenix that arose from Jimmy Valentine's ashes—ashes left by the flame of a sudden and alterative attack of love—remained in Elmore, and prospered. He opened a shoe store and secured a good run of trade.

Socially he was also a success, and made many friends. And he accomplished the wish of his heart. He met Miss Annabel Adams, and became more and more captivated by her charms.

At the end of a year the situation of Mr. Ralph Spencer was this: he had won the respect of the community, his shoe store was flourishing, and he and Annabel were engaged to be married in two weeks. Mr. Adams, the typical, plodding, country banker, approved of Spencer. Annabel's pride in him almost equaled her affection. He was as much at home in the family of Mr. Adams and that of Annabel's married sister as if he were already a member.

One day Jimmy sat down in his room and wrote this letter, which he mailed to the safe address of one of his old friends in St. Louis:

Dear Old Pal:—I want you to be at Sullivan's place, in Little Rock, next Wednesday night, at nine o'clock. I want you to wind up some little matters for me. And, also, I want to make you a present of my kit of tools. I know you'll be glad to get them—you couldn't duplicate the lot for one thousand dollars. Say, Billy, I've quit the old business—a year ago. I've got a nice store. I'm making an honest living, and I'm going to marry the finest girl on earth two weeks from now. It's the only life, Billy—the straight one. I wouldn't touch a dollar of another man's money now for a million. After I get married I'm going to sell out and go West, where there won't be so much danger of having old scores brought up against me. I tell you, Billy, she's an angel. She believes in me; and I wouldn't do another crooked thing for the whole world. Be sure to be at Sully's, for I must see you. I'll bring along the tools with me.

Your old friend, JIMMY.

On the Monday night after Jimmy wrote this letter Ben Price jogged unobtrusively into Elmore in a livery buggy. He lounged about town in his quiet way until he found out what he wanted to know. From the drugstore across the street from Spencer's shoe store he got a good look at Ralph D. Spencer.

"Going to marry the banker's daughter, are you, Jimmy?" said Ben to himself softly. "Well, I don't know!"

The next morning Jimmy took breakfast at the Adamses'. He was going to Little Rock that day to order his wedding suit and buy something nice for Annabel. That would be the first time he had left town since he came to Elmore. It had been more than a year now since those last professional "jobs," and he thought he could safely venture out.

After breakfast quite a family party went downtown together— Mr. Adams, Annabel, Jimmy, and Annabel's married sister with her two little girls, aged five and nine. They came by the hotel where Jimmy still boarded, and he ran up to his room and brought along his suitcase. Then they went on to the bank. There stood Jimmy's horse and buggy and Dolph Gibson, who was going to drive him over to the railroad station.

All went inside the high, carved-oak railings into the banking room—Jimmy included, for Mr. Adams' future son-in-law was welcome anywhere. The clerks were pleased to be greeted by the good-looking, agreeable young man who was going to marry Miss Annabel. Jimmy set his suitcase down. Annabel, whose heart was bubbling with happiness and lively youth, put on Jimmy's hat, and picked up the suitcase. "Wouldn't I make a nice drummer?" said Annabel. "My! Ralph, how heavy it is? Feels like it was full of gold bricks."

"Lot of nickel-plated shoehorns in there," said Jimmy coolly, "that I'm going to return. Thought I'd save express charges by taking them up. I'm getting awfully economical."

The Elmore Bank had just put in a new safe and vault. Mr. Adams was very proud of it, and insisted on an inspection by everyone. The vault was a small one, but it had a new, patented door. It fastened with three, solid, steel bolts thrown simultaneously with a single handle, and had a time lock. Mr. Adams beamingly explained its workings to Mr. Spencer, who showed a courteous, but not too intelligent, interest. The two children, May and Agatha, were delighted by the shining metal and funny clock and knobs.

While they were thus engaged Ben Price sauntered in and leaned on his elbow, looking casually inside between the railings. He told the teller that he didn't want anything; he was just waiting for a man he knew.

Suddenly there was a scream or two from the women, and a commotion. Unperceived by the elders, May, the nine-year-old girl, in a spirit of play, had shut Agatha in the vault. She had then shot the bolts and turned the knob of the combination as she had seen Mr. Adams do.

The old banker sprang to the handle and tugged at it for a moment. "The door can't be opened," he groaned. "The clock hasn't been wound nor the combination set."

Agatha's mother screamed again, hysterically.

"Hush!" said Mr. Adams, raising his trembling hand. "All be quiet for a moment. Agatha!" he called as loudly as he could. "Listen to me." During the following silence they could just hear the faint sound of the child wildly shrieking in the dark vault in a panic of terror.

"My precious darling!" wailed the mother. "She will die of fright! Open the door! Oh, break it open! Can't you men do something?"

"There isn't a man nearer than Little Rock who can open that door," said Mr. Adams, in a shaky voice. "My God! Spencer, what shall we do? That child—she can't stand it long in there. There isn't enough air, and, besides, she'll go into convulsions from fright."

Agatha's mother, frantic now, beat the door of the vault with her hands. Somebody wildly suggested dynamite. Annabel turned to Jimmy, her large eyes full of anguish, but not yet despairing. To a woman nothing seems quite impossible to the powers of the man she worships.

"Can't you do something, Ralph—*try*, won't you?"

He looked at her with a queer, soft smile on his lips and in his keen eyes.

"Annabel," he said, "give me that rose you are wearing, will you?"

Hardly believing that she heard him aright, she unpinned the bud from the bosom of her dress, and placed it in his hand. Jimmy stuffed it into his vestpocket, threw off his coat and pulled up his shirtsleeves. With that act Ralph D. Spencer passed away and Jimmy Valentine took his place.

"Get away from the door, all of you," he commanded shortly.

He set his suitcase on the table, and opened it out flat. From that time on he seemed to be unconscious of the presence of anyone else. He laid out the shining, queer implements swiftly and orderly, whistling softly to himself as he always did when at work. In a deep silence and immovable, the others watched him as if under a spell.

In a minute Jimmy's pet drill was biting smoothly into the steel door. In ten minutes—breaking his own burglarious record—he threw back the bolts and opened the door.

Agatha, almost collapsed, but safe, was gathered into her mother's arms.

Jimmy Valentine put on his coat, and walked outside the railings toward the front door. As he went he thought he heard a faraway voice that he once knew call "Ralph!" But he never hesitated.

At the door a big man stood somewhat in his way.

"Hello, Ben!" said Jimmy, still with his strange smile. "Got around at last, have you? Well, let's go. I don't know that it makes much difference, now."

And then Ben Price acted rather strangely.

"Guess you're mistaken, Mr. Spencer," he said. "Don't believe I recognize you. Your buggy's waiting for you, ain't it?"

And Ben Price turned and strolled down the street.

THE CABALLERO'S WAY

THE CISCO KID had killed six men in more or less fair scrimmages, had murdered twice as many (mostly Mexicans), and had winged a larger number whom he modestly forbore to count. Therefore a woman loved him.

The Kid was twenty-five, looked twenty; and a careful insurance company would have estimated the probable time of his demise at—say twenty-six. His habitat was anywhere between the Frio and the Rio Grande. He killed for the love of it—because he was quick-tempered—to avoid arrest—for his own amusement—any reason that came to his mind would suffice. He had escaped capture because he could shoot five-sixths of a second sooner than any sheriff or ranger in the service, and because he rode a speckled roan horse that knew every cowpath in the mesquite and pear thickets from San Antonio to Matamoras.

Tonia Perez, the girl who loved the Cisco Kid, was half Carmen, half Madonna, and the rest—oh, yes, a woman who is half Carmen and half Madonna can always be something more—the rest, let us say, was hummingbird. She lived in a grass-roofed jacal near a little Mexican settlement at the Lone Wolf crossing of the Frio. With her lived a father or grandfather, a lineal Aztec, somewhat less than a thousand years old, who herded a hundred goats and lived in a continuous, drunken dream from drinking mescal. Back of the jacal a tremendous forest of bristling pear, twenty feet high at its worst, crowded almost to its door. It was along the bewildering maze of this spinous thicket that the speckled roan would bring the Kid to see his girl. And once, clinging like a lizard to the ridge-pole high up under the peaked grass roof, he had heard Tonia, with her Madonna face and Carmen beauty and hummingbird soul, parley with the sheriff's posse, denying knowledge of her man in her soft mélange of Spanish and English.

One day the adjutant-general of the State, who is, ex-officio, commander of the ranger forces, wrote some sarcastic lines to Captain Duval of Company X, stationed at Laredo, relative to the serene and undisturbed existence led by murderers and desperadoes in the said captain's territory.

The captain turned the color of brick dust under his tan and forwarded the letter, after adding a few comments, per ranger Private Bill Adamson, to ranger Lieutenant Sandridge, camped at a water hole on the Nueces with a squad of five men in preservation of law and order.

Lieutenant Sandridge turned a beautiful *couleur de rose* through his ordinary strawberry complexion, tucked the letter in his hip pocket, and chewed off the ends of his gamboge mustache.

The next morning he saddled his horse and rode alone to the Mexican settlement at the Lone Wolf Crossing of the Frio, twenty miles away.

Six feet two, blond as a viking, quiet as a deacon, dangerous as a machine gun, Sandridge moved among the jacals, patiently seeking news of the Cisco Kid.

Far more than the law, the Mexicans dreaded the cold and certain vengeance of the lone rider that the ranger sought. It had been one of the Kid's pastimes to shoot Mexicans "to see them kick": if he demanded from them moribund Terpsichorean feats, simply that he might be entertained, what terrible and extreme penalties would be certain to follow should they anger him! One and all they lounged with upturned palms and shrugging shoulders, filling the air with *"quien sabes"* and denials of the Kid's acquaintance.

But there was a man named Fink who kept a store at the Crossing—a man of many nationalities, tongues, interests, and ways of thinking.

"No use to ask them Mexicans," he said to Sandridge. "They're afraid to tell. This *hombre* they call the Kid—Goodall is his name, ain't it?—he's been in my store once or twice. I have an idea you might run across him at—but I guess I don't keer to say, myself. I'm two seconds later in pulling a gun than I used to be, and the difference is worth thinking about. But this Kid's got a half-Mexican girl at the Crossing that he comes to see. She lives in that jacal a hundred yards down the arroyo at the edge of the pear. Maybe she—no, I don't suppose she would, but that jacal would be a good place to watch, anyway."

Sandridge rode down to the jacal of Perez. The sun was low, and the broad shade of the great pear thicket already covered the grass-thatched hut. The goats were enclosed for the night in a brush corral nearby. A few kids walked the top of it, nibbling the chaparral leaves. The old Mexican lay upon a blanket on the grass, already in a stupor from his mescal, and dreaming, perhaps, of the nights when he and Pizarro touched glasses to their New World fortunes—so old his wrinkled face seemed to proclaim him to be. And in the door of the jacal stood Tonia. And Lieutenant Sandridge sat in his saddle staring at her like a gannet agape at a sailorman.

The Cisco Kid was a vain person, as all eminent and successful assassins are, and his bosom would have been ruffled had he known that at a simple exchange of glances two persons, in whose minds he had been looming large, suddenly abandoned (at least for the time) all thought of him.

Never before had Tonia seen such a man as this. He seemed to be made of sunshine and blood-red tissue and clear weather. He seemed to illuminate the shadow of the pear when he smiled, as though the sun were rising again. The men she had known had been small and dark. Even the Kid, despite his achievements, was a stripling, no larger than herself, with black, straight hair and a cold, marble face that chilled the noonday.

As for Tonia, though she sends description to the poorhouse, let her make a millionaire of your fancy. Her blue-black hair, smoothly divided in the middle and bound close to her head, and her large eyes full of the Latin melancholy gave her the Madonna touch. Her motions and air spoke of the concealed fire and the desire to charm that she had inherited from the *gitanas* of the Basque province. As for the hummingbird part of her, that dwelt in her heart; you could not perceive it unless her bright red skirt and dark blue blouse gave you a symbolic hint of the vagarious bird.

The newly lighted sun god asked for a drink of water. Tonia brought it from the red jar hanging under the brush shelter. Sandridge considered it necessary to dismount so as to lessen the trouble of her ministrations.

I play no spy; nor do I assume to master the thoughts of any human heart; but I assert, by the chronicler's right, that before a quarter of an hour had sped, Sandridge was teaching her how to plait a six-strand rawhide stake-rope, and Tonia had explained to him that were it not for her little English book that the peripatetic *padre* had given her and the little crippled *chivo*, that she fed from a bottle, she would be very, very lonely indeed.

Which leads to a suspicion that the Kid's fences needed repairing, and that the adjutant-general's sarcasm had fallen upon unproductive soil.

In his camp by the water hole Lieutenant Sandridge announced and reiterated his intention either of causing the Cisco Kid to nibble the black loam of the Frio country prairies or of hauling him before a judge and jury. That sounded businesslike. Twice a week he rode over to the Lone Wolf Crossing of the Frio, and directed Tonia's slim, slightly lemon-tinted fingers among the intricacies of the slowly growing lariata. A six-strand plait is hard to learn and easy to teach.

The ranger knew that he might find the Kid there at any visit. He kept his armament ready and had a frequent eye for the pear thicket at the rear of the jacal. Thus he might bring down the kite and the hummingbird with one stone.

While the sunny-haired ornithologist was pursuing his studies, the Cisco Kid was also attending to his professional duties. He moodily shot up a saloon in a small cow village on Quintana Creek, killed the town marshal (plugging him neatly in the center of his tin badge), and then rode away, morose and unsatisfied. No true artist is uplifted by shooting an aged man carrying an old-style .38 bulldog.

On his way the Kid suddenly experienced the yearning that all men feel when wrongdoing loses its keen edge of delight. He yearned for the woman he loved to reassure him that she was his in spite of it. He wanted her to call his bloodthirstiness bravery and his cruelty devotion. He wanted Tonia to bring him water from the red jar under the brush shelter, and tell him how the *chivo* was thriving on the bottle.

The Kid turned the speckled roan's head up the ten-mile pear flat that stretches along the Arroyo Hondo until it ends at the Lone Wolf Crossing of the Frio. The roan whickered; for he had sense of locality and direction equal to that of a belt-line streetcar horse; and he knew he would be soon nibbling the rich mesquite grass at the end of a forty-foot stake-rope while Ulysses rested his head in Circe's straw-roofed hut.

More weird and lonesome than the journey of an Amazonian explorer is the ride of one through a Texas pear flat. With dismal monotony and startling variety the uncanny and multiform shapes of the cacti lift their twisted trunks and fat, bristly hands to encumber the way. The demon plant, appearing to live without soil or rain, seems to taunt the parched traveler with its lush gray-greenness. It warps itself a thousand times about what look to be open and inviting paths, only to lure the rider into blind and impassable spine-defended "bottoms of the bag," leaving him to retreat if he can, with the points of the compass whirling in his head.

To be lost in the pear is to die almost the death of the thief on the cross, pierced by nails and with grotesque shapes of all the fiends hovering about.

But it was not so with the Kid and his mount. Winding, twisting, circling, tracing the most fantastic and bewildering trail ever picked out, the good roan lessened the distance to the Lone Wolf Crossing with every coil and turn that he made.

While they fared the Kid sang. He knew but one tune and sang it, as he knew but one code and lived it and but one girl and loved her. He was a single-minded man of conventional ideas. He had a voice like a coyote with bronchitis, but whenever he chose to sing his song he sang. It was a conventional song of the camps and trail, running at its beginning as near as may be to these words:

> Don't you monkey with my Lulu girl
> Or I'll tell you what I'll do—

and so on. The roan was inured to it, and did not mind.

But even the poorest singer will, after a certain time, gain his own consent to refrain from contributing to the world's noises. So the Kid, by the time he was within a mile or two of Tonia's jacal, had reluctantly allowed his song to die away—not because his vocal performance had become less charming to his own ears, but because his laryngeal muscles were aweary.

As though he were in a circus ring the speckled roan wheeled and danced through the labyrinth of pear until at length his rider knew by certain landmarks that the Lone Wolf Crossing was close at hand. Then, where the pear was thinner, he caught sight of the grass roof of the jacal and the hackberry tree on the edge of the arroyo. A few yards farther the Kid stopped the roan and gazed intently through the prickly openings. Then he dismounted, dropped the roan's reins, and proceeded on foot, stooping and silent, like an Indian. The roan, knowing his part, stood still, making no sound.

The Kid crept noiselessly to the very edge of the pear thicket and reconnoitered between the leaves of a clump of cactus.

Ten yards from his hiding place, in the shade of the jacal, sat his Tonia calmly plaiting a rawhide lariat. So far she might surely escape condemnation; women have been known, from time to time, to engage in more mischievous occupations. But if all must be told, there is to be added that her head reposed against the broad and comfortable chest of a tall red-and-yellow man, and that his arm was about her, guiding her nimble small fingers that required so many lessons at the intricate six-strand plait.

Sandridge glanced quickly at the dark mass of pear when he heard a slight squeaking sound that was not altogether unfamiliar. A gun-scabbard will make that sound when one grasps the handle of a six-shooter suddenly. But the sound was not repeated; and Tonia's fingers needed close attention.

And then, in the shadow of death, they began to talk of their love; and in the still July afternoon every word they uttered reached the ears of the Kid.

"Remember, then," said Tonia, "you must not come again until I send for you. Soon he will be here. A *vaquero* at the *tienda* said today he saw him on the Guadalupe three days ago. When he is that near he always comes. If he comes and finds you here he will kill you. So, for my sake, you must come no more until I send you the word."

"All right," said the ranger. "And then what?"

"And then," said the girl, "you must bring your men here and kill him. If not, he will kill you."

"He ain't a man to surrender, that's sure," said Sandridge. "It's kill or be killed for the officer that goes up against Mr. Cisco Kid."

"He must die," said the girl. "Otherwise there will not be any peace in the world for thee and me. He has killed many. Let him so die. Bring your men, and give him no chance to escape."

"You used to think right much of him," said Sandridge.

Tonia dropped the lariat, twisted herself around, and curved a lemon-tinted arm over the ranger's shoulder.

"But then," she murmured in liquid Spanish, "I had not beheld thee, thou great, red mountain of a man! And thou art kind and good as well as strong. Could one choose him, knowing thee? Let him die;

for then I will not be filled with fear by day and night lest he hurt thee or me."

"How will I know when he comes?" asked Sandridge.

"When he comes," said Tonia, "he remains two days, sometimes three. Gregorio, the small son of old Luisa, the *lavandera,* has a swift pony. I will write a letter to thee and send it by him, saying how it will be best to come upon him. By Gregorio will the letter come. And bring many men with thee, and have much care, oh, dear red one, for the rattlesnake is not quicker to strike than is *'El Chivato,'* as they call him, to send a ball from his *pistola."*

"The Kid's handy with his gun, sure enough," admitted Sandridge, "but when I come for him I shall come alone. I'll get him by myself or not at all. The Cap wrote one or two things to me that make me want to do the trick without any help. You let me know when Mr. Kid arrives, and I'll do the rest."

"I will send you the message by the boy, Gregorio," said the girl. "I knew you were braver than that small slayer of men who never smiles. How could I ever have thought I cared for him?"

It was time for the ranger to ride back to his camp on the water hole. Before he mounted his horse he raised the slight form of Tonia with one arm high from the earth for a parting salute. The drowsy stillness of the torpid summer air still lay thick upon the dreaming afternoon. The smoke from the fire in the jacal, where the *frijoles* blubbered in the iron pot, rose straight as a plumb line above the clay-daubed chimney. No sound or movement disturbed the serenity of the dense pear thicket ten yards away.

When the form of Sandridge had disappeared, loping his big dun down the steep banks of the Frio crossing, the Kid crept back to his own horse, mounted him, and rode back along the tortuous trail he had come.

But not far. He stopped and waited in the silent depths of the pear until half an hour had passed. And then Tonia heard the high, untrue notes of his unmusical singing coming nearer and nearer; and she ran to the edge of the pear to meet him.

The Kid seldom smiled; but he smiled and waved his hat when he saw her. He dismounted, and his girl sprang into his arms. The Kid looked at her fondly. His thick black hair clung to his head like a wrinkled mat. The meeting brought a slight ripple of some undercurrent of feeling to his smooth, dark face that was usually as motionless as a clay mask.

"How's my girl?" he asked, holding her close.

"Sick of waiting so long for you, dear one," she answered. "My eyes are dim with always gazing into that devil's pincushion through which you come. And I can see into it such a little way, too. But you are here, beloved one, and I will not scold. *Que mal muchacho!* not to come to see your *alma* more often. Go in and rest, and let me water your horse and stake him with the long rope. There is cool water in the jar for you."

The Kid kissed her affectionately.

"Not if the court knows itself do I let a lady stake my horse for me," said he. "But if you'll run in, *chica,* and throw a pot of coffee together while I attend to the *caballo,* I'll be a good deal obliged."

Besides his marksmanship the Kid had another attribute for which he admired himself greatly. He was *muy caballero,* as the Mexicans express it, where the ladies were concerned. For them he had always gentle words and consideration. He could not have spoken a harsh word to a woman. He might ruthlessly slay their husbands and brothers, but he could not have laid the weight of a finger in anger upon a woman. Wherefore many of that interesting division of humanity who had come under the spell of his politeness declared their disbelief in the stories circulated about Mr. Kid. One shouldn't believe everything one heard, they said. When confronted by their indignant menfolk with proof of the caballero's deeds of infamy, they said maybe he'd been driven to it, and that he knew how to treat a lady, anyhow.

Considering this extremely courteous idiosyncrasy of the Kid and the pride that he took in it, one can perceive that the solution of the problem that was presented to him by what he saw and heard from his hiding place in the pear that afternoon (at least as to one of the actors) must have been obscured by difficulties. And yet one could not think of the Kid overlooking little matters of that kind.

At the end of the short twilight they gathered around a supper of *frijoles,* goat steaks, canned peaches, and coffee, by the light of a lantern in the jacal. Afterward, the ancestor, his flock corralled, smoked a cigarette and became a mummy in a gray blanket. Tonia washed the few dishes while the Kid dried them with the flour-sacking towel. Her eyes shone; she chatted volubly of the inconsequent happenings of her small world since the Kid's last visit; it was as all his other homecomings had been.

Then outside Tonia swung in a grass hammock with her guitar and sang sad *canciones de amor.*

"Do you love me just the same, old girl?" asked the Kid, hunting for his cigarette papers.

"Always the same, little one," said Tonia, her dark eyes lingering upon him.

"I must go over to Fink's," said the Kid, rising, "for some tobacco. I thought I had another sack in my coat. I'll be back in a quarter of an hour."

"Hasten," said Tonia. "And tell me—how long shall I call you my own this time? Will you be gone again tomorrow, leaving me to grieve, or will you be longer with your Tonia?"

"Oh, I might stay two or three days this trip," said the Kid, yawning. "I've been on the dodge for a month, and I'd like to rest up."

He was gone half an hour for his tobacco. When he returned Tonia was still lying in the hammock.

"It's funny," said the Kid, "how I feel. I feel like there was somebody lying behind every bush and tree waiting to shoot me. I never had mullygrubs like them before. Maybe it's one of them presumptions. I've got half a notion to light out in the morning before day. The Guadalupe country is burning up about that old Dutchman I plugged down there."

"You're not afraid—no one could make my brave little one fear."

"Well, I haven't been usually regarded as a jack rabbit when it comes to scrapping; but I don't want a posse smoking me out when I'm in your jacal. Somebody might get hurt that oughtn't to."

"Remain with your Tonia; no one will find you here."

The Kid looked keenly into the shadows up and down the arroyo and toward the dim lights of the Mexican village.

"I'll see how it looks later on," was his decision.

At midnight a horseman rode into the rangers' camp, blazing his way by noisy "hallos" to indicate a pacific mission. Sandridge and one or two others turned out to investigate the row. The rider announced himself to be Domingo Sales, from the Lone Wolf Crossing. He bore a letter for Señor Sandridge. Old Luisa, the *lavandera,* had persuaded him to bring it, he said, her son Gregorio being too ill of a fever to ride.

Sandridge lighted the camp lantern and read the letter. These were its words:

Dear One: He has come. Hardly had you ridden away when he came out of the pear. When he first talked he said he would stay three days or more. Then as it grew later he was like a wolf or a fox, and walked about without rest, looking and listening. Soon he said he must leave before daylight when it is darkest and stillest. And then he seemed to suspect that I be not true to him. He looked at me so strange that I am frightened. I swear to him that I love him, his own Tonia. Last of all he said I must prove to him I am true. He thinks that even now men are waiting to kill him as he rides from my house. To escape he says he will dress in my clothes, my red skirt and the blue waist I wear and the brown mantilla over the head, and thus ride away. But before that he says I must put on his clothes, his pantalones and camisa *and hat, and ride away on his horse from the jacal as far as the big road beyond the crossing and back again. This before he goes, so he can tell if I am true and if men are hidden to shoot him. It is a terrible thing. An hour before daybreak this is to be. Come, my dear one, and kill this man and take me for your Tonia. Do not try to take hold of him alive, but kill him quickly. Knowing all, you should do that. You must come alone before the time and hide near the jacal where the wagon and saddles are kept. It is dark in there. He will wear my red skirt and blue waist and brown mantilla. I send you a hundred kisses. Come surely and shoot quickly and straight.*

Thine Own Tonia

Sandridge quickly explained to his men the official part of the missive. The rangers protested against his going alone.

"I'll get him easy enough," said the lieutenant. "The girl's got him trapped. And don't ever think he'll get the drop on me."

Sandridge saddled his horse and rode to the Lone Wolf Crossing. He tied his big dun in a clump of brush on the arroyo, took his Winchester from its scabbard, and carefully approached the Perez jacal. There was only the half of a high moon drifted over by ragged, milk-white gulf clouds.

The wagon shed was an excellent place for ambush; and the ranger got inside it safely. In the black shadow of the brush shelter in front of the jacal he could see a horse tied and hear him impatiently pawing the hard-trodden earth.

He waited almost an hour before two figures came out of the jacal. One, in men's clothes, quickly mounted the horse and galloped past the wagon shed toward the crossing and village. And then the other figure, in skirt, waist, and mantilla over its head, stepped out into the faint moonlight, gazing after the rider. Sandridge thought he would take his chance then before Tonia rode back. He fancied she might not care to see it.

"Throw up your hands," he ordered loudly, stepping out of the wagon shed with his Winchester at his shoulder.

There was a quick turn of the figure, but no movement to obey, so the ranger pumped in the bullets—one—two—three—and then twice more; for you never could be too sure of bringing down the Cisco Kid. There was no danger of missing at ten paces, even in that half moonlight.

The old ancestor, asleep on his blanket, was awakened by the shots. Listening further, he heard a great cry from some man in mortal distress or anguish, and rose up grumbling at the disturbing ways of moderns.

The tall, red ghost of a man burst into the jacal, reaching one hand, shaking like a *tule* reed, for the lantern hanging on its nail. The other spread a letter on the table.

"Look at this letter, Perez," cried the man. "Who wrote it?"

"*Ah, Dios!* It is Señor Sandridge," mumbled the old man, approaching. *"Pues, senor,* that letter was written by *'El Chivato,'* as he is called—by the man of Tonia. They say he is a bad man; I do not know. While Tonia slept he wrote the letter and sent it by this old hand of mine to Domingo Sales to be brought to you. Is there anything wrong in the letter? I am very old; and I did not know. *Valgame Dios!* It is a very foolish world; and there is nothing in the house to drink—nothing to drink."

Just then all that Sandridge could think of to do was to go outside and throw himself face downward in the dust by the side of his hummingbird, of whom not a feather fluttered. He was not a caballero by instinct, and he could not understand the niceties of revenge.

A mile away the rider who had ridden past the wagon shed struck up a harsh, untuneful song, the words of which began:

> Don't you monkey with my Lulu girl,
> Or I'll tell you what I'll do—

WHILE THE AUTO WAITS

PROMPTLY AT THE beginning of twilight, came again to that quiet corner of that quiet, small park the girl in gray. She sat upon a bench and read a book, for there was yet to come a half hour in which print could be accomplished.

To repeat: Her dress was gray, and plain enough to mask its impeccancy of style and fit. A large-meshed veil imprisoned her turban hat and a face that shone through it with a calm and unconscious beauty. She had come there at the same hour on the day previous, and on the day before that; and there was one who knew it.

The young man who knew it hovered near, relying upon burnt sacrifices to the great joss, Luck. His piety was rewarded, for, in turning a page, her book slipped from her fingers and bounded from the bench a full yard away.

The young man pounced upon it with instant avidity, returning it to its owner with that air that seems to flourish in parks and public places—a compound of gallantry and hope, tempered with respect for the policeman on the beat. In a pleasant voice, he risked an inconsequent remark upon the weather—that introductory topic responsible for so much of the world's unhappiness—and stood poised for a moment, awaiting his fate.

The girl looked him over leisurely; at his ordinary, neat dress and his features distinguished by nothing particular in the way of expression.

"You may sit down, if you like," she said, in a full, deliberate contralto. "Really, I would like to have you do so. The light is too bad for reading. I would prefer to talk."

The vassal of Luck slid upon the seat by her side with complaisance.

"Do you know," he said, speaking the formula with which park chairmen open their meetings, "that you are quite the stunningest girl I have seen in a long time? I had my eye on you yesterday. Didn't know somebody was bowled over by those pretty lamps of yours, did you, honeysuckle?"

"Whoever you are," said the girl in icy tones, "you must remember that I am a lady. I will excuse the remark you have just made because the mistake was, doubtless, not an unnatural one—in your circle. I asked you to sit down; if the invitation must constitute me your honeysuckle, consider it withdrawn."

"I earnestly beg your pardon," pleaded the young man. His expression of satisfaction had changed to one of penitence and humility. "It was my fault, you know—I mean, there are girls in parks, you know—that is, of course, you don't know, but——"

"Abandon the subject, if you please. Of course I know. Now, tell me about these people passing and crowding, each way, along these paths. Where are they going? Why do they hurry so? Are they happy?"

The young man had promptly abandoned his air of coquetry. His cue was now for a waiting part; he could not guess the role he would be expected to play.

"It *is* interesting to watch them," he replied, postulating her mood. "It is the wonderful drama of life. Some are going to supper and some to—er—other places. One wonders what their histories are."

"I do not," said the girl; "I am not so inquisitive. I come here to sit because here, only, can I be near the great, common, throbbing heart of humanity. My part in life is cast where its beats are never felt. Can you surmise why I spoke to you, Mr.——?"

"Parkenstacker," supplied the young man. Then he looked eager and hopeful.

"No," said the girl, holding up a slender finger, and smiling slightly. "You would recognize it immediately. It is impossible to keep one's name out of print. Or even one's portrait. This veil and this hat of my maid furnish me with an *incog.* You should have seen the chauffeur stare at it when he thought I did not see. Candidly, there are five or six names that belong in the holy of holies, and mine, by the accident of birth, is one of them. I spoke to you, Mr. Stackenpot——"

"Parkenstacker," corrected the young man, modestly.

"Mr. Parkenstacker, because I wanted to talk, for once, with a natural man—one unspoiled by the despicable gloss of wealth and supposed social superiority. Oh! You do not know how weary I am of it—money, money, money! And of the men who surround me, dancing like little marionettes all cut by the same pattern. I am sick of pleasure, of jewels, of travel, of society, of luxuries of all kinds."

"I always had an idea," ventured the young man, hesitatingly, "that money must be a pretty good thing."

"A competence is to be desired. But when you have so many millions that——!" She concluded the sentence with a gesture of despair. "It is the monotony of it," she continued, "that palls. Drives, dinners, theaters, balls, suppers, with the gilding of superfluous wealth over it all. Sometimes the very tinkle of the ice in my champagne glass nearly drives me mad."

Mr. Parkenstacker looked ingenuously interested.

"I have always liked," he said, "to read and hear about the ways of wealthy and fashionable folks. I suppose I am a bit of a snob. But I like to have my information accurate. Now, I had formed the opinion that champagne is cooled in the bottle and not by placing ice in the glass."

The girl gave a musical laugh of genuine amusement.

"You should know," she explained in an indulgent tone, "that we of the non-useful class depend for our amusement upon departure from precedent. Just now it is a fad to put ice in champagne. The idea was originated by a visiting Prince of Tartary while dining at the Waldorf. It will soon give way to some other whim. Just as at a dinner party this week on Madison Avenue a green kid glove was laid by the plate of each guest to be put on and used while eating olives."

"I see," admitted the young man, humbly. "These special diversions of the inner circle do not become familiar to the common public."

"Sometimes," continued the girl, acknowledging his confession of error by a slight bow, "I have thought that if I ever should love a man it would be one of lowly station. One who is a worker and not a drone. But, doubtless, the claims of caste and wealth will prove stronger than my inclination. Just now I am besieged by two. One is a Grand Duke of a German principality. I think he has, or has had, a wife, somewhere, driven mad by his intemperance and cruelty. The other is an English Marquis, so cold and mercenary that I even prefer the diabolism of the Duke. What is it that impels me to tell you these things, Mr. Packenstaker?"

"Parkenstacker," breathed the young man. "Indeed, you cannot know how much I appreciate your confidences."

The girl contemplated him with a calm, impersonal regard that befitted the difference in their stations.

"What is your line of business, Mr. Parkenstacker?" she asked.

"A very humble one. But I hope to rise in the world. Were you really in earnest when you said that you could love a man of lowly position?"

"Indeed I was. But I said 'might.' There is the Grand Duke and the Marquis, you know. Yes; no calling could be too humble were the man what I would wish him to be."

"I work," declared Mr. Parkenstacker, "in a restaurant."

The girl shrank slightly.

"Not as a waiter?" she said a little imploringly. "Labor is noble, but—personal attendance, you know—valets and——"

"I am not a waiter. I am cashier in"—on the street they faced that bounded the opposite side of the park was the brilliant electric sign "RESTAURANT"—"I am cashier in that restaurant you see there."

The girl consulted a tiny watch set in a bracelet of rich design upon her left wrist, and rose, hurriedly. She thrust her book into a glittering reticule suspended from her waist, for which, however, the book was too large.

"Why are you not at work?" she asked.

"I am on the night turn," said the young man; "it is yet an hour before my period begins. May I not hope to see you again?"

"I do not know. Perhaps—but the whim may not seize me again. I must go quickly now. There is a dinner, and a box at the play—and, oh! the same old round. Perhaps you noticed an automobile at the upper corner of the park as you came. One with a white body."

"And red running gear?" asked the young man, knitting his brows reflectively.

"Yes. I always come in that. Pierre waits for me there. He supposes me to be shopping in the department store across the square. Conceive of the bondage of the life wherein we must deceive even our chauffeurs. Good-night."

"But it is dark now," said Mr. Parkenstacker, "and the park is full of rude men. May I not walk——?"

"If you have the slightest regard for my wishes," said the girl firmly, "you will remain at this bench for ten minutes after I have left. I do not mean to accuse you, but you are probably aware that autos generally bear the monogram of their owner. Again, good-night."

Swift and stately she moved away through the dusk. The young man watched her graceful form as she reached the pavement at the park's edge, and turned up along it toward the corner where stood the automobile. Then he treacherously and unhesitatingly began to dodge and skim among the park trees and shrubbery in a course parallel to her route, keeping her well in sight.

When she reached the corner she turned her head to glance at the motor car, and then passed it, continuing on across the street. Sheltered behind a convenient standing cab, the young man followed her movements closely with his eyes. Passing down the sidewalk of the street opposite the park, she entered the restaurant with the blazing sign. The place was one of those frankly glaring establishments, all white paint and glass, where one may dine cheaply and conspicuously. The girl penetrated the restaurant to some retreat at its rear, whence she quickly emerged without her hat and veil.

The cashier's desk was well to the front. A red-haired girl on the stool climbed down, glancing pointedly at the clock as she did so. The girl in gray mounted in her place.

The young man thrust his hands into his pockets and walked slowly back along the sidewalk. At the corner his foot struck a small, paper-covered volume lying there, sending it sliding to the edge of the turf. By its picturesque cover he recognized it as the book the girl had been reading. He picked it up carelessly, and saw that its title was "New Arabian Nights," the author being of the name of Stevenson. He dropped it again upon the grass, and lounged, irresolute, for a minute. Then he stepped into the automobile, reclined upon the cushions, and said two words to the chauffeur:

"Club, Henri."

Suite Homes and Their Romance

Few young couples in the Big-City-of-Bluff began their married existence with greater promise of happiness than did Mr. and Mrs. Claude Turpin. They felt no especial animosity toward each other; they were comfortably established in a handsome apartment house that had a name and accommodations like those of a sleeping car; they were living as expensively as the couple on the next floor above who had twice their income; and their marriage had occurred on a wager, a ferryboat, and first acquaintance, thus securing a sensational newspaper notice of their names attached to pictures of the Queen of Roumania and M. Santos-Dumont.

Turpin's income was $200 per month. On payday, after calculating the amounts due for rent, installments on furniture and piano, gas, and bills owed to the florist, confectioner, milliner, tailor, wine merchant, and cab company, the Turpins would find that they still had $200 left to spend. How to do this is one of the secrets of metropolitan life.

The domestic life of the Turpins was a beautiful picture to see. But you couldn't gaze upon it as you could at an oleograph of "Don't Wake Grandma," or "Brooklyn by Moonlight."

You had to blink when you looked at it; and you heard a fizzing sound just like the machine with a "scope" at the end of it. Yes; there wasn't much repose about the picture of the Turpin's domestic life. It was something like "Spearing Salmon in the Columbia River," or "Japanese Artillery in Action."

Every day was just like another; as the days are in New York. In the morning Turpin would take bromo seltzer, his pocket change from under the clock, his hat, no breakfast, and his departure for the office. At noon Mrs. Turpin would get out of bed and humor, put on a kimono, airs, and the water to boil for coffee.

Turpin lunched downtown. He came home at six to dress for dinner. They always dined out. They strayed from the chophouse to chop-sueydom, from terrace to table d'hôte, from rathskeller to road-house, from café to casino, from Maria's to Martha Washington. Such is domestic life in the great city. Your vine is the mistletoe; your fig tree bears dates. Your household gods are Mercury and John Howard Payne. For the wedding march you now hear only "Come with the Gypsy Bride." You rarely dine at the same place twice in succession. You tire of the food; and besides, you want to give them time for the question of that souvenir silver sugar bowl to blow over.

The Turpins were therefore happy. They made many warm and delightful friends, some of whom they remembered the next day. Their home life was an ideal one, according to the rules and regulations of the Book of Bluff.

There came a time when it dawned upon Turpin that his wife was getting away with too much money. If you belong to the near-swell class in the Big City, and your income is $200 per month, and you find at the end of the month, after looking over the bills for current expenses, that you, yourself, have spent $150, you very naturally wonder what has become of the other $50. So you suspect your wife. And perhaps you give her a hint that something needs explanation.

"I say, Vivien," said Turpin one afternoon when they were enjoying in rapt silence the peace and quiet of their cozy apartment, "you've been creating a hiatus big enough for a dog to crawl through in this month's honorarium. You haven't been paying your dressmaker anything on account, have you?"

There was a moment's silence. No sounds could be heard except the breathing of the fox terrier, and the subdued, monotonous sizzling of Vivien's fulvous locks against the insensate curling irons. Claude Turpin, sitting upon a pillow that he had thoughtfully placed upon the convolutions of the apartment sofa, narrowly watched the riante, lovely face of his wife.

"Claudie, dear," said she, touching her finger to her ruby tongue and testing the unresponsive curling irons, "you do me an injustice. Mme. Toinette has not seen a cent of mine since the day you paid your tailor ten dollars on account."

Turpin's suspicions were allayed for the time. But one day soon there came an anonymous letter to him that read:

Watch your wife. She is blowing in your money secretly. I was a sufferer just as you are. The place is No. 345 Blank Street. A word to the wise, etc.

A Man Who Knows

Turpin took this letter to the captain of the police precinct that he lived in.

"My precinct is as clean as a hound's tooth," said the captain. "The lid's shut down as close there as it is over the eye of a Williamsburg girl when she's kissed at a party. But if you think there's anything queer at the address, I'll go there with ye."

On the next afternoon at three, Turpin and the captain crept softly up the stairs of No. 345 Blank Street. A dozen plainclothes men, dressed in full police uniforms, so as to allay suspicion, waited in the hall below.

At the top of the stairs was a door, which was found to be locked. The captain took a key from his pocket and unlocked it. The two men entered.

They found themselves in a large room, occupied by twenty or twenty-five elegantly clothed ladies. Racing charts hung against the walls, a ticker clicked in one corner; with a telephone receiver to his ear a man was calling out the various positions of the horses in a very exciting race. The occupants of the room looked up at the intruders; but, as if reassured by the sight of the captain's uniform, they reverted their attention to the man at the telephone.

"You see," said the captain to Turpin, "the value of an anonymous letter! No high-minded and self-respecting gentleman should consider one worthy of notice. Is your wife among this assembly, Mr. Turpin?"

"She is not," said Turpin.

"And if she was," continued the captain, "would she be within the reach of the tongue of slander? These ladies constitute a Browning Society. They meet to discuss the meaning of the great poet. The telephone is connected with Boston, whence the parent society transmits frequently its interpretations of the poems. Be ashamed of yer suspicions, Mr. Turpin."

"Go soak your shield," said Turpin. "Vivien knows how to take care of herself in a poolroom. She's not dropping anything on the ponies. There must be something queer going on here."

"Nothing but Browning," said the captain. "Hear that?"

"Thanatopsis by a nose," drawled the man at the telephone.

"That's not Browning; that's Longfellow," said Turpin, who sometimes read books.

"Back to the pasture!" exclaimed the captain. "Longfellow made the pacing-to-wagon record of 7.53 'way back in 1868."

"I believe there's something queer about this joint," repeated Turpin.

"I don't see it," said the captain.

"I know it looks like a poolroom, all right," persisted Turpin, "but that's all a blind. Vivien has been dropping a lot of coin somewhere. I believe there's some underhanded work going on here."

A number of racing sheets were tacked close together, covering a large space on one of the walls. Turpin, suspicious, tore several of them down. A door, previously hidden, was revealed. Turpin placed an ear to the crack and listened intently. He heard the soft hum of many voices, low and guarded laughter, and a sharp, metallic clicking and scraping as if from a multitude of tiny but busy objects.

"My God! It is as I feared!" whispered Turpin to himself. "Summon your men at once!" he called to the captain. "She is in there, I know."

At the blowing of the captain's whistle the uniformed plain-clothes men rushed up the stairs into the poolroom. When they saw the betting paraphernalia distributed around they halted, surprised and puzzled to know why they had been summoned.

But the captain pointed to the locked door and bade them break it down. In a few moments they demolished it with the axes they carried. Into the other room sprang Claude Turpin, with the captain at his heels.

The scene was one that lingered long in Turpin's mind. Nearly a score of women—women expensively and fashionably clothed, many beautiful and of refined appearance—had been seated at little marble-topped tables. When the police burst open the door they shrieked and ran here and there like gaily plumed birds that had been disturbed in a tropical grove. Some became hysterical; one or two fainted; several knelt at the feet of the officers and besought them for mercy on account of their families and social position.

A man who had been seated behind a desk had seized a roll of currency as large as the ankle of a Paradise Roof Gardens chorus girl and jumped out of the window. Half a dozen attendants huddled at one end of the room, breathless from fear.

Upon the tables remained the damning and incontrovertible evidences of the guilt of the habituées of that sinister room—dish after dish heaped high with ice cream, and surrounded by stacks of empty ones, scraped to the last spoonful.

"Ladies," said the captain to his weeping circle of prisoners, "I'll not hold any of yez. Some of yez I recognize as having fine houses and good standing in the community, with hardworking husbands and childer at home. But I'll read ye a bit of lecture before ye go. In the next room there's a twenty-to-one shot just dropped in under the wire three lengths ahead of the field. Is this the way we waste your husbands' money instead of helping earn it? Home wid yez! The lid's on the ice-cream freezer in this precinct."

Claude Turpin's wife was among the patrons of the raided room. He led her to the apartment in stern silence. There she wept so remorsefully and besought his forgiveness so pleadingly that he forgot his just anger, and soon he gathered his penitent golden-haired Vivien in his arms and forgave her.

"Darling," she murmured, half sobbingly, as the moonlight drifted through the open window, glorifying her sweet, upturned face. "I know I done wrong. I will never touch ice cream again. I forgot you were not a millionaire. I used to go there every day. But today I felt some strange, sad presentiment of evil, and I was not myself. I ate only eleven saucers."

"Say no more," said Claude gently, as he fondly caressed her waving curls.

"And you are sure that you fully forgive me?" asked Vivien, gazing at him entreatingly with dewy eyes of heavenly blue.

"Almost sure, little one," answered Claude, stooping and lightly touching her snowy forehead with his lips. "I'll let you know later on. I've got a month's salary down on Vanilla to win the three-year-old steeplechase tomorrow; and if the ice-cream hunch is to the good you are It again—see?"

Hearts and Hands

At Denver there was an influx of passengers into the coaches on the eastbound B. & M. express. In one coach there sat a very pretty young woman dressed in elegant taste and surrounded by all the luxurious comforts of an experienced traveler. Among the new-comers were two young men, one of handsome presence, with a bold, frank countenance and manner; the other a ruffled, glum-faced person, heavily built and roughly dressed. The two were handcuffed together.

As they passed down the aisle of the coach the only vacant seat offered was a reversed one facing the attractive young woman. Here the linked couple seated themselves. The young woman's glance fell upon them with a distant, swift disinterest; then, with a lovely smile brightening her countenance and a tender pink tingeing her rounded cheeks, she held out a little gray-gloved hand. When she spoke her voice, full, sweet and deliberate, proclaimed that its owner was accustomed to speak and be heard.

"Well, Mr. Easton, if you *will* make me speak first, I suppose I must. Don't you ever recognize old friends when you meet them in the West?"

The younger man roused himself sharply at the sound of her voice, seemed to struggle with a slight embarrassment which he threw off instantly, and then clasped her fingers with his left hand.

"It's Miss Fairchild," he said with a smile. "I'll ask you to excuse the other hand; it's otherwise engaged just at present."

He slightly raised his right hand, bound at the wrist by the shining "bracelet" to the left one of his companion. The glad look in the girl's eyes slowly changed to a bewildered horror. The glow faded from her cheeks. Her lips parted in a vague, relaxing distress. Easton, with a little laugh as if amused, was about to speak again when the other forestalled him. The glum-faced man had been watching the girl's countenance with veiled glances from his keen, shrewd eyes.

"You'll excuse me for speaking, miss, but I see you're acquainted with the marshal here. If you'll ask him to speak a word for me when we get to the pen he'll do it, and it'll make things easier for me there. He's taking me to Leavenworth prison. It's seven years for counterfeiting."

"Oh!" said the girl with a deep breath and returning color. "So, that is what you are doing out here? A marshal!"

"My dear Miss Fairchild," said Easton calmly, "I had to do something. Money has a way of taking wings unto itself, and you know it takes money to keep step with our crowd in Washington. I saw this opening in the West, and—well, a marshalship isn't quite as high a position as that of ambassador, but——"

"The ambassador," said the girl warmly, "doesn't call any more. He needn't ever have done so. You ought to know that. And so now you are one of these dashing Western heroes, and you ride and shoot and go into all kinds of dangers. That's different from the Washington life. You have been missed from the old crowd."

The girl's eyes, fascinated, went back, widening a little, to rest upon the glittering handcuffs.

"Don't you worry about them, miss," said the other man. "All marshals handcuff themselves to their prisoners to keep them from getting away. Mr. Easton knows his business."

"Will we see you again soon in Washington?" asked the girl.

"Not soon, I think," said Easton. "My butterfly days are over, I fear."

"I love the West," said the girl, irrelevantly. Her eyes were shining softly. She looked away out the car window. She began to speak truly and simply, without the gloss of style and manner. "Mamma and I spent the Summer in Denver. She went home a week ago because father was slightly ill. I could live and be happy in the West. I think the air here agrees with me. Money isn't everything. But people always misunderstand things and remain stupid——"

"Say, Mr. Marshal," growled the glum-faced man, "This isn't quite fair. I'm needin' a drink, and haven't had a smoke all day.

Haven't you talked long enough? Take me in the smoker now, won't you? I'm half dead for a pipe."

The bound travelers rose to their feet, Easton with the same slow smile on his face.

"I can't deny a petition for tobacco," he said lightly. "It's the one friend of the unfortunate. Good-bye, Miss Fairchild. Duty calls, you know." He held out his hand for a farewell.

"It's too bad you are not going East," she said, reclothing herself with manner and style. "But you must go on to Leavenworth, I suppose?"

"Yes," said Easton, "I must go on to Leavenworth."

The two men sidled down the aisle into the smoker.

Two passengers in a seat nearby had heard most of the conversation. Said one of them: "That's marshal's a good sort of chap. Some of these Western fellows are all right."

"Pretty young to hold an office like that, isn't he?" asked the other.

"Young!" exclaimed the first speaker, "why—— Oh! didn't you catch on? Say—did you ever know an officer to handcuff a prisoner to his *right* hand?"

The Trimmed Lamp

Of course there are two sides to the question. Let us look at the other. We often hear "shopgirls" spoken of. No such persons exist. There are girls who work in shops. They make their living that way. But why turn their occupation into an adjective? Let us be fair. We do not refer to the girls who live on Fifth Avenue as "marriage girls."

Lou and Nancy were chums. They came to the big city to find work because there was not enough to eat at home to go around. Nancy was nineteen; Lou was twenty. Both were pretty, active, country girls who had no ambition to go on the stage.

The little cherub that sits up aloft guided them to a cheap and respectable boarding house. Both found positions and became wage-earners. They remained chums. It is at the end of six months that I would beg you to step forward and be introduced to them. Gentle Reader: My lady friends, Miss Nancy and Miss Lou. While you are shaking hands please take notice—cautiously—of their attire. Yes, cautiously; for they are as quick to resent a stare as a lady in a box at the horse show.

Lou is a piecework ironer in a hand laundry. She is clothed in a badly fitting purple dress, and her hat plume is four inches too long; but her ermine muff and scarf cost $25, and its fellow beasts will be ticketed in the windows at $7.98 before the season is over. Her cheeks are pink, and her light blue eyes bright. Contentment radiates from her.

Nancy you would call a shopgirl—because you have the habit. There is no type; but a perverse generation is always seeking a type; so this is what the type should be. She has the high-ratted pompadour, and the exaggerated straight front. Her skirt is shoddy, but has the correct flare. No furs protect her against the bitter spring air, but she wears her short broadcloth jacket as jauntily as though it were Persian lamb! On her face and in her eyes, remorseless type-seeker, is the typical shopgirl expression. It is a look of silent but contemptuous revolt against cheated womanhood; of sad prophecy of the vengeance to come. When she laughs her loudest the look is still there. The same look can be seen in the eyes of Russian peasants; and those of us left will see it someday on Gabriel's face when he comes to blow us up. It is a look that should wither and abash man; but he has been known to smirk at it and offer flowers—with a string tied to them.

Now lift your hat and come away, while you receive Lou's cheery "See you again," and the sardonic, sweet smile of Nancy that seems, somehow, to miss you and go fluttering like a white moth up over the housetops to the stars.

The two waited on the corner for Dan. Dan was Lou's steady company. Faithful? Well he was on hand when Mary would have had to hire a dozen subpoena servers to find her lamb.

"Ain't you cold, Nance?" said Lou. "Say, what a chump you are for working in that old store for eight dollars a week! I made eighteen fifty last week. Of course ironing ain't as swell work as selling lace behind a counter, but it pays. None of us ironers make less than ten dollars. And I don't know that it's any less respectful work, either."

"You can have it," said Nancy with uplifted nose. "I'll take my eight a week and hall bedroom. I like to be among nice things and swell people. And look what a chance I've got! Why, one of our glove girls married a Pittsburg—steel maker, or blacksmith or something—the other day worth a million dollars. I'll catch a swell myself sometime. I ain't bragging on my looks or anything; but I'll take my chances where there's big prizes offered. What show would a girl have in a laundry?"

"Why, that's where I met Dan," said Lou triumphantly. "He came in for his Sunday shirt and collars and saw me at the first board, ironing. We all try to get to work at the first board. Ella Maginnis was sick that day, and I had her place. He said he noticed my arms first, how round and white they was. I had my sleeves rolled up. Some nice fellows come into laundries. You can tell 'em by their bringing their clothes in suitcases, and turning in the door sharp and sudden."

"How can you wear a waist like that, Lou?" said Nancy, gazing down at the offending article with sweet scorn in her heavy-lidded eyes. "It shows fierce taste."

"This waist?" cried Lou with wide-eyed indignation. "Why, I paid sixteen dollars for this waist. It's worth twenty-five. A woman left it to be laundered, and never called for it. The boss sold it to me. It's got yards and yards of hand embroidery on it. Better talk about that ugly, plain thing you've got on."

"This ugly, plain thing," said Nancy calmly, "was copied from one that Mrs. Van Alstyne Fisher was wearing. The girls say her bill in the store last year was twelve thousand dollars. I made mine, myself. It cost me a dollar fifty. Ten feet away you couldn't tell it from hers."

"Oh, well," said Lou good-naturedly, "if you want to starve and put on airs, go ahead. But I'll take my job and good wages; and after hours give me something as fancy and attractive to wear as I am able to buy."

But just then Dan came—a serious young man with a ready-made necktie, who had escaped the city's brand of frivolity—an electrician earning $30 per week who looked upon Lou with the sad eyes of Romeo, and thought her embroidered waist a web in which any fly should delight to be caught.

"My friend, Mr. Owens—shake hands with Miss Danforth," said Lou.

"I'm mighty glad to know you, Miss Danforth," said Dan with outstretched hand. "I've heard Lou speak of you so often."

"Thanks," said Nancy, touching his fingers with the tips of her cool ones. "I've heard her mention you—a few times."

Lou giggled.

"Did you get that handshake from Mrs. Van Alstyne Fisher, Nance?" she asked.

"If I did, you can feel safe in copying it," said Nancy.

"Oh, I couldn't use it at all. It's too stylish for me. It's intended to set off diamond rings, that high shake is. Wait till I get a few and then I'll try it."

"Learn it first," said Nancy wisely, "and you'll be more likely to get the rings."

"Now, to settle this argument," said Dan, with his ready, cheerful smile, "let me make a proposition. As I can't take both of you up to Tiffany's and do the right thing, what do you say to a little vaudeville? I've got the tickets. How about looking at stage diamonds, since we can't shake hands with the real sparklers?"

The faithful squire took his place close to the curb; Lou next, a little peacocky in her bright and pretty clothes; Nancy on the inside, slender, and soberly clothed as the sparrow, but with the true Van Alstyne Fisher walk—thus they set out for their evening's moderate diversion.

I do not suppose that many look upon a great department store as an educational institution. But the one in which Nancy worked was something like that to her. She was surrounded by beautiful things that breathed of taste and refinement. If you live in an atmosphere of luxury, luxury is yours whether your money pays for it, or another's.

The people she served were mostly women whose dress, manners, and position in the social world were quoted as criterions. From them Nancy began to take toll—the best from each according to her view.

From one she would copy and practice a gesture, from another an eloquent lifting of an eyebrow, from others, a manner of walking, of carrying a purse, of smiling, of greeting a friend, of addressing "inferiors in station." From her best beloved model, Mrs. Van Alstyne Fisher, she made requisition for that excellent thing, a soft, low voice as clear as silver and as perfect in articulation as the notes of a thrush. Suffused in the aura of this high social refinement and good breeding, it was impossible for her to escape a deeper effect of it. As good habits are said to be better than good principles, so, perhaps, good manners are better than good habits. The teachings of your parents may not keep alive your New England conscience; but if you sit on a straight-back chair and repeat the words "prisms and pilgrims" forty times the devil will flee from you. And when Nancy spoke in the Van Alstyne Fisher tones she felt the thrill of *noblesse oblige* to her very bones.

There was another source of learning in the great departmental school. Whenever you see three or four shopgirls gather in a bunch, and jingle their wire bracelets as an accompaniment to apparently frivolous conversation, do not think that they are there for the purpose of criticizing the way Ethel does her back hair. The meeting may lack the dignity of the deliberative bodies of man; but it has all the importance of the occasion on which Eve and her first daughter first put their heads together to make Adam understand his proper place in the household. It is Woman's Conference for Common Defense and Exchange of Strategical Theories of Attack and Repulse upon and against the World, which is a Stage, and Man, its Chief Usher, who Persists in Throwing Bouquets Thereupon. Woman, the most helpless of the young of any animal—with the fawn's grace but without its fleetness; with the bird's beauty but without its power of flight; with the honeybee's burden of sweetness but without its—Oh, let's drop the similes —some of us may have been stung.

During this council of war they pass weapons one to another, and exchange stratagems that each has devised and formulated out of the tactics of life.

"I says to 'im," says Sadie, "ain't you the fresh thing! Who do you suppose I am, to be addressing such a remark to me? And what do you think he says back to me?"

The heads, brown, black, flaxen, red, and yellow bob together; the answer is given; and the parry to the thrust is decided upon, to be used by each thereafter in passages-at-arms with the common enemy, man.

Thus Nancy learned the art of defense; and to a woman successful defense means victory.

The curriculum of a department store is a wide one. Perhaps no other college could have fitted her as well for her life's ambition—the drawing of a matrimonial prize.

Her station in the store was a favored one. The music room was near enough for her to hear and become familiar with the works of the best composers—at least to acquire the familiarity that passed for appreciation in the social world in which she was vaguely trying to set a tentative and aspiring foot. She absorbed the educating influence of art wares of costly and dainty fabrics, of adornments that are almost culture to women.

The other girls soon became aware of Nancy's ambition. "Here comes your millionaire, Nance," they would call to her whenever any man who looked the role approached her counter. It got to be a habit of men, who were hanging about while their womenfolk were shopping, to stroll over the handkerchief counter and dawdle over the cambric squares. Nancy's imitation, high-bred air and genuine dainty beauty was what attracted. Many men thus came to display their graces before her. Some of them may have been millionaires; others were certainly no more than their sedulous apes. Nancy learned to discriminate. There was a window at the end of the handkerchief counter; and she could see the rows of vehicles waiting for the shoppers in the street below. She looked, and perceived that automobiles differ as well as do their owners.

Once a fascinating gentleman bought four dozen handkerchiefs, and wooed her across the counter with a King Cophetua air. When he had gone one of the girls said: "What's wrong, Nance, that you didn't warm up to that fellow? He looks the swell article, all right, to me."

"Him?" said Nancy with her coolest, sweetest, most impersonal, Van Alstyne Fisher smile; "not for mine. I saw him drive up outside. A twelve H.P. machine and an Irish chauffeur! And you saw what kind of handkerchiefs he bought—silk! And he's got dactylis on him. Give me the real thing or nothing, if you please."

Two of the most "refined" women in the store—a forelady and a cashier—had a few "swell gentlemen friends" with whom they now and then dined. Once they included Nancy in an invitation. The dinner took place in a spectacular café whose tables are engaged for New Year's Eve a year in advance. There were two "gentlemen friends"—one without any hair on his head—high living ungrew it; and we can prove it—the other a young man whose worth and sophistication he impressed upon you in two convincing ways—he swore that all the wine was corked; and he wore diamond cuff buttons. This young man perceived irresistible excellencies in Nancy. His taste ran to shopgirls; and here was one that added the voice and manners of his high social world to the franker charms of her own caste. So, on the following day, he appeared in the store and made her a serious proposal of marriage over a box of hemstitched, grass-bleached Irish linens. Nancy declined. A brown pompadour ten feet away had been using her eyes and ears. When the rejected suitor had gone she heaped carboys of upbraidings and horror upon Nancy's head.

"What a terrible little fool you are! That fellow's a millionaire—he's a nephew of old Van Skittles himself. And he was talking on the level, too. Have you gone crazy, Nance?"

"Have I?" said Nancy. "I didn't like him, did I? He isn't a millionaire so much that you could notice it, anyhow. His family only allows him twenty thousand dollars a year to spend. The bald-headed fellow was guying him about it the other night at supper."

The brown pompadour came nearer and narrowed her eyes.

"Say, what do you want?" she inquired, in a voice hoarse for lack of chewing gum. "Ain't that enough for you? Do you want to be a Mormon, and marry Rockefeller and Gladstone Dowie and the King of Spain and the whole bunch? Ain't twenty thousand a year good enough for you?"

Nancy flushed a little under the level gaze of the black, shallow eyes.

"It wasn't altogether the money, Carrie," she explained. "His friend caught him in a rank lie the other night at dinner. It was about some girl he said he hadn't been to the theater with. Well, I can't stand a liar. Put everything together—I don't like him; and that settles it. When I sell out it's not going to be on any bargain day. I've got to have something that sits up in a chair like a man, anyhow. Yes, I'm looking out for a catch; but it's got to be able to do something more than make a noise like a toy bank."

"The physiopathic ward for yours!" said the brown pompadour, walking away.

These high ideas, if not ideals, Nancy continued to cultivate on $8 per week. She bivouacked on the trail of the great unknown "catch," eating her dry bread and tightening her belt day by day. On her face was the faint, soldierly, sweet, grim smile of the preordained man-hunter. The store was her forest; and many times she raised her rifle at game that seemed broad-antlered and big; but always some deep unerring instinct—perhaps of the huntress, perhaps of the woman—made her hold her fire and take up the trail again.

Lou flourished in the laundry. Out of her $18.50 per week she paid $6 for her room and board. The rest went mainly for clothes. Her opportunities for bettering her taste and manners were few compared with Nancy's. In the steaming laundry there was nothing but work, work and her thoughts of the evening pleasures to come. Many costly and showy fabrics passed under her iron; and it may be that her growing fondness for dress was thus transmitted to her through the conducting metal.

When the day's work was over Dan awaited her outside, her faithful shadow in whatever light she stood.

Sometimes he cast an honest and troubled glance at Lou's clothes, that increased in conspicuity rather than in style; but this was no disloyalty; he deprecated the attention they called to her in the streets.

And Lou was no less faithful to her chum. There was a law that Nancy should go with them on whatsoever outings they might take. Dan bore the extra burden heartily and in good cheer. It might be said that Lou furnished the color, Nancy the tone, and Dan the weight of the distraction-seeking trio. The escort, in his neat but obviously ready-made suit, his ready-made tie and unfailing, genial, ready-made wit never startled or clashed. He was of that good kind that you are likely to forget while they are present, but remember distinctly after they are gone.

To Nancy's superior taste the flavor of these ready-made pleasures was sometimes a little bitter: but she was young; and youth is a gourmand when it cannot be a gourmet.

"Dan is always wanting me to marry him right away," Lou told her once. "But why should I? I'm independent. I can do as I please with the money I earn; and he never would agree for me to keep on working afterward. And say, Nance, what do you want to stick to that old store for, and half starve and half dress yourself? I could get you a place in the laundry right now if you'd come. It seems to me that you could afford to be a little less stuck-up if you could make a good deal more money."

"I don't think I'm stuck-up, Lou," said Nancy, "but I'd rather live on half rations and stay where I am. I suppose I've got the habit. It's the chance that I want. I don't expect to be always behind a counter. I'm learning something new every day. I'm right up against refined and rich people all the time—even if I do only wait on them; and I'm not missing any pointers that I see passing around."

"Caught your millionaire yet?" asked Lou with her teasing laugh.

"I haven't selected one yet," answered Nancy. "I've been looking them over."

"Goodness! The idea of picking over 'em! Don't you ever let one get by you Nance—even if he's a few dollars shy. But of course you're joking—millionaires don't think about working girls like us."

"It might be better for them if they did," said Nancy, with cool wisdom. "Some of us could teach them how to take care of their money."

"If one was to speak to me," laughed Lou, "I know I'd have a duck fit."

"That's because you don't know any. The only difference between swells and other people is you have to watch 'em closer. Don't you think that red silk lining is just a little bit too bright for that coat, Lou?"

Lou looked at the plain, dull olive jacket of her friend.

"Well, no I don't—but it may seem so beside that faded-looking thing you've got on."

"This jacket," said Nancy compacently, "has exactly the cut and fit of one that Mrs. Van Alstyne Fisher was wearing the other day.

The material cost me three ninety-eight. I suppose hers cost about a hundred dollars more.

"Oh, well," said Lou lightly, "it don't strike me as millionaire bait. Shouldn't wonder if I catch one before you do, anyway."

Truly it would have taken a philosopher to decide upon the values of the theories held by the two friends. Lou, lacking that certain pride and fastidiousness that keeps stores and desks filled with girls working for the barest living, thumped away gaily with her iron in the noisy and stifling laundry. Her wages supported her even beyond the point of comfort; so that her dress profited until sometimes she cast a sidelong glance of impatience at the neat but inelegant apparel of Dan—Dan the constant, the immutable, the undeviating.

As for Nancy, her case was one of tens of thousands. Silk and jewels and laces and ornaments and the perfume and music of the fine world of good-breeding and taste—these were made for woman; they are her equitable portion. Let her keep near them if they are a part of life to her, and if she will. She is no traitor to herself, as Esau was; for she keeps her birthright and the pottage she earns is often very scant.

In this atmosphere Nancy belonged; and she throve in it and ate her frugal meals and schemed over her cheap dresses with a determined and contented mind. She already knew woman; and she was studying man, the animal, both as to his habits and eligibility. Someday she would bring down the game that she wanted; but she promised herself it would be what seemed to her the biggest and the best, and nothing smaller.

Thus she kept her lamp trimmed and burning to receive the bridegroom when he should come.

But another lesson she learned, perhaps unconsciously. Her standard of values began to shift and change. Sometimes the dollar-mark grew blurred in her mind's eye, and shaped itself into letters that spelled such words as "truth" and "honor" and now and then just "kindness." Let us make a likeness of one who hunts the moose or elk in some mighty wood. He sees a little dell, mossy and embowered, where a rill trickles, babbling to him of rest and comfort. At these times the spear of Nimrod himself grows blunt.

So Nancy wondered sometimes if Persian lamb was always quoted at its market value by the hearts that it covered.

One Thursday evening Nancy left the store and turned across Sixth Avenue westward to the laundry. She was expected to go with Lou and Dan to a musical comedy.

Dan was just coming out of the laundry when she arrived. There was a queer, strained look on his face.

"I thought I would drop around to see if they had heard from her," he said.

"Heard from who?" asked Nancy. "Isn't Lou there?"

"I thought you knew," said Dan. "She hasn't been here or at the house where she lived since Monday. She moved all her things from there. She told one of the girls in the laundry she might be going to Europe."

"Hasn't anybody seen her anywhere?" asked Nancy.

Dan looked at her with his jaw set grimly and a steely gleam in his steady gray eyes.

"They told me in the laundry," he said harshly, "that they saw her pass yesterday—in an automobile. With one of the millionaires, I suppose, that you and Lou were forever busying your brains about."

For the first time Nancy quailed before a man. She laid her hand that trembled slightly on Dan's sleeve.

"You've no right to say such a thing to me Dan—as if I had anything to do with it!"

"I didn't mean it that way," said Dan, softening. He fumbled in his vest pocket.

"I've got the tickets for the show tonight," he said with a gallant show of lightness. "If you——"

Nancy admired pluck whenever she saw it.

"I'll go with you, Dan," she said.

THREE MONTHS WENT by before Nancy saw Lou again.

At twilight one evening the shopgirl was hurrying home along the border of a little quiet park. She heard her name called, and wheeled about in time to catch Lou rushing into her arms.

After the first embrace they drew their heads back as serpents do, ready to attack or to charm, with a thousand questions trembling on their swift tongues. And then Nancy noticed that prosperity had descended upon Lou, manifesting itself in costly furs, flashing gems, and creations of the tailors' art.

"You little fool!" cried Lou loudly and affectionately. "I see you are still working in that store, and as shabby as ever. And how about that big catch you were going to make—nothing doing yet, I suppose?"

And then Lou looked, and saw that something better than prosperity had descended upon Nancy—something that shone brighter than gems in her eyes and redder than a rose in her cheeks, and that danced like electricity anxious to be loosed from the tip of her tongue.

"Yes, I'm still in the store," said Nancy, "but I'm going to leave it next week. I've made my catch—the biggest catch in the world. You won't mind now Lou, will you?—I'm going to be married to Dan—to Dan!—he's my Dan now—why, Lou!"

Around the corner of the park strolled one of those new-crop, smooth-faced young policemen that are making the force more endurable—at least to the eye. He saw a woman with an expensive fur coat and diamond-ringed hands crouching down against the iron fence of the park sobbing turbulently, while a slender, plainly dressed working girl leaned close, trying to console her. But the Gibsonian cop, being of the new order, passed on, pretending not to notice, for he was wise enough to know that these matters are beyond help, so far as the power he represents is concerned, though he rap the pavement with his nightstick till the sound goes up to the furthermost stars.

CONFESSIONS OF A HUMORIST

THERE WAS A painless stage of incubation that lasted twenty-five years, and then it broke out on me, and people said I was It.

But they called it humor instead of measles.

The employees in the store bought a silver inkstand for the senior partner on his fiftieth birthday. We crowded into his private office to present it.

I had been selected for spokesman, and I made a little speech that I had been preparing for a week.

It made a hit. It was full of puns and epigrams and funny twists that brought down the house (which was a very solid one in the whole-sale hardware line). Old Marlowe himself actually grinned, and the employees took their cue and roared.

My reputation as a humorist dates from half-past nine o'clock on that morning.

For weeks afterward my fellow clerks fanned the flame of my self-esteem. One by one they came to me, saying what an awfully clever speech that was, old man, and carefully explained to me the point of each one of my jokes.

Gradually I found that I was expected to keep it up. Others might speak sanely on business matters and the day's topics, but from me something gamesome and airy was required.

I was expected to crack jokes about the crockery and lighten up the granite ware with *persiflage*. I was second bookkeeper, and if I failed to show up a balance sheet without something comic about the footings or could find no cause for laughter in an invoice of plows, the other clerks were disappointed.

By degrees my fame spread, and I became a local "character." Our town was small enough to make this possible. The daily newspaper often quoted my sayings. At social gatherings I was indispensable.

I believe I did possess considerable wit and a facility for quick and spontaneous repartee. This gift I cultivated and improved by practice. And the nature of it was kindly and genial, not running to sarcasm or offending others. People began to smile when they saw me coming, and by the time we had met I generally had the word ready to broaden the smile into a laugh.

I had married early. We had a charming boy of three and a girl of five. Naturally, we lived in a vine-covered cottage, and were happy. My salary as bookkeeper in the hardware concern kept at a distance those ills attendant upon superfluous wealth.

At sundry times I had written out a few jokes and conceits that I considered peculiarly happy, and had sent them to certain periodicals that print such things. All of them had been instantly accepted. Several of the editors had written to request further contributions.

One day I received a letter from the editor of a famous weekly publication. He suggested that I submit to him a humorous composition to fill a column of space; hinting that he would make it a regular feature of each issue if the work proved satisfactory. I did so, and at the end of two weeks he offered to make a contract with me for a year at a figure that was considerably higher than the amount paid me by the hardware firm.

I was filled with delight. My wife already crowned me in her mind with the imperishable evergreens of literary success. We had lobster croquettes and a bottle of blackberry wine for supper that night. Here was the chance to liberate myself from drudgery. I talked over the matter very seriously with Louisa. We agreed that I must resign my place at the store and devote myself to humor.

I resigned. My fellow clerks gave me a farewell banquet. The speech I made there coruscated. It was printed in full by the *Gazette*. The next morning I awoke and looked at the clock.

"Late, by George!" I exclaimed, and grabbed for my clothes. Louisa reminded me that I was no longer a slave to hardware and contractors' supplies. I was now a professional humorist.

After breakfast she proudly led me to the little room off the kitchen. Dear girl! There was my table and chair, writing pad, ink and pipe tray. And all the author's trappings—the celery stand full of fresh roses and honeysuckle, last year's calendar on the wall, the dictionary, and a little bag of chocolates to nibble between inspirations. Dear girl!

I sat me to work. The wallpaper is patterned with arabesques or odalisks or—perhaps—it is trapezoids. Upon one of the figures I fixed my eyes. I bethought me of humor.

A voice startled me—Louisa's voice.

"If you aren't too busy, dear," it said, "come to dinner."

I looked at my watch. Yes, five hours had been gathered in by the grim scytheman. I went to dinner.

"You mustn't work too hard at first," said Louisa. "Goethe—or was it Napoleon?—said five hours a day is enough for mental labor. Couldn't you take me and the children to the woods this afternoon?"

"I *am* a little tired," I admitted. So we went to the woods.

But I soon got the swing of it. Within a month I was turning out copy as regular as shipments of hardware.

And I had success. My column in the weekly made some stir, and I was referred to in a gossipy way by the critics as something fresh in the line of humorists. I augmented my income considerably by contributing to other publications.

I picked up the tricks of the trade. I could take a funny idea and make a two-line joke of it, earning a dollar. With false whiskers on, it would serve up cold as a quatrain, doubling its producing value. By turning the skirt and adding a ruffle of rhyme you would hardly recognize it as *vers de société* with neatly shod feet and a fashion plate illustration.

I began to save up money, and we had new carpets and a parlor organ. My townspeople began to look upon me as a citizen of some consequence instead of the merry trifler I had been when I clerked in the hardware store.

After five or six months the spontaneity seemed to depart from my humor. Quips and droll sayings no longer fell carelessly from my lips. I was sometimes hard run for material. I found myself listening to catch available ideas from the conversation of my friends. Sometimes I chewed my pencil and gazed at the wallpaper for hours trying to build up some gay little bubble of unstudied fun.

And then I became a harpy, a Moloch, a Jonah, a vampire to my acquaintances. Anxious, haggard, greedy, I stood among them like a veritable killjoy. Let a bright saying, a witty comparison, a piquant phrase fall from their lips and I was after it like a hound springing upon a bone. I dared not trust my memory; but, turning aside guiltily and meanly I would make a note of it in my ever-present memorandum book or upon my cuff for my own future use.

My friends regarded me in sorrow and wonder. I was not the same man. Where once I had furnished them entertainment and jollity, I now preyed upon them. No jests from me ever bid for their smiles now. They were too precious. I could not afford to dispense gratuitously the means of my livelihood.

I was a lugubrious fox praising the singing of my friends, the crows, that they might drop from their beaks the morsels of wit that I coveted.

Nearly everyone began to avoid me. I even forgot how to smile, not even paying that much for the sayings I appropriated.

No persons, places, times, or subjects were exempt from my plundering in search of material. Even in church my demoralized fancy went hunting among the solemn aisles and pillars for spoil.

Did the minister give out the longmeter doxology, at once I began: "Doxology—sockdology—sockdolager—meter—meet her."

The sermon ran through my mental sieve, its precepts filtering unheeded, could I but glean a suggestion of a pun or a *bon mot*. The solemnest anthems of the choir were but an accompaniment to my thoughts as I conceived new changes to ring upon the ancient comicalities concerning the jealousies of soprano, tenor, and basso.

My own home became a hunting ground. My wife is a singularly feminine creature, candid, sympathetic, and impulsive. Once her conversation was my delight, and her ideas a source of unfailing pleasure. Now I worked her. She was a gold mine of those amusing but lovable inconsistencies that distinguish the female mind.

I began to market those pearls of unwisdom and humor that should have enriched only the sacred precincts of home. With devilish cunning I encouraged her to talk. Unsuspecting, she laid her heart bare. Upon the cold, conspicuous, common, printed page I offered it to the public gaze.

A literary Judas, I kissed her and betrayed her. For pieces of silver I dressed her sweet confidences in the pantalettes and frills of folly and made them dance in the market place.

Dear Louisa! Of nights I have bent over her, cruel as a wolf above a tender lamb, hearkening even to her soft words murmured in sleep, hoping to catch an idea for my next day's grind. There is worse to come.

God help me! Next my fangs were buried deep in the neck of the fugitive sayings of my little children.

Guy and Viola were two bright fountains of childish, quaint thoughts and speeches. I found a ready sale for this kind of humor, and was furnishing a regular department in a magazine with "Funny Fancies of Childhood." I began to stalk them as an Indian stalks the antelope. I would hide behind sofas and doors, or crawl on my hands and knees among the bushes in the yard to eavesdrop while they were at play. I had all the qualities of a Harpy except remorse.

Once, when I was barren of ideas, and my copy must leave in the next mail, I covered myself in a pile of autumn leaves in the yard, where I knew they intended to come to play. I cannot bring myself to believe that Guy was aware of my hiding place, but even if he was I would be loath to blame him for his setting fire to the leaves, causing the destruction of my new suit of clothes, and nearly cremating a parent.

Soon my own children began to shun me as a pest. Often, when I was creeping upon them like a melancholy ghoul, I would hear them say to each other: "Here comes papa," and they would gather their toys and scurry away to some safer hiding place. Miserable wretch that I was!

And yet I was doing well financially. Before the first year had passed I had saved a thousand dollars, and we had lived in comfort.

But at what a cost! I am not quite clear as to what a Pariah is, but I was everything that it sounds like. I had no friends, no amusements, no enjoyment of life. The happiness of my family had been sacrificed. I was a bee, sucking sordid honey from life's fairest flowers, dreaded and shunned on account of my sting.

One day a man spoke to me with a pleasant and friendly smile. Not in months had the thing happened. I was passing the undertaking establishment of Peter Heffelbower. Peter stood in the door and saluted me. I stopped, strangely wrung in my heart by his greeting. He asked me inside.

The day was chill and rainy. We went into the back room, where a fire burned in a little stove. A customer came, and Peter left me alone for a while. Presently I felt a new feeling stealing over me—a sense of beautiful calm and content. I looked around the place. There were rows of shining rosewood caskets, black palls, trestles, hearse plumes, mourning streamers, and all the paraphernalia of the solemn trade. Here was peace, order, silence, the abode of grave and dignified reflections. Here, on the brink of life, was a little niche pervaded by the spirit of eternal rest.

When I entered it the follies of the world abandoned me at the door. I felt no inclination to wrest a humorous idea from those somber and stately trappings. My mind seemed to stretch itself to grateful repose upon a couch draped with gentle thoughts.

A quarter of an hour ago I was an abandoned humorist. Now I was a philosopher, full of serenity and ease. I had found a *refuge* from humor, from the hot chase of the shy quip, from the degrading pursuit of the panting joke, from the restless reach after the nimble repartee.

I had not known Heffelbower well. When he came back I let him talk, fearful that he might prove to be a jarring note in the sweet, dirge-like harmony of his establishment.

But, no. He chimed truly. I gave a long sigh of happiness. Never have I known a man's talk to be as magnificently dull as Peter's was. Compared with it the Dead Sea is a geyser. Never a sparkle or a glimmer of wit marred his words. Commonplaces as trite and as plentiful as blackberries flowed from his lips no more stirring in quality than a last week's tape running from a ticker. Quaking a little I tried upon him one of my best pointed jokes. It fell back ineffectual, with the point broken. I loved that man from then on.

Two or three evenings each week I would steal down to Heffelbower's and revel in his back room. That was my only joy. I began to rise early and hurry through my work, that I might spend more time in my haven. In no other place could I throw off my habit of extracting humorous ideas from my surroundings. Peter's talk left me no openings had I besieged it ever so hard.

Under this influence I began to improve in spirits. It was the recreation from one's labor which every man needs. I surprised one or two of my former friends by throwing them a smile and a cheery word as I passed them on the streets. Several times I dumbfounded my family by relaxing long enough to make a jocose remark in their presence.

I had so long been ridden by the incubus of humor that I seized my hours of holiday with a schoolboy's zest.

My work began to suffer. It was not the pain and burden to me that it had been. I often whistled at my desk, and wrote with far more fluency than before. I accomplished my tasks impatiently, as anxious to be off to my helpful retreat as a drunkard is to get to his tavern.

My wife had some anxious hours in conjecturing where I spent my afternoons. I thought it best not to tell her; women do not understand these things. Poor girl!—she had one shock out of it.

One day I brought home a silver coffin handle for a paperweight and a fine, fluffy hearse plume to dust my papers with.

I loved to see them on my desk, and think of the beloved back room down at Heffelbower's. But Louisa found them, and she shrieked with horror. I had to console her with some lame excuse for having them, but I saw in her eyes that the prejudice was not removed. I had to remove the articles, though, at double-quick time.

One day Peter Heffelbower laid before me a temptation that swept me off my feet. In his sensible, uninspired way he showed me his books, and explained that his profits and his business were increasing rapidly. He had thought of taking in a partner with some cash. He would rather have me than anyone he knew. When I left his place that afternoon Peter had my check for the thousand dollars I had in the bank, and I was a partner in his undertaking business.

I went home with feelings of delirious joy, mingled with a certain amount of doubt. I was dreading to tell my wife about it. But I walked on air. To give up the writing of humorous stuff, once more to enjoy the apples of life, instead of squeezing them to a pulp for a few drops of hard cider to make the public feel funny—what a boon that would be!

At the supper table Louisa handed me some letters that had come during my absence. Several of them contained rejected manuscripts. Ever since I first began going to Heffelbower's my stuff had been coming back with alarming frequency. Lately I had been dashing off my jokes and articles with the greatest fluency. Previously I had labored like a bricklayer, slowly and with agony.

Presently I opened a letter from the editor of the weekly with which I had a regular contract. The checks for that weekly article were still our main dependence. The letter ran thus:

> Dear Sir: As you are aware, our contract for the year expires with the present month. While regretting the necessity for so doing, we must say that we do not care to renew same for the coming year. We were quite pleased with your style of humor, which seems to have delighted quite a large proportion of our readers. But for the past two months we have noticed a decided falling off in its quality.
>
> Your earlier work showed a spontaneous, easy, natural flow of fun

and wit. Of late it is labored, studied, and unconvincing, giving painful evidence of hard toil and drudging mechanism.

Again regretting that we do not consider your contributions available any longer, we are, yours sincerely,

THE EDITOR

I handed this letter to my wife. After she had read it her face grew extremely long, and there were tears in her eyes.

"The mean old thing!" she exclaimed, indignantly. "I'm sure your pieces are just as good as they ever were. And it doesn't take you half as long to write them as it did." And then, I suppose, Louisa thought of the checks that would cease coming. "Oh, John," she wailed, "what will you do now?"

For an answer I got up and began to do a polka step around the supper table. I am sure Louisa thought the trouble had driven me mad; and I think the children hoped it had, for they tore after me, yelling with glee and emulating my steps. I was now something like their old playmate as of yore.

"The theater for us tonight!" I shouted, "nothing less. And a late, wild, disreputable supper for all of us at the Palace Restaurant. Lumty-diddle-de-dee-de-dum!"

And then I explained my glee by declaring that I was now a partner in a prosperous undertaking establishment, and that written jokes might go hide their heads in sackcloth and ashes for all of me.

With the editor's letter in her hand to justify the deed I had done, my wife could advance no objections save a few mild ones based on the feminine inability to appreciate a good thing such as the little back room of Peter Hef—no, of Heffelbower & Co.'s undertaking establishment.

In conclusion, I will say that today you will find no man in our town as well liked, as jovial and full of merry sayings as I. My jokes are again noised about and quoted; once more I take pleasure in my wife's confidential chatter without a mercenary thought, while Guy and Viola play at my feet distributing gems of childish humor without fear of the ghastly tormentor who used to dog their steps, notebook in hand.

Our business has prospered finely. I keep the books and look after the shop, while Peter attends to outside matters. He says that my levity and high spirits would simply turn any funeral into a regular Irish wake.

THE ETHICS OF PIG

On an eastbound train I went into the smoker and found Jefferson Peters, the only man with a brain west of the Wabash River who can use his cerebrum, cerebellum, and medulla oblongata at the same time.

Jeff is in the line of unillegal graft. He is not to be dreaded by widows and orphans; he is a reducer of surplusage. His favorite disguise is that of the targetbird at which the spendthrift or the reckless investor may shy a few inconsequential dollars. He is readily vocalized by tobacco; so, with the aid of two thick and easy-burning brevas, I got the story of his latest Autolycan adventure.

"In my line of business," said Jeff, "the hardest thing is to find an upright, trustworthy, strictly honorable partner to work a graft with. Some of the best men I ever worked with in a swindle would resort to trickery at times.

"So, last summer, I thinks I will go over into this section of country where I hear the serpent has not yet entered, and see if I can find a partner naturally gifted with a talent for crime, but not yet contaminated by success.

"I found a village that seemed to show the right kind of a layout. The inhabitants hadn't found out that Adam had been dispossessed, and were going right along naming the animals and killing snakes just as if they were in the Garden of Eden. They call this town Mount Nebo, and it's up near the spot where Kentucky and West Virginia and North Carolina corner together. Them States don't meet? Well, it was in that neighborhood, anyway.

"After putting in a week proving I wasn't a revenue officer, I went over to the store where the rude fourflushers of the hamlet lied, to see if I could get a line on the kind of man I wanted.

" 'Gentlemen,' says I, after we had rubbed noses and gathered 'round the dried-apple barrel, 'I don't suppose there's another community in the whole world into which sin and chicanery has less extensively permeated than this. Life here, where all the women are brave and propitious and all the men honest and expedient, must, indeed, be an idol. It reminds me,' says I, 'of Goldstein's beautiful ballad entitled "The Deserted Village," which says:

> Ill fares the land, to hastening ills a prey;
>   What art can drive its charms away?
> The judge rode slowly down the lane, mother,
>   For I'm to be Queen of the May.'

" 'Why, yes, Mr. Peters,' says the storekeeper. 'I reckon we air about as moral and torpid a community as there be on the mounting, according to censuses of opinion; but I reckon you ain't ever met Rufe Tatum.'

" 'Why, no,' says the town constable, 'he can't hardly have ever. That air Rufe is shore the monstrousest scalawag that has escaped hangin' on the galluses. And that puts me in mind that I ought to have turned Rufe out of the lockup day before yesterday. The thirty days he got for killin' Yance Goodloe was up then. A day or two more won't hurt Rufe any, though.'

" 'Shucks, now,' says I, in the mountain idiom, 'don't tell me there's a man in Mount Nebo as bad as that.'

" 'Worse,' says the storekeeper. 'He steals hogs.'

"I thinks I will look up this Mr. Tatum; so a day or two after the constable turned him out I got acquainted with him and invited him out on the edge of town to sit on a log and talk business.

"What I wanted was a partner with a natural rural make-up to play a part in some little one-act outrages that I was going to book with the Pitfall & Gin circuit in some of the Western towns; and this R. Tatum was born for the role as sure as nature cast Fairbanks for the stuff that kept *Eliza* from sinking into the river.

"He was about the size of a first baseman; and he had ambiguous blue eyes like the china dog on the mantelpiece that Aunt Harriet used to play with when she was a child. His hair waved a little bit like the statue of the dinkus-thrower in the Vacation at Rome, but the color of it reminded you of the 'Sunset in the Grand Cañon, by an American Artist,' that they hang over the stovepipe holes in the salongs. He was the Reub, without needing a touch. You'd have known him for one, even if you'd seen him on the vaudeville stage with one cotton suspender and a straw over his ear.

"I told him what I wanted, and found him ready to jump at the job.

" 'Overlooking such a trivial little peccadillo as the habit of manslaughter,' says I, 'what have you accomplished in the way of indirect brigandage or nonactionable thriftiness that you could point to, with or without pride, as an evidence of your qualifications for the position?'

" 'Why,' says he, in his kind of Southern system of procrastinated accents, 'hain't you heard tell? There ain't any man, black or white, in the Blue Ridge that can tote off a shoat as easy as I can without bein' heard, seen, or cotched. I can lift a shoat,' he goes on, 'out of a pen, from under a piazza, at the trough, in the woods, day or night, anywhere or anyhow, and I guarantee nobody won't hear a squeal. It's all in the way you grap hold of 'em and carry 'em atterwards. Someday,' goes on this gentle despoiler of pigpens, 'I hope to become reckernized as the champion shoat-stealer of the world.'

" 'It's proper to be ambitious,' says I; 'and hog-stealing will do very well for Mount Nebo; but in the outside world, Mr. Tatum, it would be considered as crude a piece of business as a bear raid on Bay State Gas. However, it will do as a guarantee of good faith. We'll go into partnership. I've got a thousand dollars cash capital; and with that homeward-plods atmosphere of yours we ought to be able to win out a few shares of Soon Parted, preferred, in the money market.'

"So I attaches Rufe, and we go away from Mount Nebo down into the lowlands. And all the way I coach him for his part in the grafts I had in mind. I had idled away two months on the Florida coast, and was feeling all to the Ponce de Leon, besides having so many new schemes up my sleeve that I had to wear kimonos to hold 'em.

"I intended to assume a funnel shape and mow a path nine miles wide through the farming belt of the Middle West; so we headed in that direction. But when we got as far as Lexington we found Binkley Brothers' circus there, and the blue-grass peasantry romping into town and pounding the Belgian blocks with their hand-pegged sabots as artless and arbitrary as an extra session of a Datto Bryan duma. I never pass a circus without pulling the valve-cord and coming down for a little Key West money; so I engaged a couple of rooms and board for Rufe and me at a house near the circus grounds run by a widow lady named Peevy. Then I took Rufe to a clothing store and gents'-outfitted him. He showed up strong, as I knew he would, after he was rigged up in the ready-made rutabaga regalia. Me and old Misfitzky stuffed him into a bright blue suit with a Nile green visible plaid effect, and riveted on a fancy vest of a light Tuskegee Normal tan color, a red necktie, and the yellowest pair of shoes in town. They were the first clothes Rufe had ever worn except the gingham layette and the butternut topdressing of his native kraal, and he looked as self-conscious as an Igorrote with a new nose ring.

"That night I went down to the circus tents and opened a small shell game. Rufe was to be the capper. I gave him a roll of phony currency to bet with and kept a bunch of it in a special pocket to pay his winnings out of. No; I didn't mistrust him; but I simply can't manipulate the ball to lose when I see real money bet. My fingers go on a strike every time I try it.

"I set up my little table and began to show them how easy it was to guess which shell the little pea was under. The unlettered hinds gathered in a thick semicircle and began to nudge elbows and banter one another to bet. Then was when Rufe ought to have singlefooted up and called the turn on the little joker for a few tens and fives to get them started. But, no Rufe. I'd seen him two or three times walking about and looking at the sideshow pictures with his mouth full of peanut candy; but he never came nigh.

"The crowd piked a little; but trying to work the shells without a capper is like fishing without bait. I closed the game with only forty-two dollars of the unearned increment, while I had been counting on yanking the yeomen for two hundred at least. I went home at eleven and went to bed. I supposed that the circus had proved too alluring for Rufe, and that he had succumbed to it, concert and all; but I meant to give him a lecture on general business principles in the morning.

"Just after Morpheus had got both my shoulders to the shuck mattress I hears a houseful of unbecoming and ribald noises like a youngster screeching with green-apple colic. I opens my door and calls out in the hall for the widow lady, and when she sticks her head out, I says: 'Mrs. Peevy, ma'am, would you mind choking off that kid of yours so that honest people can get their rest?'

" 'Sir,' says she, 'it's no child of mine. It's the pig squealing that your friend Mr. Tatum brought home to his room a couple of hours ago. And if you are uncle or second cousin or brother to it, I'd appreciate your stopping its mouth, sir, yourself, if you please.'

"I put on some of the polite outside habiliments of external society and went into Rufe's room. He had gotten up and lit his lamp, and was pouring some milk into a tin pan on the floor for a dingy-white, half-grown, squealing pig.

" 'How is this, Rufe?' says I. 'You flimflammed in your part of the work tonight, and put the game on crutches. And how do you explain the pig? It looks like backsliding to me.'

" 'Now, don't be too hard on me, Jeff,' says he. 'You know how long I've been used to stealing shoats. It's got to be a habit with me. And tonight, when I see such a fine chance, I couldn't help takin' it.'

" 'Well,' says I, 'maybe you've really got kleptopigia. And maybe when we get out of the pig belt you'll turn your mind to higher and more remunerative misconduct. Why you should want to stain your soul with such a distasteful, feeble-minded, perverted, roaring beast as that I can't understand.'

" 'Why, Jeff,' says he, 'you ain't in sympathy with shoats. You don't understand 'em like I do. This here seems to me to be an animal of more than common powers of ration and intelligence. He walked half across the room on his hind legs a while ago.'

" 'Well, I'm going back to bed,' says I. 'See if you can impress it upon your friend's ideas of intelligence that he's not to make so much noise.'

" 'He was hungry,' says Rufe. 'He'll go to sleep and keep quiet now.'

"I always get up before breakfast and read the morning paper whenever I happen to be within the radius of a Hoe cylinder or a Washington hand press. The next morning I got up early, and found the Lexington daily on the front porch where the carrier had thrown it. The first thing I saw in it was a double-column ad on the front page that read like this:

FIVE THOUSAND DOLLARS REWARD

The above amount will be paid, and no questions asked, for the return, alive and uninjured, of Beppo, the famous European educated pig, that strayed or was stolen from the sideshow tents of Binkley Bros.' circus last night.

GEO. B. TAPLEY
Business Manager
At the circus grounds

"I folded up the paper flat, put it into my inside pocket, and went to Rufe's room. He was nearly dressed, and was feeding the pig the rest of the milk and some apple-peelings.

" 'Well, well, well, good morning all,' I says, hearty and amiable. 'So we are up? And piggy is having his breakfast. What had you intended doing with that pig, Rufe?'

" 'I'm going to crate him up,' says Rufe, 'and express him to ma in Mount Nebo. He'll be company for her while I am away.'

" 'He's a mighty fine pig,' says I, scratching him on the back.

" 'You called him a lot of names last night,' says Rufe.

" 'Oh, well,' says I, 'he looks better to me this morning. I was raised on a farm, and I'm very fond of pigs. I used to go to bed at sundown, so I never saw one by lamplight before. Tell you what I'll do, Rufe,' I says. 'I'll give you ten dollars for that pig.'

" 'I reckon I wouldn't sell this shoat,' says he. 'If it was any other one I might.'

" 'Why not this one?' I asked, fearful that he might know something.

" 'Why, because,' says he, 'it was the grandest achievement of my life. There ain't airy other man that could have done it. If I ever have a fireside and children, I'll sit beside it and tell 'em how their daddy toted off a shoat from a whole circus full of people. And maybe my grandchildren, too. They'll certainly be proud a whole passel. Why,' says he, 'there was two tents, one openin' into the other. This shoat was on a platform, tied with a little chain. I seen a giant and a lady with a fine chance of bushy white hair in the other tent. I got the shoat and crawled out from under the canvas again without him squeakin' as loud as a mouse. I put him under my coat, and I must have passed a hundred folks before I got out where the streets was dark. I reckon I wouldn't sell that shoat, Jeff. I'd want ma to keep it, so there'd be a witness to what I done.'

" 'The pig won't live long enough,' I says, 'to use as an exhibit in your senile fireside mendacity. Your grandchildren will have to take your word for it. I'll give you one hundred dollars for the animal.'

"Rufe looked at me astonished.

" 'The shoat can't be worth anything like that to you,' he says. 'What do you want him for?'

" 'Viewing me casuistically,' says I, with a rare smile, 'you wouldn't think that I've got an artistic side to my temper. But I have. I'm a collector of pigs. I've scoured the world for unusual pigs. Over in the Wabash Valley I've got a hog ranch with most every specimen on it, from a Merino to a Poland China. This looks like a blooded pig to me, Rufe,' says I. 'I believe it's a genuine Berkshire. That's why I'd like to have it.'

" 'I'd shore like to accommodate you,' says he, 'but I've got the artistic tenement, too. I don't see why it ain't art when you can steal a shoat better than anybody else can. Shoats is a kind of inspiration and genius with me. Specially this one. I wouldn't take two hundred and fifty for that animal.'

" 'Now, listen,' says I, wiping off my forehead. 'It's not so much a matter of business with me as it is art; and not so much art as it is philanthropy. Being a connoisseur and disseminator of pigs, I wouldn't feel like I'd done my duty to the world unless I added that Berkshire to my collection. Not intrinsically, but according to the ethics of pigs as friends and coadjutors of mankind, I offer you five hundred dollars for the animal.'

" 'Jeff,' says this pork esthete, 'it ain't money; it's sentiment with me.'

" 'Seven hundred,' says I.

" 'Make it eight hundred,' says Rufe, 'and I'll crush the sentiment out of my heart.'

"I went under my clothes for my money-belt, and counted him out forty twenty-dollar certificates.

" 'I'll just take him into my own room,' says I, 'and lock him up till after breakfast.'

"I took the pig by the hind leg. He turned on a squeal like the steam calliope at the circus.

" 'Let me tote him in for you,' says Rufe; and he picks up the beast under one arm, holding his snout with the other hand, and packs him into my room like a sleeping baby.

"After breakfast Rufe, who had a chronic case of haberdashery ever since I got his trousseau, says he believes he will amble down to Misfitzky's and look over some royal-purple socks. And then I got as busy as a one-armed man with the nettle-rash pasting on wallpaper. I found an old man with an express wagon to hire; and we tied the pig in a sack and drove down to the circus grounds.

"I found George B. Tapley in a little tent with a window open. He was a fattish man with an immediate eye, in a black skullcap, with a four-ounce diamond screwed into the bosom of his red sweater.

" 'Are you George B. Tapley?' I asks.

" 'I swear it,' says he.

" 'Well, I've got it,' says I.

" 'Designate,' says he. 'Are you the guinea pigs for the Asiatic python or the alfalfa for the sacred buffalo?'

" 'Neither,' says I. 'I've got Beppo, the educated hog, in a sack in that wagon. I found him rooting up the flowers in my front yard this morning. I'll take the five thousand dollars in large bills, if it's handy.'

"George B. hustles out of his tent, and asks me to follow. We go into one of the sideshows. In there was a jet black pig with a pink ribbon around his neck lying on some hay and eating carrots that a man was feeding to him.

" 'Hey, Mac,' calls G. B. 'Nothing wrong with the worldwide this morning, is there?'

" 'Him? No,' says the man. 'He's got an appetite like a chorus girl at 1 A.M.'

" 'How'd you get this pipe?' says Tapley to me. 'Eating too many porkchops last night?'

"I pulls out the paper and shows him the ad.

" 'Fake,' says he. 'Don't know anything about it. You've beheld with your own eyes the marvelous, worldwide porcine wonder of the four-footed kingdom eating with preternatural sagacity his matutinal meal, unstrayed and unstole. Good morning.'

"I was beginning to see. I got in the wagon and told Uncle Ned to drive to the most adjacent orifice of the nearest alley. There I took out my pig, got the range carefully for the other opening, set his sights, and gave him such a kick that he went out the other end of the alley twenty feet ahead of his squeal.

"Then I paid Uncle Ned his fifty cents, and walked down to the newspaper office. I wanted to hear it in cold syllables. I got the advertising man to his window.

" 'To decide a bet,' says I, 'wasn't the man who had this ad put in last night short and fat, with long, black whiskers and a clubfoot?'

" 'He was not,' says the man. 'He would measure about six feet by four and a half inches with cornsilk hair, and dressed like the pansies of the conservatory.'

"At dinnertime I went back to Mrs. Peevy's.

" 'Shall I keep some soup hot for Mr. Tatum till he comes back?' she asks.

" 'If you do, ma'am,' says I, 'you'll more than exhaust for firewood all the coal in the bosom of the earth and all the forests on the outside of it.'

"So there, you see," said Jefferson Peters, in conclusion, "how hard it is ever to find a fair-minded and honest business partner."

"But," I began, with the freedom of long acquaintance, "the rule should work both ways. If you had offered to divide the reward you would not have lost—"

Jeff's look of dignified reproach stopped me.

"That don't involve the same principles at all," said he. "Mine was a legitimate and moral attempt at speculation. Buy low and sell high—don't Wall Street indorse it? Bulls and bears and pigs—what's the difference? Why not bristles as well as horns and fur?"

THE PIMIENTA PANCAKES

WHILE WE WERE rounding up a bunch of the Triangle-O cattle in the Frio bottoms, a projecting branch of a dead mesquite caught my wooden stirrup and gave my ankle a wrench that laid me up in camp for a week.

On the third day of my compulsory idleness I crawled out near the grub wagon, and reclined helpless under the conversational fire of Judson Odom, the camp cook. Jud was a monologist by nature, whom Destiny, with customary blundering, had set in a profession wherein he was bereaved, for the greater portion of his time, of an audience.

Therefore, I was manna in the desert of Jud's obmutescence.

Betimes I was stirred by invalid longings for something to eat that did not come under the caption of "grub." I had visions of the maternal pantry "deep as first love, and wild with all regret," and then I asked, "Jud, can you make pancakes?"

Jud laid down his six-shooter, with which he was preparing to pound an antelope steak, and stood over me in what I felt to be a menacing attitude. He further endorsed my impression that his pose was resentful by fixing upon me with his light blue eyes a look of cold suspicion.

"Say, you," he said, with candid though not excessive choler, "did you mean that straight, or was you trying to throw the gaff into me? Some of the boys been telling you about me and that pancake racket?"

"No, Jud," I said sincerely, "I meant it. It seems to me I'd swap my pony and saddle for a stack of buttered brown pancakes with some

98

first crop, open kettle New Orleans sweetening. Was there a story about pancakes?"

Jud was mollified at once when he saw that I had not been dealing in allusions. He brought some mysterious bags and tin boxes from the grub wagon and set them in the shade of the hackberry where I lay reclined. I watched him as he began to arrange them leisurely and untie their many strings.

"No, not a story," said Jud as he worked, "but just the logical disclosures in the case of me and that pink-eyed snoozer from Mired Mule Cañada and Miss Willella Learight. I don't mind telling you.

"I was punching them for Old Bill Toomey, on the San Miguel. One day I gets all ensnared up in aspirations for to eat some canned grub that hasn't ever mooed or baaed or grunted or been in peck measures. So, I gets on my bronc and pushes the wind for Uncle Emsley Telfair's store at the Pimienta Crossing on the Nueces.

"About three in the afternoon I throwed my bridle rein over a mesquite limb, and walked the last twenty yards into Uncle Emsley's store. I got up on the counter and told Uncle Emsley that the signs pointed to the devastation of the fruit crop of the world. In a minute I had a bag of crackers and a long-handled spoon, with an open can each of apricots and pineapples and cherries and green gages beside of me, with Uncle Emsley busy chopping away with the hatchet at the yellow clings. I was feeling like Adam before the apple stampede, and was digging my spurs into the side of the counter and working with my twenty-four-inch spoon when I happened to look out of the window into the yard of Uncle Emsley's house, which was next to the store.

"There was a girl standing there—an imported girl with fixings on—philandering with a croquet maul and amusing herself by watching my style of encouraging the fruit canning industry.

"I slid off the counter and delivered up my shovel to Uncle Emsley.

" 'That's my niece,' says he; 'Miss Willella Learight, down from Palestine on a visit. Do you want that I should make you acquainted?'

" 'The Holy Land,' I says to myself, my thoughts milling some as I tried to run 'em into the corral. 'Why not? There was sure angels in Pales— Why, yes, Uncle Emsley,' I says out loud, 'I'd be awful edified to meet Miss Learight.'

"So Uncle Emsley took me out in the yard and gave us each other's entitlements.

"I never was shy about women. I never could understand why some men who can break a mustang before breakfast and shave in the dark, get all left-handed and full of perspiration and excuses when they see a bolt of calico draped around what belongs in it. Inside of eight minutes me and Miss Willella was aggravating the croquet balls around as amiable as second cousins. She gave me a dig about the quantity of canned fruit I had eaten, and I got back at her, flat-footed, about how a certain lady named Eve started the fruit trouble in the first free-grass pasture—'Over in Palestine, wasn't it?' says I, as easy and pat as roping a one-year-old.

"That was how I acquired cordiality for the proximities of Miss Willella Learight; and the disposition grew larger as time passed. She was stopping at Pimienta Crossing for her health, which was very good, and for the climate, which was forty percent hotter than Palestine. I rode over to see her once every week for a while; and then I figured it out that if I doubled the number of trips I would see her twice as often.

"One week I slipped in a third trip; and that's where the pancakes and the pink-eyed snoozer busted into the game.

"That evening, while I set on the counter with a peach and two damsons in my mouth, I asked Uncle Emsley how Miss Willella was.

" 'Why,' says Uncle Emsley, 'she's gone riding with Jackson Bird, the sheep man from over at Mired Mule Cañada.'

"I swallowed the peach seed and the two damson seeds. I guess somebody held the counter by the bridle while I got off; and then I walked out straight ahead till I butted against the mesquite where my roan was tied.

" 'She's gone riding,' I whispers in the bronc's ear, 'with Birdstone Jack, the hired mule from Sheep Man's Cañada. Did you get that, Old Leather-and-Gallops?'

"That bronc of mine wept, in his way. He'd been raised a cow pony and he didn't care for snoozers.

"I went back and said to Uncle Emsley: 'Did you say a sheep man?'

" 'I said a sheep man,' says Uncle again. 'You must have heard tell of Jackson Bird. He's got eight sections of grazing and four thousand head of the finest Cotswolds south of the Arctic Circle.'

"I went out and sat on the ground in the shade of the store and leaned against a prickly pear. I sifted sand into my boot with unthinking hands while I soliloquized a quantity about this bird with the Jackson plumage to his name.

"I never had believed in harming sheep men. I see one, one day, reading a Latin grammar on hossback, and I never touched him! They never irritated me like they do most cowmen. You wouldn't go to work now, and impair and disfigure snoozers, would you, that eat on tables and wear little shoes and speak to you on subjects? I had always let 'em pass, just as you would a jack rabbit; with a polite word and a guess about the weather, but no stopping to swap canteens. I never thought it was worthwhile to be hostile with a snoozer. And because I'd been lenient, and let 'em live, here was one going around riding with Miss Willella Learight!

"An hour by sun they come loping back, and stopped at Uncle Emsley's gate. The sheep person helped her off; and they stood throwing each other sentences all sprightful and sagacious for a while. And then this feathered Jackson flies up in his saddle and raises his little stewpot of a hat, and trots off in the direction of his mutton ranch. By this time I had turned the sand out of my boots and unpinned myself from the prickly pear; and by the time he gets half a mile out of Pimienta, I singlefoots up beside him on my bronc.

"I said that snoozer was pink-eyed, but he wasn't. His seeing arrangement was gray enough, but his eyelashes was pink and his hair was sandy, and that gave you the idea. Sheep man?—he wasn't more than a lamb man, anyhow—a little thing with his neck involved in a yellow silk handkerchief, and shoes tied up in bowknots.

" 'Afternoon!' says I to him. 'You now ride with a equestrian who is commonly called Dead-Moral-Certainty Judson, on account of the way I shoot. When I want a stranger to know me I always introduce myself before the draw, for I never did like to shake hands with ghosts.'

" 'Ah,' says he, just like that— 'Ah, I'm glad to know you, Mr. Judson. I'm Jackson Bird, from over at Mired Mule Ranch.'

"Just then one of my eyes saw a roadrunner skipping down the hill with a young tarantula in his bill, and the other eye noticed a rabbit hawk sitting on a dead limb in a water elm. I popped over one after the other with my forty-five, just to show him. 'Two out of three,' says I. 'Birds just naturally seem to draw my fire wherever I go.'

" 'Nice shooting,' says the sheep man, without a flutter. 'But don't you sometimes ever miss the third shot? Elegant fine rain that

was last week for the young grass, don't you think, Mr. Judson?'
says he.

" 'Willie,' says I, riding over close to his palfrey, 'your infatuated
parents may have denounced you by the name of Jackson, but you
sure molted into a twittering Willie—let us slough off this here analysis
of rain and the elements, and get down to talk that is outside the
vocabulary of parrots. That is a bad habit you have got of riding with
young ladies over at Pimienta. I've known birds,' says I, 'to be served
on toast for less than that. Miss Willella,' says I, 'don't ever want any
nest made out of sheep's wool by a tomtit of the Jacksonian branch of
ornithology. Now, are you going to quit, or do you wish for to gallop
up against this Dead-Moral-Certainty attachment to my name, which is
good for two hyphens and at least one set of funeral obsequies?'

"Jackson Bird flushed up some, and then he laughed.

" 'Why, Mr. Judson,' says he, 'you've got the wrong idea. I've
called on Miss Learight a few times; but not for the purpose you
imagine. My object is purely a gastronomical one.'

"I reached for my gun.

" 'Any coyote,' says I, 'that would boast of dishonorable——'

" 'Wait a minute,' says this Bird, 'till I explain. What would I do
with a wife? If you ever saw that ranch of mine! I do my own cooking
and mending. Eating—that's all the pleasure I get out of sheep raising.
Mr. Judson, did you ever taste the pancakes that Miss Learight
makes?'

" 'Me? No,' I told him. 'I never was advised that she was up to
any culinary maneuvres.'

" 'They're golden sunshine,' says he; 'honey-browned by the am-
brosial fires of Epicurus. I'd give two years of my life to get the recipe
for making them pancakes. That's what I went to see Miss Learight
for,' says Jackson Bird, 'but I haven't been able to get it from her. It's
an old recipe that's been in the family for seventy-five years. They
hand it down from one generation to another, but they don't give it
away to outsiders. If I could get that recipe, so I could make them
pancakes for myself on my ranch, I'd be a happy man,' says Bird.

" 'Are you sure,' I says to him, 'that it ain't the hand that mixes
the pancakes that you're after?'

" 'Sure,' says Jackson. 'Miss Learight is a mighty nice girl, but I
can assure you my intentions go no further than the gastro—' but he
seen my hand going down to my holster and changed his similitude—
'than the desire to procure a copy of the pancake recipe,' he finishes.

" 'You ain't such a bad little man,' says I, trying to be fair. 'I was thinking some of making orphans of your sheep, but I'll let you fly away this time. But you stick to pancakes,' says I, 'as close as the middle one of a stack; and don't go and mistake sentiments for syrup, or there'll be singing at your ranch, and you won't hear it.'

" 'To convince you that I am sincere,' says the sheep man, 'I'll ask you to help me. Miss Learight and you being closer friends, maybe she would do for you what she wouldn't for me. If you will get me a copy of that pancake recipe, I give you my word that I'll never call upon her again.'

" 'That's fair,' I says, and I shook hands with Jackson Bird. 'I'll get it for you if I can, and glad to oblige.' And he turned off down the big pear flat on the Piedra, in the direction of Mired Mule; and I steered northwest for old Bill Toomey's ranch.

"It was five days afterward when I got another chance to ride over to Pimienta. Miss Willella and me passed a gratifying evening at Uncle Emsley's. She sang some, and exasperated the piano quite a lot with quotations from the operas. I gave imitations of a rattlesnake, and told her about Snaky McFee's new way of skinning cows, and described the trip I made to Saint Louis once. We was getting along in one another's estimations fine. Thinks I, if Jackson Bird can now be persuaded to migrate, I win. I recollect his promise about the pancake receipt, and I thinks I will persuade it from Miss Willella and give it to him; and then if I catches Birdie off of Mired Mule again, I'll make him hop the twig.

"So, along about ten o'clock, I put on a wheedling smile and says to Miss Willella: 'Now, if there's anything I do like better than the sight of a red steer on green grass it's the taste of a nice hot pancake smothered in sugarhouse molasses.'

"Miss Willella gave a little jump on the piano stool, and looked at me curious.

" 'Yes,' says she, 'they're real nice. What did you say was the name of that street in Saint Louis, Mr. Odom, where you lost your hat?'

" 'Pancake Avenue,' says I, with a wink, to show her that I was on about the family receipt, and couldn't be side-corraled off of the subject. 'Come, now, Miss Willella,' I says; 'let's hear how you make 'em. Pancakes is just whirling in my head like wagon wheels. Start her off, now—pound of flour, eight dozen eggs, and so on. How does the catalog of constituents run?'

" 'Excuse me for a moment, please,' says Miss Willella, and she gives me a quick kind of sideways look, and slides off the stool. She ambled out into the other room, and directly Uncle Emsley comes in, in his shirtsleeves, with a pitcher of water. He turns around to get a glass on the table, and I see a forty-five in his hip pocket. 'Great postholes!' thinks I, 'but here's a family thinks a heap of cooking receipts, protecting it with firearms. I've known outfits that wouldn't do that much by a family feud.'

" 'Drink this here down,' says Uncle Emsley, handing me the glass of water. 'You've rid too far today, Jud, and got yourself over-excited. Try to think about something else now.'

" 'Do you know how to make them pancakes, Uncle Emsley?' I asked.

" 'Well, I'm not as apprized in the anatomy of them as some,' says Uncle Emsley, 'but I reckon you take a sifter of plaster of Paris and a little dough and saleratus and cornmeal, and mix 'em with eggs and buttermilk as usual. Is old Bill going to ship beeves to Kansas City again this spring, Jud?'

"That was all the pancake specifications I could get that night. I didn't wonder that Jackson Bird found it uphill work. So I dropped the subject and talked with Uncle Emsley a while about hollow-horn and cyclones. And then Miss Willella came and said 'good night,' and I hit the breeze for the ranch.

"About a week afterwards, I met Jackson Bird riding out of Pimienta as I rode in, and we stopped in the road for a few frivolous remarks.

" 'Got the bill of particulars for them flapjacks yet?' I asked him.

" 'Well, no,' says Jackson. 'I don't seem to have any success in getting hold of it. Did you try?'

" 'I did,' says I, 'and 'twas like trying to dig a prairie dog out of his hole with a peanut hull. That pancake receipt must be a jookalorum, the way they hold on to it.'

" 'I'm most ready to give it up,' says Jackson, so discouraged in his pronunciations that I felt sorry for him; 'but I did want to know how to make them pancakes to eat on my lonely ranch,' says he. 'I lie awake of nights thinking how good they are.'

" 'You keep on trying for it,' I tells him, 'and I'll do the same. One of us is bound to get a rope over its horns before long. Well, so long, Jackey.'

"You see, by this time we was on the peacefullest of terms. When

I saw that he wasn't after Miss Willella I had more endurable contemplations of that sand-haired snoozer. In order to help out the ambitions of his appetite I kept on trying to get that receipt from Miss Willella. But every time I would say 'pancakes' she would get sort of remote and fidgety about the eye, and try to change the subject. If I held her to it she would slide out and round up Uncle Emsley with his pitcher of water and hip-pocket howitzer.

"One day I galloped over to the store with a fine bunch of blue verbenas that I cut out of a herd of wild flowers over on Poisoned Dog Prairie. Uncle Emsley looked at 'em with one eye shut and says, 'Haven't ye heard the news?'

" 'Cattle up?' I asks.

" 'Willella and Jackson Bird was married in Palestine yesterday,' says he. 'Just got a letter this morning.'

"I dropped them flowers in a cracker barrel, and let the news trickle in my ears and down toward my upper left-hand shirt pocket until it got to my feet.

" 'Would you mind saying that over again once more, Uncle Emsley?' says I. 'Maybe my hearing has got wrong, and you only said that prime heifers was 4.80 on the hoof, or something like that.'

" 'Married yesterday,' says Uncle Emsley, 'and gone to Waco and Niagara Falls on a wedding tour. Why, didn't you see none of the signs all along? Jackson Bird has been courting of Willella ever since that day he took her out riding.'

" 'Then,' says I, in a kind of yell, 'what was all this zizzaparoola he give me about pancakes? Tell me *that*.'

"When I said 'pancakes' Uncle Emsley sort of dodged and stepped back.

" 'Somebody's been dealing me pancakes from the bottom of the deck,' I says, 'and I'll find out. I believe you know. Talk up,' says I, 'or we'll mix a panful of batter right here.'

"I slid over the counter after Uncle Emsley. He grabbed at his gun, but it was in a drawer, and he missed it two inches. I got him by the front of his shirt and shoved him in a corner.

" 'Talk pancakes,' says I, 'or be made into one. Does Miss Willella make 'em?'

" 'She never made one in her life and I never saw one,' says Uncle Emsley, soothing. 'Calm down now, Jud—calm down. You've got excited, and that wound in your head is contaminating your sense of intelligence. Try not to think about pancakes.'

" 'Uncle Emsley,' says I, 'I'm not wounded in the head except so far as my natural cogitative instincts run to runts. Jackson Bird told me he was calling on Miss Willella for the purpose of finding out her system of producing pancakes, and he asked me to help him get the bill of lading of the ingredients. I done so, with the results as you see. Have I been sodded down with Johnson grass by a pink-eyed snoozer, or what?'

"Slack up your grip on my dress shirt,' says Uncle Emsley, 'and I'll tell you. Yes, it looks like Jackson Bird has gone and humbugged you some. The day after he went riding with Willella, he came back and told me and her to watch out for you whenever you got to talking about pancakes. He said you was in camp once where they was cooking flapjacks, and one of the fellows cut you over the head with a frying pan. Jackson said that whenever you got overhot or excited, that wound hurt you and made you kind of crazy, and you went to raving about pancakes. He told us to just get you worked off of the subject and soothed down, and you wouldn't be dangerous. So, me and Willella done the best by you we knew how. Well, well,' says Uncle Emsley, 'that Jackson Bird is sure a seldom kind of a snoozer.' "

During the progress of Jud's story he had been slowly but deftly combining certain portions of the contents of his sacks and cans. Toward the close of it he set before me the finished product—a pair of red-hot, rich-hued pancakes on a tin plate. From some secret hoarding place he also brought a lump of excellent butter and a bottle of golden syrup.

"How long ago did these things happen?" I asked him.

"Three years," said Jud. "They're living on the Mired Mule Ranch now. But I haven't seen either of 'em since. They say Jackson Bird was fixing his ranch up fine with rocking chairs and window curtains all the time he was putting me up the pancake tree. Oh, I got over it after a while. But the boys kept the racket up."

"Did you make these cakes by the famous recipe?" I asked.

"Didn't I tell you there wasn't no receipt?" said Jud. "The boys hollered pancakes till they got pancake hungry, and I cut this receipt out of a newspaper. How does the truck taste?"

"They're delicious," I answered. "Why don't you have some too, Jud?"

I was sure I heard a sigh.

"Me?" said Jud. "I don't never eat 'em."

Compliments of the Season

THERE ARE NO more Christmas stories to write. Fiction is exhausted; and newspaper items, the next best, are manufactured by clever young journalists who have married early and have an engagingly pessimistic view of life. Therefore, for seasonable diversion, we are reduced to two very questionable sources—facts and philosophy. We will begin with—whichever you choose to call it.

Children are pestilential little animals with which we have to cope under a bewildering variety of conditions. Especially when childish sorrows overwhelm them are we put to our wits' end. We exhaust our paltry store of consolation; and then beat them, sobbing, to sleep. Then we grovel in the dust of a million years, and ask God why. Thus we call out of the rattrap. As for the children, no one understands them except old maids, hunchbacks, and shepherd dogs.

Now come the facts in the case of the Rag Doll, the Tatterdemalion, and the Twenty-fifth of December.

On the tenth of that month the Child of the Millionaire lost her rag doll. There were many servants in the Millionaire's palace on the Hudson, and these ransacked the house and grounds, but without finding the lost treasure. The Child was a girl of five, and one of those perverse little beasts that often wound the sensibilities of wealthy parents by fixing their affections upon some vulgar, inexpensive toy instead of upon diamond-studded automobiles and pony phaetons.

The Child grieved sorely and truly, a thing inexplicable to the Millionaire, to whom the rag-doll market was about as interesting as Bay State Gas; and to the Lady, the Child's mother, who was all for form—that is, nearly all, as you shall see.

The Child cried inconsolably, and grew hollow-eyed, knock-kneed, spindling, and corykilverty in many other respects. The Millionaire smiled and tapped his coffers confidently. The pick of the output of the French and German toymakers was rushed by special delivery to the mansion; but Rachel refused to be comforted. She was weeping for her rag child, and was for a high protective tariff against all foreign foolishness. Then doctors with the finest bedside manners and stopwatches were called in. One by one they chattered futilely about pepto-manganate of iron and sea voyages and hypophosphites until their stopwatches showed that Bill Rendered was under the wire for show or place. Then, as men, they advised that the rag doll be found as soon as possible and restored to its mourning parent. The Child sniffed at therapeutics, chewed a thumb, and wailed for her Betsy. And all this time cablegrams were coming from Santa Claus saying that he would soon be there and enjoining us to show a true Christian spirit and let up on the poolrooms and tontine policies and platoon systems long enough to give him a welcome. Everywhere the spirit of Christmas was diffusing itself. The banks were refusing loans, the pawnbrokers had doubled their gang of helpers, people bumped your shins on the streets with red sleds, Thomas and Jeremiah bubbled before you on the bars while you waited on one foot, holly wreaths of hospitality were hung in windows of the stores, they who had 'em were getting out their furs. You hardly knew which was the best bet in balls—three, high, moth, or snow. It was no time at which to lose the rag doll of your heart.

If Doctor Watson's investigating friend had been called in to solve this mysterious disappearance he might have observed on the Millionaire's wall a copy of "The Vampire." That would have quickly suggested, by induction, "A rag and a bone and a hank of hair." "Flip," a Scotch terrier, next to the rag doll in the Child's heart, frisked through the halls. The hank of hair! Aha! X, the unfound quantity, represented the rag doll. But the bone? Well, when dogs find bones they——Done! It were an easy and a fruitful task to examine Flip's forefeet. Look, Watson! Earth—dried earth between the toes. Of course, the dog—but Sherlock was not there. Therefore it devolves. But topography and architecture must intervene.

The Millionaire's palace occupied a lordly space. In front of it was a lawn close-mowed as a South Ireland man's face two days after a shave. At one side of it and fronting on another street was a pleasance trimmed to a leaf, and the garage and stables. The Scotch pup had ravished the rag doll from the nursery, dragged it to a corner of the lawn, dug a hole, and buried it after the manner of careless undertakers. There you have the mystery solved, and no checks to write for the hypodermical wizard of fi'-pun notes to toss to the sergeant. Then let's get down to the heart of the thing, tiresome readers—the Christmas heart of the thing.

Fuzzy was drunk. Not riotously or helplessly or loquaciously, as you or I might get, but decently, appropriately, and inoffensively, as becomes a gentleman down on his luck.

Fuzzy was a soldier of misfortune. The road, the haystack, the park bench, the kitchen door, the bitter round of eleemosynary beds-with-shower-bath-attachment, the petty pickings and ignobly garnered largess of great cities—these formed the chapters of his history.

Fuzzy walked toward the river, down the street that bounded one side of the Millionaire's house and grounds. He saw a leg of Betsy, the lost rag doll, protruding, like the clue to a Liliputian murder mystery, from its untimely grave in a corner of the fence. He dragged forth the maltreated infant, tucked it under his arm, and went on his way crooning a road song of his brethren that no doll that has been brought up to the sheltered life should hear. Well for Betsy that she had no ears. And well that she had no eyes save unseeing circles of black; for the faces of Fuzzy and the Scotch terrier were those of brothers, and the heart of no rag doll could withstand twice to become the prey of such fearsome monsters.

Though you may not know it, Grogan's saloon stands near the river and near the foot of the street down which Fuzzy traveled. In Grogan's, Christmas cheer was already rampant.

Fuzzy entered with his doll. He fancied that as a mummer at the feast of Saturn he might earn a few drops from the wassail cup.

He set Betsy on the bar and addressed her loudly and humorously, seasoning his speech with exaggerated compliments and endearments, as one entertaining his lady friend. The loafers and bibbers around caught the farce of it, and roared. The bartender gave Fuzzy a drink. Oh, many of us carry rag dolls.

"One for the lady?" suggested Fuzzy impudently, and tucked another contribution to Art beneath his waistcoat.

He began to see possibilities in Betsy. His first night had been a success. Visions of a vaudeville circuit about town dawned upon him.

In a group near the stove sat "Pigeon" McCarthy, Black Riley, and "One-ear" Mike, well and unfavorably known in the tough shoestring district that blackened the left bank of the river. They passed a newspaper back and forth among themselves. The item that each solid and blunt forefinger pointed out was an advertisement headed "One Hundred Dollars Reward." To earn it, one must return the rag doll lost, strayed, or stolen from the Millionaire's mansion. It seemed that grief still ravaged, unchecked, in the bosom of the too faithful Child. Flip, the terrier, capered and shook his absurd whiskers before her, powerless to distract. She wailed for her Betsy in the faces of walking, talking, ma-ma-ing, and eye-closing French Mabelles and Violettes. The advertisement was a last resort.

Black Riley came from behind the stove and approached Fuzzy in his one-sided, parabolic way.

The Christmas mummer, flushed with his success, had tucked Betsy under his arm, and was about to depart to the filling of im-promptu dates elsewhere.

"Say, 'Bo," said Black Riley to him, "where did you cop out dat doll?"

"This doll?" asked Fuzzy, touching Betsy with his forefinger to be sure that she was the one referred to. "Why, this doll was presented to me by the Emperor of Beloochistan. I have seven hundred others in my country home in Newport. This doll—"

"Cheese the funny business," said Riley. "You swiped it or picked it up at de house on de hill where—but never mind dat. You want to take fifty cents for de rags, and take it quick. Me brother's kid at home might be wantin' to play wid it. Hey—what?"

He produced the coin.

Fuzzy laughed a gurgling, insolent, alcoholic laugh in his face. Go to the office of Sarah Bernhardt's manager and propose to him that she be released from a night's performance to entertain the Tackytown Lyceum and Literary Coterie. You will hear the duplicate of Fuzzy's laugh.

Black Riley gaged Fuzzy quickly with his blueberry eye as a wres-tler does. His hand was itching to play the Roman and wrest the rag Sabine from the extemporaneous merry-andrew who was entertaining an angel unaware. But he refrained. Fuzzy was fat and solid and big. Three inches of well-nourished corporeity, defended from the winter winds by dingy linen, intervened between his vest and trousers. Count-less small, circular wrinkles running around his coatsleeves and knees guaranteed the quality of his bone and muscle. His small blue eyes, bathed in the moisture of altruism and wooziness, looked upon you kindly yet without abashment. He was whiskerly, whiskyly, fleshily formidable. So, Black Riley temporized.

"Wot'll you take for it, den?" he asked.

"Money," said Fuzzy, with husky firmness, "cannot buy her."

He was intoxicated with the artist's first sweet cup of attainment. To set a faded-blue, earth-stained rag doll on a bar, to hold mimic converse with it, and to find his heart leaping with the sense of plaudits earned and his throat scorching with free libations poured in his honor—could base coin buy him from such achievements? You will perceive that Fuzzy had the temperament.

Fuzzy walked out with the gait of a trained sea lion in search of other cafés to conquer.

Though the dusk of twilight was hardly yet apparent, lights were beginning to spangle the city like popcorn bursting in a deep skillet. Christmas Eve, impatiently expected, was peeping over the brink of the hour. Millions had prepared for its celebration. Towns would be painted red. You, yourself, have heard the horns and dodged the capers of the Saturnalians.

"Pigeon" McCarthy, Black Riley, and "One-ear" Mike held a hasty converse outside Grogan's. They were narrow-chested, pallid striplings, not fighters in the open, but more dangerous in their ways of warfare than the most terrible of Turks. Fuzzy, in a pitched battle, could have eaten the three of them. In a go-as-you-please encounter he was already doomed.

They overtook him just as he and Betsy were entering Costigan's Casino. They deflected him, and shoved the newspaper under his nose. Fuzzy could read—and more.

"Boys," said he, "you are certainly damn true friends. Give me a week to think it over."

The soul of a real artist is quenched with difficulty.

The boys carefully pointed out to him that advertisements were soulless, and that the deficiencies of the day might not be supplied by the morrow.

"A cool hundred," said Fuzzy thoughtfully and mushily.

"Boys," said he, "you are true friends. I'll go up and claim the reward. The show business is not what it used to be."

Night was falling more surely. The three tagged at his sides to the foot of the rise on which stood the Millionaire's house. There Fuzzy turned upon them acrimoniously.

"You are a pack of putty-faced beagle hounds," he roared. "Go away."

They went away—a little way.

In "Pigeon" McCarthy's pocket was a section of two-inch gas-pipe eight inches long. In one end of it and in the middle of it was a lead plug. One-half of it was packed tight with solder. Black Riley carried a slungshot, being a conventional thug. "One-ear" Mike relied upon a pair of brass knucks—an heirloom in the family.

"Why fetch and carry," said Black Riley, "when someone will do it for ye? Let him bring it out to us. Hey—what?"

"We can chuck him in the river," said "Pigeon" McCarthy, "with a stone tied to his feet."

"Youse guys make me tired," said "One-ear" Mike sadly. "Ain't progress ever appealed to none of yez? Sprinkle a little gasoline on 'im, and drop 'im on the Drive—well?"

Fuzzy entered the Millionaire's gate and zigzagged toward the softly glowing entrance of the mansion. The three goblins came up to the gate and lingered—one on each side of it, one beyond the roadway. They fingered their cold metal and leather, confident.

Fuzzy rang the doorbell, smiling foolishly and dreamily. An atavistic instinct prompted him to reach for the button of his right glove. But he wore no gloves; so his left hand dropped, embarrassed.

The particular menial whose duty it was to open doors to silks and laces shied at first sight of Fuzzy. But a second glance took in his passport, his card of admission, his surety of welcome—the lost rag doll of the daughter of the house dangling under his arm.

Fuzzy was admitted into a great hall, dim with the glow from unseen lights. The hireling went away and returned with a maid and the Child. The doll was restored to the mourning one. She clasped her lost darling to her breast; and then, with the inordinate selfishness and candor of childhood, stamped her foot and whined hatred and fear of the odious being who had rescued her from the depths of sorrow and despair. Fuzzy wriggled himself into an ingratiatory attitude and essayed the idiotic smile and blattering small talk that is supposed to charm the budding intellect of the young. The Child bawled, and was dragged away, hugging her Betsy close.

There came the Secretary, pale, poised, polished, gliding in pumps, and worshiping pomp and ceremony. He counted out into Fuzzy's hand ten ten-dollar bills; then dropped his eye upon the door, transferred it to James, its custodian, indicated the obnoxious earner of the reward with the other, and allowed his pumps to waft him away to secretarial regions.

James gathered Fuzzy with his own commanding optic and swept him as far as the front door.

When the money touched Fuzzy's dingy palm his first instinct was to take to his heels; but a second thought restrained him from that blunder of etiquette. It was his; it had been given him. It—and, oh, what an elysium it opened to the gaze of his mind's eye! He had tumbled to the foot of the ladder; he was hungry, homeless, friendless, ragged, cold, drifting; and he held in his hand the key to a paradise of the mud honey that he craved. The fairy doll had waved a wand with her rag-stuffed hand; and now wherever he might go the enchanted palaces with shining footrests and magic red fluids in gleaming glassware would be open to him.

He followed James to the door.

He paused there as the flunky drew open the great mahogany portal for him to pass into the vestibule.

Beyond the wrought-iron gates in the dark highway Black Riley and his two pals casually strolled, fingering under their coats the inevitably fatal weapons that were to make the reward of the rag doll theirs.

Fuzzy stopped at the Millionaire's door and bethought himself. Like little sprigs of mistletoe on a dead tree, certain living green thoughts and memories began to decorate his confused mind. He was quite drunk, mind you, and the present was beginning to fade. Those wreaths and festoons of holly with their scarlet berries making the great hall gay—where had he seen such things before? Somewhere he had known polished floors and odors of fresh flowers in winter, and—and someone was singing a song in the house that he thought he had heard before. Someone singing and playing a harp. Of course it was Christmas—Fuzzy thought he must have been pretty drunk to have overlooked that.

And then he went out of the present, and there came back to him out of some impossible, vanished, and irrevocable past a little, pure-white, transient, forgotten ghost—the spirit of noblesse oblige. Upon a gentleman certain things devolve.

James opened the outer door. A stream of light went down the graveled walk to the iron gate. Black Riley, McCarthy, and One-ear Mike saw, and carelessly drew their sinister cordon closer about the gate.

With a more imperious gesture than James's master had ever

used or could ever use, Fuzzy compelled the menial to close the door. Upon a gentleman certain things devolve. Especially at the Christmas season.

"It is cust—customary," he said to James, the flustered, "when a gentleman calls on Christmas Eve to pass the compliments of the season with the lady of the house. You und'stand? I shall not move shtep till I pass compl'ments season with lady of the house. Und'stand?"

There was an argument. James lost. Fuzzy raised his voice and sent it through the house unpleasantly. I did not say he was a gentleman. He was simply a tramp being visited by a ghost.

A sterling-silver bell rang. James went back to answer it, leaving Fuzzy in the hall. James explained somewhere to someone.

Then he came and conducted Fuzzy into the library.

The Lady entered a moment later. She was more beautiful and holy than any picture that Fuzzy had seen. She smiled, and said something about a doll. Fuzzy didn't understand that; he remembered nothing about a doll.

A footman brought in two small glasses of sparkling wine on a stamped sterling-silver waiter. The Lady took one. The other was handed to Fuzzy.

As his fingers closed on the slender glass stem his disabilities dropped from him for one brief moment. He straightened himself; and Time, so disobliging to most of us, turned backward to accommodate Fuzzy.

Forgotten Christmas ghosts whiter than the false beards of the most opulent Kriss Kringle were rising in the fumes of Grogan's whisky. What had the Millionaire's mansion to do with a long, wainscoted Virginia hall, where the riders were grouped around a silver punchbowl, drinking the ancient toast of the House? And why should the patter of the cab horses' hoofs on the frozen street be in any wise related to the sound of the saddled hunters stamping under the shelter of the west veranda? And what had Fuzzy to do with any of it?

The Lady, looking at him over her glass, let her condescending smile fade away like a false dawn. Her eyes turned serious. She saw something beneath the rags and Scotch terrier whiskers that she did not understand. But it did not matter.

Fuzzy lifted his glass and smiled vacantly.

"P-pardon, lady," he said, "but couldn't leave without exchangin' comp'ments sheason with lady th' house. 'Gainst princ'ples gen'leman do sho."

And then he began the ancient salutation that was a tradition in the House when men wore lace ruffles and powder.

"The blessings of another year——"

Fuzzy's memory failed him. The Lady prompted:

"Be upon this hearth."

"The guest——" stammered Fuzzy.

"And upon her who——" continued the Lady, with a leading smile.

"Oh, cut it out," said Fuzzy ill-manneredly. "I can't remember. Drink hearty."

Fuzzy had shot his arrow. They drank. The Lady smiled again the smile of her caste. James enveloped Fuzzy and reconducted him toward the front door. The harp music still softly drifted through the house.

Outside, Black Riley breathed on his cold hands and hugged the gate.

"I wonder," said the Lady to herself, musing, "who—but there were so many who came. I wonder whether memory is a curse or a blessing to them after they have fallen so low."

Fuzzy and his escort were nearly at the door. The Lady called: "James!"

James stalked back obsequiously, leaving Fuzzy waiting unsteadily, with his brief spark of the divine fire gone.

Outside, Black Riley stamped his cold feet and got a firmer grip on his section of gaspipe.

"You will conduct this gentleman," said the Lady, "downstairs. Then tell Louis to get out the Mercedes and take him to whatever place he wishes to go."

GIFTS OF THE MAGI

ONE DOLLAR AND eighty-seven cents. That was all. And 60 cents of it was in pennies. Pennies saved one and two at a time by bulldozing the grocer and the vegetable man and the butcher until one's cheeks burned with the silent imputation of parsimony that such close dealing implied. Three times Della counted it. One dollar and eighty-seven cents. And the next day would be Christmas.

There was clearly nothing to do but flop down on the shabby little couch and howl. So Della did it. Which instigates the moral reflection that life is made up of sobs, sniffles, and smiles, with sniffles predominating.

While the mistress of the home is gradually subsiding from the first stage to the second take a look at the home. A furnished flat at $8 per week. It did not exactly beggar description, but it certainly had that word on the lookout for the mendicancy squad.

In the vestibule below belonged to this flat a letterbox into which no letter would go, and an electric button from which no mortal finger could coax a ring. Also appertaining thereunto was a card bearing the name "Mr. James Dillingham Young."

The "Dillingham" had been flung to the breeze during a former period of prosperity when its possessor was being paid $30 per week. Now, when the income was shrunk to $20, the letters of "Dillingham" looked blurred, as though they were thinking seriously of contracting to a modest and unassuming D. But whenever Mr. James Dillingham Young came home and reached his flat above he was called "Jim" and greatly hugged by Mrs. James Dillingham Young, already introduced to you as Della. Which is all very good.

Della finished her cry and attended to her cheeks with the powder rag. She stood by the window and looked out dully at a gray cat walking a gray fence in a gray backyard. Tomorrow would be Christmas Day, and she had only $1.87 with which to buy Jim a present. She had been saving every penny she could for months, with this result. Twenty dollars a week doesn't go far. Expenses had been greater than she had calculated. They always are. Only $1.87 to buy a present for Jim. Her Jim. Many a happy hour she had spent planning for something nice for him. Something fine and rare and sterling—something just a little bit near to being worthy of the honor of being owned by Jim.

There was a pier glass between the windows of the room. Perhaps you have seen a pier glass in an $8 flat. A very thin and very agile person may, by observing his reflection in a rapid sequence of longitudinal strips, obtain a fairly accurate conception of his looks. Della, being slender, had mastered the art.

Suddenly she whirled from the window and stood before the glass. Her eyes were shining brilliantly, but her face had lost its color within twenty seconds. Rapidly she pulled down her hair and let it fall to its full length.

Now, there were two possessions of the James Dillingham Youngs in which they both took a mighty pride. One was Jim's gold watch that had been his father's and his grandfather's. The other was Della's hair. Had the Queen of Sheba lived in the flat across the airshaft Della would have let her hair hang out the window someday to dry and mocked at Her Majesty's jewels and gifts. Had King Solomon been the janitor, with all his treasures piled up in the basement, Jim would have pulled out his watch every time he passed, just to see him pluck at his beard from envy.

So now Della's beautiful hair fell about her, rippling and shining like a cascade of brown waters. It reached below her knee and made itself almost a garment for her. And then she did it up again nervously and quickly. Once she faltered for a minute and stood still while a tear or two splashed on the worn red carpet.

On went her old brown jacket; on went her old brown hat. With a whirl of skirts and with the brilliant sparkle still in her eyes, she fluttered out the door and down the stairs to the street.

Where she stopped the sign read: "Mme. Sofronie. Hair Goods of All Kinds." One flight up Della ran, and collected herself, panting, before Madame, large, too white, chilly and hardly looking the "Sofronie."

"Will you buy my hair?" asked Della.

"I buy hair," said Madame. "Take yer hat off and let's have a sight at the looks of it."

Down rippled the brown cascade.

"Twenty dollars," said Madame, lifting the mass with a practiced hand.

"Give it to me quick," said Della.

Oh, and the next two hours tripped by on rosy wings. Forget the hashed metaphor. She was ransacking the stores for Jim's present.

She found it at last. It surely had been made for Jim and no one else. There was none other like it in any of the stores, and she had turned all of them inside out. It was a platinum fob chain simple and chaste in design, properly proclaiming its value by substance alone and not by meretricious ornamentation—as all good things should do. It was even worthy of The Watch. As soon as she saw it she knew that it must be Jim's. It was like him. Quietness and value—the description applied to both. Twenty-one dollars they took from her for it, and she hurried home with the 87 cents. With that chain on his watch Jim might be properly anxious about the time in any company. Grand as the watch was, he sometimes looked at it on the sly on account of the old leather strap that he used in place of a chain.

When Della reached home her intoxication gave way a little to prudence and reason. She got out her curling irons and lighted the gas and went to work repairing the ravages made by generosity added to love. Which is always a tremendous task, dear friends—a mammoth task.

Within forty minutes her head was covered with tiny, close-lying curls that made her look wonderfully like a truant schoolboy. She looked at her reflection in the mirror long, carefully and critically.

"If Jim doesn't kill me," she said to herself, "before he takes a second look at me, he'll say I look like a Coney Island chorus girl. But what could I do—oh, what could I do with a dollar and eighty-seven cents!"

At 7 o'clock the coffee was made and the frying pan was on the back of the stove hot and ready to cook the chops.

Jim was never late. Della doubled the fob chain in her hand and sat on the corner of the table near the door that he always entered.

Then she heard his step on the stair away down on the first flight, and she turned white for just a moment. She had a habit of saying little silent prayers about the simplest everyday things, and now she whispered: "Please, God, make him think I am still pretty."

The door opened and Jim stepped in and closed it. He looked thin and very serious. Poor fellow, he was only twenty-two—and to be burdened with a family! He needed a new overcoat and he was without gloves.

Jim stopped inside the door, as immovable as a setter at the scent of quail. His eyes were fixed upon Della, and there was an expression in them that she could not read, and it terrified her. It was not anger, nor surprise, nor disapproval, nor horror, nor any of the sentiments that she had been prepared for. He simply stared at her fixedly with that peculiar expression on his face.

Della wriggled off the table and went for him.

"Jim, darling," she cried, "don't look at me that way. I had my hair cut off and sold it because I couldn't have lived through Christmas without giving you a present. It'll grow again—you won't mind, will you? I just had to do it. My hair grows awfully fast. Say 'Merry Christmas!' Jim, and let's be happy. You don't know what a nice—what a beautiful, nice gift I've got for you."

"You've cut off your hair?" asked Jim laboriously, as if he had not arrived at that patent fact yet even after the hardest mental labor.

"Cut it off and sold it," said Della. "Don't you like me just as well, anyhow? I'm me without my hair, ain't I?"

Jim looked about the room curiously.

"You say your hair is gone?" he said with an air almost of idiocy.

"You needn't look for it," said Della. "It's sold, I tell you—sold and gone too. It's Christmas Eve, boy. Be good to me, for it went for you. Maybe the hairs of my head were numbered," she went on with a sudden serious sweetness, "but nobody could ever count my love for you. Shall I put the chops on, Jim?"

Out of his trance Jim seemed to quickly wake. He enfolded his Della. For ten seconds let us regard with discreet scrutiny some inconsequential object in the other direction. Eight dollars a week or a million a year—what is the difference? A mathematician or a wit would give you the wrong answer. The magi brought valuable gifts, but that was not among them. This dark assertion will be illuminated later on.

Jim drew a package from his overcoat pocket and threw it upon the table.

"Don't make any mistake, Dell," he said, "about me. I don't think there's anything in the way of a haircut or a shave or a shampoo that could make me like my girl any less. But if you'll unwrap that package you may see why you had me going awhile at first."

White fingers and nimble tore at the string and paper. And then an ecstatic scream of joy; and then, alas! a quick feminine change to hysterical tears and wails, necessitating the immediate employment of all the comforting powers of the lord of the flat.

For there lay The Combs—the set of combs, side and back, that Della had worshiped for long in a Broadway window. Beautiful combs, pure tortoiseshell, with jeweled rims—just the shade to wear in the beautiful vanished hair. They were expensive combs, she knew, and her heart had simply craved and yearned over them without the least hope of possession. And now, they were hers, but the tresses that should have adorned the coveted adornments were gone.

But she hugged them to her bosom, and at length she was able to look up with dim eyes and a smile and say: "My hair grows so fast, Jim!"

And then Della leaped up like a little singed cat and cried, "Oh, oh!"

Jim had not yet seen his beautiful present. She held it out to him eagerly upon her open palm. The dull, precious metal seemed to flash with a reflection of her bright and ardent spirit.

"Isn't it a dandy, Jim? I hunted all over town to find it. You'll have to look at the time a hundred times a day now. Give me your watch. I want to see how it looks on it."

Instead of obeying, Jim tumbled down on the couch and put his hands under the back of his head and smiled.

"Dell," said he, "let's put our Christmas presents away and keep 'em a while. They're too nice to use just at present. I sold the watch to get the money to buy your combs. And now suppose you put the chops on."

The magi, as you know, were wise men—wonderfully wise men—who brought gifts to the Babe in the manger. They invented the art of giving Christmas gifts. Being wise, their gifts were no doubt wise ones, possibly bearing the privilege of exchange in case of duplication. And here I have lamely related to you the uneventful chronicle of two foolish children in a flat who most unwisely sacrificed for each other the greatest treasures of their house. But in a last word to the wise of these days let it be said that of all who give gifts these two were of the wisest. Of all who give and receive gifts, such as they are the wisest. Everywhere they are the wisest. They are the magi.

THE ADVENTURES OF
SHAMROCK JOLNES

I AM SO fortunate as to count Shamrock Jolnes, the great New York detective, among my muster of friends. Jolnes is what is called the "inside man" of the city detective force. He is an expert in the use of the typewriter, and it is his duty, whenever there is a "murder mystery" to be solved, to sit at a desk telephone at headquarters and take down the message of "cranks" who phone in their confessions to having committed the crime.

But on certain "off" days when confessions are coming in slowly and three or four new papers have run to earth as many different guilty persons, Jolnes will knock about the town with me, exhibiting, to my great delight and instruction, his marvelous powers of observation and deduction.

The other day I dropped in at Headquarters and found the great detective gazing thoughtfully at a string that was tied tightly around his little finger.

"Good morning, Whatsup," he said without turning his head. "I'm glad to notice that you've had your house fitted up with electric lights at last."

"Will you please tell me," I said in surprise, "how you knew that? I am sure that I never mentioned the fact to anyone, and the wiring was a rush order not completed until this morning."

"Nothing easier," said Jolnes genially. "As you came in I caught the odor of the cigar you are smoking. I know an expensive cigar; and I know that not more than three men in New York can afford to smoke cigars and pay gas bills too at the present time. That was an easy one. But I am working just now on a little problem of my own."

"Why have you that string on your finger?" I asked.

"That's the problem," said Jolnes. "My wife tied that on this morning to remind me of something I was to send up to the house. Sit down, Whatsup, and excuse me for a few moments."

The distinguished detective went to a wall telephone, and stood with the receiver to his ear for probably ten minutes.

"Were you listening to a confession?" I asked when he had returned to his chair.

"Perhaps," said Jolnes with a smile, "it might be called something of the sort. To be frank with you, Whatsup, I've cut out the dope. I've been increasing the quantity for so long that morphine doesn't have much effect on me anymore. I've got to have something more powerful. That telephone I just went to is connected with a room in the Waldorf where there's an author's reading in progress. Now, to get at the solution of this string."

After five minutes of silent pondering, Jolnes looked at me with a smile, and nodded his head.

"Wonderful man!" I exclaimed. "Already?"

"It is quite simple," he said, holding up his finger. "You see that knot? That is to prevent my forgetting. It is, therefore, a forget-me-knot. A forget-me-not is a flower. It was a sack of flour that I was to send home!"

"Beautiful!" I could not help crying out in admiration.

"Suppose we go out for a ramble," suggested Jolnes.

"There is only one case of importance on hand now. Old man McCarty, one hundred and four years old, died from eating too many bananas. The evidence points so strongly to the Mafia that the police have surrounded the Second Avenue Katzenjammer Gambrinus Club No. 2, and the capture of the assassin in only the matter of a few hours. The detective force has not yet been called on for assistance."

Jolnes and I went out and up the street toward the corner, where we were to catch a surface car.

Halfway up the block we met Rheingelder, an acquaintance of ours, who held a City Hall position.

"Good morning, Rheingelder," said Jolnes, halting.

"Nice breakfast that was you had this morning."

Always on the lookout for the detective's remarkable feats of deduction, I saw Jolnes's eyes flash for an instant upon a long yellow splash on the shirt bosom and a smaller one upon the chin of Rheingelder—both undoubtedly made by the yolk of an egg.

"Oh, dot is some of your detectiveness," said Rheingelder, shaking all over with a smile. "Vell, I bet you trinks and cigars all around dot you cannot tell vot I haf eaten for breakfast."

"Done," said Jolnes. "Sausage, pumpernickel, and coffee."

Rheingelder admitted the correctness of the surmise and paid the bet. When we had proceeded on our way I said to Jolnes, "I thought you looked at the egg spilled on his chin and shirt front."

"I did," said Jolnes. "That is where I began my deduction. Rheingelder is a very economical, saving man. Yesterday eggs dropped in the market to twenty-eight cents per dozen. Today they are quoted at forty-two. Rheingelder ate eggs yesterday, and today he went back to his usual fare. A little thing like this isn't anything, Whatsup; it belongs to the primary arithmetic class."

When we boarded the streetcar we found the seats all occupied —principally by ladies. Jolnes and I stood on the rear platform.

About the middle of the car there sat an elderly man with a short, gray beard, who looked to be the typical, well-dressed New Yorker. At successive corners other ladies climbed aboard, and soon three or four of them were standing over the man, clinging to straps and glaring meaningly at the man who occupied the coveted seat. But he resolutely retained his place.

"We New Yorkers," I remarked to Jolnes, "have about lost our manners, as far as the exercise of them in public goes."

"Perhaps so," said Jolnes lightly; "but the man you evidently refer to happens to be a very chivalrous and courteous gentleman from Old Virginia. He is spending a few days in New York with his wife and two daughters, and he leaves for the South tonight."

"You know him, then?" I said in amazement.

"I never saw him before we stepped on the car," declared the detective smilingly.

"By the gold tooth of the Witch of Endor!" I cried. "If you can construe all that from his appearance you are dealing in nothing else than black art."

"The habit of observation—nothing more," said Jolnes. "If the old gentleman gets off the car before we do, I think I can demonstrate to you the accuracy of my deduction."

Three blocks farther along the gentleman rose to leave the car. Jolnes addressed him at the door:

"Pardon me, sir, but are you not Colonel Hunter, of Norfolk, Virginia?"

"No, suh," was the extremely courteous answer. "My name, suh, is Ellison—Major Winfield R. Ellison, from Fairfax County, in the same state. I know a good many people, suh, in Norfolk—the Goodriches, the Tollivers, and the Crabtrees, suh, but I never had the pleasure of meeting yo' friend, Colonel Hunter. I am happy to say, suh, that I am going back to Virginia tonight, after having spent a week in yo' city with my wife and three daughters. I shall be in Norfolk in about ten days, and if you will give me yo' name, suh, I will take pleasure in looking up Colonel Hunter and telling him that you inquired after him, suh."

"Thank you," said Jolnes. "Tell him that Reynolds sent his regards, if you will be so kind."

I glanced at the great New York detective and saw that a look of intense chagrin had come upon his clear-cut features. Failure in the slightest point always galled Shamrock Jolnes.

"Did you say your *three* daughters?" he asked of the Virginia gentleman.

"Yes, suh, my three daughters, all as fine girls as there are in Fairfax County," was the answer.

With that Major Ellison stopped the car and began to descend the step.

Shamrock Jolnes clutched his arm.

"One moment, sir," he begged, in an urbane voice in which I alone detected the anxiety—"am I not right in believing that one of the young ladies is an *adopted* daughter?"

"You are, suh," admitted the major, from the ground, "but how the devil you knew it, suh, is mo' than I can tell."

"And mo' than I can tell, too," I said, as the car went on.

Jolnes was restored to his calm, observant serenity by having wrested victory from his apparent failure; so after we got off the car he invited me into a café promising to reveal the process of his latest wonderful feat.

"In the first place," he began after we were comfortably seated, "I knew the gentleman was no New Yorker because he was flushed and uneasy and restless on account of the ladies that were standing, although he did not rise and give them his seat. I decided from his appearance that he was a Southerner rather than a Westerner.

"Next I began to figure out his reason for not relinquishing his seat to a lady when he evidently felt strongly, but not overpoweringly, impelled to do so. I very quickly decided upon that. I noticed that one of his eyes had received a severe jab in one corner, which was red and inflamed, and that all over his face were tiny round marks about the size of the end of an uncut lead pencil. Also upon both of his patent-leather shoes were a number of deep imprints shaped like ovals cut off square at one end.

"Now, there is only one district in New York City where a man is bound to receive scars and wounds and indentations of that sort—and that is along the sidewalks of Twenty-third Street and a portion of Sixth Avenue south of there. I knew from the imprints of trampling French heels on his feet and the marks of countless jabs in the face from umbrellas and parasols carried by women in the shopping district that he had been in conflict with the amazonian troops. And as he was a man of intelligent appearance, I knew he would not have braved such dangers unless he had been dragged thither by his own folk. Therefore, when he got on the car his anger at the treatment he had received was sufficient to make him keep his seat in spite of his traditions of Southern chivalry."

"That is all very well," I said, "but why did you insist upon daughters—and especially two daughters? Why couldn't a wife alone have taken him shopping?"

"There had to be daughters," said Jolnes calmly. "If he had only a wife, and she near his own age, he could have bluffed her into going alone. If he had a young wife she would prefer to go alone. So there you are."

"I'll admit that," I said. "But, now, why two daughters? And how, in the name of all the prophets, did you guess that one was adopted when he told you he had three?"

"Don't say guess," said Jolnes, with a touch of pride in his air. "There is no such word in the lexicon of ratiocination. In Major Ellison's buttonhole there was a carnation and a rosebud backed by a geranium leaf. No woman ever combined a carnation and a rosebud into a boutonnière. Close your eyes, Whatsup, and give the logic of your imagination a chance. Cannot you see the lovely Adele fastening the carnation to the lapel so that Papa may be gay upon the street? And then the romping Edith May dancing up with sisterly jealousy to add her rosebud to the adornment?"

"And then," I cried, beginning to feel enthusiasm, "when he declared that he had three daughters——"

"I could see," said Jolnes, "one in the background who added no flower; and I knew that she must be——"

"Adopted!" I broke in. "I give you every credit; but how did you know he was leaving for the South tonight?"

"In his breast pocket," said the great detective, "something large and oval made a protuberance. Good liquor is scarce on trains, and it is a long journey from New York to Fairfax County."

"Again, I must bow to you," I said. "And tell me this, so that my last shred of doubt will be cleared away; why did you decide that he was from Virginia?"

"It was very faint, I admit," answered Shamrock Jolnes, "but no trained observer could have failed to detect the odor of mint in the car."

The Last Leaf

The Pathetic Story of Two Girl Artists in Old New York and a Gray-Haired Failure Who Made Successful Sacrifice at the End.

IN A LITTLE district west of Washington Square the streets have run crazy and broken themselves into small strips called "places." These "places" make strange angles and curves. One street crosses itself a time or two. An artist once discovered a valuable possibility in this street. Suppose a collector with a bill for paints, paper, and canvas should, in traversing this route, suddenly meet himself coming back, without a cent having been paid on account!

So, to quaint old Greenwich Village the art people soon came prowling, hunting for north windows and eighteenth-century gables and Dutch attics and low rents. Then they imported some pewter mugs and a chafing dish or two from Sixth Avenue, and become a "colony."

At the top of a squatty, three-story brick Sue and Johnsy had their studio. "Johnsy" was familiar for Joanna. One was from Maine; the other from California. They had met at the table d'hote of an Eighth Street "Delmonico's," and found their tastes in art, chicory salad, and bishop sleeves so congenial that the joint studio resulted.

That was in May. In November a cold, unseen stranger, whom the doctors called Pneumonia, stalked about the colony, touching one here and there with his icy finger. Over on the East Side this ravager strode boldly, smiting his victims by scores, but his feet trod slowly through the maze of the narrow and moss-grown "places."

Mr. Pneumonia was not what you would call a chivalric old gentleman. A mite of a little woman with blood thinned by California zephyrs was hardly fair game for the red-fisted, short-breathed old duffer. But Johnsy he smote; and she lay, scarcely moving, on her painted iron bedstead, looking through the small Dutch windowpanes at the blank side of the next brick house.

One morning the busy doctor invited Sue into the hallway with a shaggy, gray eyebrow.

"She has one chance in—let us say, ten," he said, as he shook down the mercury in his clinical thermometer. "And that chance is for her to want to live. This way people have of lining up on the side of the undertaker makes the entire pharmacopeia look silly. Your little lady has made up her mind that she's not going to get well. Has she anything on her mind?"

She—she wanted to paint the Bay of Naples someday," said Sue.

"Paint?—bosh! Has she anything on her mind worth thinking about twice—a man, for instance?"

"A man?" said Sue, with a jew's harp twang in her voice. "Is a man worth—but, no, doctor; there is nothing of the kind."

"Well, it is the weakness then," said the doctor. "I will do all that science, so far as it may filter through my efforts, can accomplish. But whenever my patient begins to count the carriages in her funeral procession I subtract 50 percent from the curative power of medicines. If you will get her to ask one question about the new winter styles in cloak sleeves I will promise you a one-in-five chance for her, instead of one in ten."

After the doctor had gone Sue went into the workroom and cried a Japanese napkin to a pulp. Then she swaggered into Johnsy's room with her drawing board, whistling ragtime.

Johnsy lay, scarcely making a ripple under the bedclothes, with her face toward the window. Sue stopped whistling, thinking she was asleep.

She arranged her board and began a pen-and-ink drawing to illustrate a magazine story. Young artists must pave their way to Art by drawing pictures for magazine stories that young authors write to pave their way to Literature.

As Sue was sketching a pair of elegant horse-show riding trousers and a monocle on the figure of the hero, an Idaho cowboy, she heard a low sound, several times repeated. She went quickly to the bedside.

Johnsy's eyes were open wide. She was looking out the window and counting—counting backward.

"Twelve," she said, and a little later "eleven"; and then "ten," and "nine"; and then "eight" and "seven" almost together.

Sue looked solicitously out of the window. What was there to count? There was only a bare, dreary yard to be seen, and the blank side of the brick house forty feet away. An old, old ivy vine, gnarled and decayed at the roots, climbed halfway up the brick wall. The cold breath of autumn had stricken its leaves from the vine until its skeleton branches clung, almost bare, to the crumbling bricks.

"What is it, dear?" asked Sue.

"Six," said Johnsy in almost a whisper. "They're falling faster now. Three days ago there were almost a hundred. It made my head ache to count them. But now it's easy. There goes another one. There are only five left now."

"Five what, dear. Tell your Sudie."

"Leaves. On the ivy vine. When the last one falls I must go, too. I've known that for three days. Didn't the doctor tell you?"

"Oh, I never heard of such nonsense," complained Sue with magnificent scorn. "What have old ivy leaves to do with your getting well? And you used to love that vine so, you naughty girl. Don't be a goosey. Why, the doctor told me this morning that your chances for getting well real soon were—let's see exactly what he said—he said the chances were ten to one! Why, that's almost as good a chance as we have in New York when we ride on the streetcars or walk past a new building. Try to take some broth now, and let Sudie go back to her drawing, so she can sell the editor man with it, and buy port wine for her sick child, and porkchops for her greedy self."

"You needn't get any more wine," said Johnsy, keeping her eyes fixed out the window. "There goes another. No, I don't want any broth. That leaves just four. I want to see the last one fall before it gets dark. Then I'll go, too."

"Johnsy, dear," said Sue, bending over her, "will you promise me to keep your eyes closed, and not look out the window until I am done working? I must hand those drawings in by tomorrow. I need the light, or I would draw the shade down."

"Couldn't you draw in the other room?" asked Johnsy coldly.

"I'd rather be here by you," said Sue. "Besides, I don't want you to keep looking at those silly ivy leaves."

"Tell me as soon as you have finished," said Johnsy, closing her eyes, and lying white and still as a fallen statue, "because I want to see the last one fall. I'm tired of waiting. I'm tired of thinking. I want to turn loose my hold on everything, and go sailing down, down, just like one of those poor, tired leaves."

"Try to sleep," said Sue. "I must call Behrman up to be my

model for the old hermit miner. I'll not be gone a minute. Don't try to move 'till I come back."

Old Behrman was a painter who lived on the ground floor beneath them. He was past sixty and had a Michael Angelo's Moses beard curling down from the head of a satyr along the body of an imp. Behrman was a failure in art. Forty years he had wielded the brush without getting near enough to touch the hem of his Mistress's robe. He had been always about to paint a masterpiece, but had never yet begun it. For several years he had painted nothing except now and then a daub in the line of commerce or advertising. He earned a little by serving as a model to those young artists in the colony who could not pay the price of a professional. He drank gin to excess, and still talked of his coming masterpiece. For the rest he was a fierce little old man, who scoffed terribly at softness in anyone, and who regarded himself as especial mastiff-in-waiting to protect the two young artists in the studio above.

Sue found Behrman smelling strongly of juniper berries in his dimly lighted den below. In one corner was a blank canvas on an easel that had been waiting there for twenty-five years to receive the first line of the masterpiece. She told him of Johnsy's fancy, and how she feared she would, indeed, light and fragile as a leaf herself, float away when her slight hold upon the world grew weaker.

Old Behrman, with his red eyes plainly streaming, shouted his contempt and derision for such idiotic imaginings.

"Vass!" he cried. "Is dere people in de world mit der foolishness to die because leafs dey drop off from a confounded vine? I haf not heard of such a thing. No, I will not bose as a model for your fool hermit-dunderhead. Vy do you allow dot silly pusiness to come in der prain of her? Ach, dot poor leetle Miss Johnsy."

"She is very ill and weak," said Sue, "and the fever has left her mind morbid and full of strange fancies. Very well, Mr. Behrman, if you do not care to pose for me, you needn't. But I think you are a horrid old—old flibbertigibbet."

"You are just like a woman!" yelled Behrman. "Who said I vill not bose? Go on. I come mit you. For half an hour I haf peen trying to say dot I am ready to bose. Gott! dis is not any blace in which one so schones at Miss Yohnsy shall lie sick. Someday I vill baint a masterpiece, and ve shall all go away. Gott! yes."

Johnsy was sleeping when they went upstairs. Sue pulled the shade down to the windowsill, and motioned Behrman into the other room. In there they peered out the window fearfully at the ivy vine. Then they looked at each other for a moment without speaking. A persistent, cold rain was falling, mingled with snow. Behrman, in his old blue shirt, took his seat as the hermit miner on an upturned kettle for a rock.

When Sue awoke from an hour's sleep the next morning she found Johnsy with dull, wide-open eyes staring at the drawn green shade.

"Pull it up; I want to see," she ordered in a whisper.

Wearily she obeyed.

But, lo! after the beating rain and fierce gusts of wind that had endured through the livelong night, there yet stood out against the brick wall one ivy leaf. It was the last on the vine. Still dark green near its stem, but with its serrated edges tinted with the yellow of dissolution and decay, it hung bravely from a branch some twenty feet above the ground.

"It is the last one," said Johnsy. "I thought it would surely fall during the night. I heard the wind. It will fall today, and I shall die at the same time."

"Dear, dear!" said Sue, leaning her worn face down to the pillow, "think of me, if you won't think of yourself. What would I do?"

But Johnsy did not answer. The lonesomest thing in all the world is a soul when it is making ready to go on its mysterious, far journey. The fancy seemed to possess her more strongly as one by one the ties that bound her to friendship and to earth were loosed.

The day wore away, and even through the twilight they could see the lone ivy leaf clinging to its stem against the wall. And then, with the coming of the night the north wind was again loosed, while the rain still beat against the windows and pattered down from the low Dutch eaves.

When it was light enough Johnsy, the merciless, commanded that the shade be raised.

The ivy leaf was still there.

Johnsy lay for a long time looking at it. And then she called to Sue, who was stirring her chicken broth over the gas stove.

"I've been a bad girl, Sudie," said Johnsy. "Something has made the last leaf stay there to show me how wicked I was. It is a sin to want to die. You may bring me a little broth now, and some milk with a little port in it, and—no; bring me a hand mirror first; and then pack some pillows about me, and I will sit up and watch you cook."

An hour later she said, "Sudie, someday I hope to paint the Bay of Naples."

The doctor came in the afternoon, and Sue had an excuse to go into the hallway as he left.

"Even chances," said the doctor, taking Sue's thin, shaking hand in his. "With good nursing you'll win. And now I must see another case I have downstairs. Behrman, his name is—some kind of an artist, I believe. Pneumonia, too. He is an old, weak man, and the attack is acute. There is no hope for him; but he goes to the hospital today to be made more comfortable."

The next day the doctor said to Sue: "She's out of danger. You've won. Nutrition and care now—that's all."

And that afternoon Sue came to the bed where Johnsy lay, contentedly knitting a very blue and very useless woolen shoulder scarf, and put one arm around her, pillows and all.

"I have something to tell you, white mouse," she said. "Mr. Behrman died of pneumonia today in the hospital. He was ill only two days. The janitor found him on the morning of the first day in his room downstairs helpless with pain. His shoes and clothing were wet through and icy cold. They couldn't imagine where he had been on such a dreadful night. And then they found a lantern, still lighted, and a ladder that had been dragged from its place, and some scattered brushes, and a palette with green and yellow colors mixed on it, and— look out the window, dear, at the last ivy leaf on the wall. Didn't you wonder why it never fluttered or moved when the wind blew? Ah, darling, it's Behrman's masterpiece—he painted it there the night that the last leaf fell."

Makes the Whole World Kin

THE BURGLAR STEPPED inside the window quickly, and then he took his time. A burglar who respects his art always takes his time before taking anything else.

The house was a private residence. By its boarded front door and untrimmed Boston ivy the burglar knew that the mistress of it was sitting on some oceanside piazza telling a sympathetic man in a yachting cap that no one had ever understood her sensitive, lonely heart. He knew by the light in the third-story front windows, and by the lateness of the season, that the master of the house had come home, and would soon extinguish his light and retire. For it was September of the year and of the soul, in which season the house's good man comes to consider roof gardens and stenographers as vanities, and to desire the return of his mate and the more durable blessings of decorum and the moral excellencies.

The burglar lighted a cigarette. The guarded glow of the match illuminated his salient points for a moment. He belonged to the third type of burglars.

This third type has not yet been recognized and accepted. The police have made us familiar with the first and second. Their classification is simple. The collar is the distinguishing mark.

When a burglar is caught who does not wear a collar he is described as a degenerate of the lowest type, singularly vicious and depraved, and is suspected of being the desperate criminal who stole the handcuffs out of Patrolman Hennessy's pocket in 1878 and walked away to escape arrest.

The other well-known type is the burglar who wears a collar. He is always referred to as a Raffles in real life. He is invariably a gentleman by daylight, breakfasting in a dress suit, and posing as a paperhanger, while after dark he plies his nefarious occupation of burglary. His mother is an extremely wealthy and respected resident of Ocean Grove, and when he is conducted to his cell he asks at once for a nail file and the *Police Gazette.* He always has a wife in every State in the Union and fiancees in all the Territories, and the newspapers print his matrimonial gallery out of their stock of cuts of the ladies who were cured by only one bottle after having been given up by five doctors, experiencing great relief after the first dose.

The burglar wore a blue sweater. He was neither a Raffles nor one of the chefs from Hell's Kitchen. The police would have been baffled had they attempted to classify him. They have not yet heard of the respectable, unassuming burglar who is neither above nor below his station.

This burglar of the third class began to prowl. He wore no masks, dark lanterns, or gum shoes. He carried a 38-caliber revolver in his pocket, and he chewed peppermint gum thoughtfully.

The furniture of the house was swathed in its summer dust protectors. The silver was far away in safe-deposit vaults. The burglar expected no remarkable "haul." His objective point was that dimly lighted room where the master of the house should be sleeping heavily after whatever solace he had sought to lighten the burden of his loneliness. A "touch" might be made there to the extent of legitimate, fair professional profits—loose money, a watch, a jeweled stickpin—nothing exorbitant or beyond reason. He had seen the window left open and had taken the chance.

The burglar softly opened the door of the lighted room. The gas was turned low. A man lay in the bed asleep. On the dresser lay many things in confusion—a crumpled roll of bills, a watch, keys, three poker chips, crushed cigars, a pink silk hair bow, and an unopened bottle of bromo seltzer for a bulwark in the morning.

The burglar took three steps toward the dresser. The man in the bed suddenly uttered a squeaky groan and opened his eyes. His right hand slid under his pillow, but remained there.

"Lay still," said the burglar in conversational tone. Burglars of the third type do not hiss. The citizen in the bed looked at the round end of the burglar's pistol and lay still.

"Now hold up both your hands," commanded the burglar.

The citizen had a little, pointed, brown-and-gray beard, like that of a painless dentist. He looked solid, esteemed, irritable, and disgusted. He sat up in bed and raised his right hand above his head.

"Up with the other one," ordered the burglar. "You might be amphibious and shoot with your left. You can count two, can't you? Hurry up, now."

"Can't raise the other one," said the citizen with a contortion of his lineaments.

"What's the matter with it?"

"Rheumatism in the shoulder."

"Inflammatory?"

"Was. The inflammation has gone down."

The burglar stood for a moment or two, holding his gun on the afflicted one. He glanced at the plunder on the dresser and then, with a half-embarrassed air back at the man in the bed. Then he, too, made a sudden grimace.

"Don't stand there making faces," snapped the citizen, bad-humoredly. "If you've come to burgle why don't you do it? There's some stuff lying around."

"'Scuse me," said the burglar with a grin, "but it just socked me one, too. It's good for you that rheumatism and me happens to be old pals. I got it in my left arm, too. Most anybody but me would have popped you when you wouldn't hoist that left claw of yours."

"How long have you had it?" inquired the citizen.

"Four years. I guess that ain't all. Once you've got it, it's you for a rheumatic life—that's my judgment."

"Ever try rattlesnake oil?" asked the citizen interestedly.

"Gallons," said the burglar. "If all the snakes I've used the oil of was strung out in a row they'd reach eight times as far as Saturn, and the rattles could be heard at Valparaiso, Indiana, and back."

"Some use Chiselum's Pills," remarked the citizen.

"Fudge!" said the burglar. "Took 'em five months. No good. I had some relief the year I tried Finkelham's Extract, Balm of Gilead poultices, and Pott's Pain Pulverizer; but I think it was the buckeye I carried in my pocket what done the trick."

"Is yours worse in the morning or at night?" asked the citizen.

"Night," said the burglar. "Just when I'm busiest. Say, take down that arm of yours—I guess you won't— Say! did you ever try Blicker-staff's Blood Builder?"

"I never did. Does yours come in paroxysms or is it a steady pain?"

The burglar sat down on the foot of the bed and rested his gun on his crossed knee.

"It jumps," said he. "It strikes me when I ain't looking for it. I had to give up second-story work because I got stuck sometimes half-way up. Tell you what—I don't believe the bloomin' doctors know what is good for it."

"Same here. I've spent a thousand dollars without getting any relief. Yours swell any?"

"Of mornings. And when it's goin' to rain—great Christopher!"

"Me, too," said the citizen. "I can tell when a streak of humidity the size of a tablecloth starts from Florida on its way to New York. And if I pass a theater where there's an 'East Lynne' matinee going on, the moisture starts my left arm jumping like a toothache."

"It's undiluted—hades!" said the burglar.

"You're dead right," said the citizen.

The burglar looked down at his pistol and thrust it into his pocket with an awkward attempt at ease.

"Say, old man," he said constrainedly, "ever try opodeldoc?"

"Slop!" said the citizen angrily. "Might as well rub on restaurant butter."

"Sure," concurred the burglar. "It's a salve suitable for little Minnie when the kitty scratches her finger. I'll tell you what! We're up against it. I only find one thing that eases her up. Hey? Little old sanitary, ameliorating, lest-we-forgot Booze. Say—this job's off— 'scuse me—get on your clothes and let's go out and have some. 'Scuse the liberty, but—ouch! There she goes again!"

"For a week," said the citizen, "I haven't been able to dress myself without help. I'm afraid Thomas is in bed, and——"

"Climb out," said the burglar, "I'll help you get into your duds."

The conventional returned as a tidal wave and flooded the citizen. He stroked his brown-and-gray beard.

"It's very unusual——" he began.

"Here's your shirt," said the burglar, "fall out. I know a man who said Omberry's Ointment fixed him in two weeks so he could use both hands in tying his four-in-hand."

As they were going out the door the citizen turned and started back.

" 'Liked to forgot my money," he explained; "laid it on the dresser last night."

The burglar caught him by the right sleeve.

"Come on," he said bluffly. "I ask you. Leave it alone. I've got the price. Ever try witch hazel and oil of wintergreen?"

Buried Treasure

There are many kinds of fools. Now, will everybody please sit still until they are called upon specifically to rise?

I had been every kind of fool except one. I had expended my patrimony, pretended my matrimony, played poker, lawn tennis, and bucket shops—parted soon with my money in many ways. But there remained one role of the wearer of cap and bells that I had not played. That was the Seeker after Buried Treasure. To few does the delectable furor come. But of all the would-be followers in the hoofprints of King Midas, none has found a pursuit so rich in pleasurable promise.

But, going back from my theme a while—as lame pens must do—I was a fool of the sentimental sort. I saw May Martha Mangum, and was hers. She was eighteen, the color of the white ivory keys of a new piano, beautiful, and possessed by the exquisite solemnity and pathetic witchery of an unsophisticated angel doomed to live in a small, dull, Texas prairie town. She had a spirit and charm that could have enabled her to pluck rubies like raspberries from the crown of Belgium or any other sporty kingdom, but she did not know it, and I did not paint the picture for her.

You see, I wanted May Martha Mangum for to have and to hold. I wanted her to abide with me, and put my slippers and pipe away every day in places where they cannot be found of evenings.

May Martha's father was a man hidden behind whiskers and spectacles. He lived for bugs and butterflies and all insects that fly or crawl or buzz or get down your back or in the butter. He was an etymologist, or words to that effect. He spent his life seining the air for

139

flying fish of the June-bug order, and then sticking pins through 'em and calling 'em names.

He and May Martha were the whole family. He prized her highly as a fine specimen of the racibus humanus because she saw that he had food at times, and put his clothes on right side before, and kept his alcohol-bottles filled. Scientists, they say, are apt to be absentminded.

There was another besides myself who thought May Martha Mangum one to be desired. That was Goodloe Banks, a young man just home from college. He had all the attainments to be found in books—Latin, Greek, philosophy, and especially the higher branches of mathematics and logic.

If it hadn't been for his habit of pouring out this information and learning on everyone that he addressed I'd have liked him pretty well. But, even as it was, he and I were, you would have thought, great pals.

We got together every time we could because each of us wanted to pump the other for whatever straws we could to find which way the wind blew from the heart of May Martha Mangum—rather a mixed metaphor: Goodloe Banks would never have been guilty of that. That is the way of rivals.

You might say that Goodloe ran to books, manners, culture, rowing, intellect, and clothes. I would have put you in mind more of baseball and Friday-night debating societies—by way of culture—and maybe of a good horseback rider.

But in our talks together and in our visits and conversation with May Martha neither Goodloe Banks nor I could find out which one of us she preferred. May Martha was natural-born noncommittal; and knew in her cradle how to keep people guessing.

As I said, old man Mangum was absentminded. After a long time he found out one day—a little butterfly must have told him—that two young men were trying to throw a net over the head of the young person, a daughter, or some such technical appendage, who looked after his comforts.

I never knew scientists could rise to such occasions. Old Mangum orally labeled and classified Goodloe and myself easily among the lowest orders of the vertebrates; and in English, too, without going any further into Latin than the simple references to Orgetorix, Rex Helvetii—which is as far as I ever went, myself. And he told us that if he ever caught us around his house again he would add us to his collection.

Goodloe Banks and I remained away five days, expecting the

storm to subside. When we dared to call at the house again May Martha Mangum and her father were gone. Gone! The house they had rented was closed. Their little store of goods and chattel was gone also.

And not a word of farewell to either of us from May Martha—not a white, fluttering note pinned to the hawthorn bush; not a chalkmark on the gatepost nor a postcard in the post office to give us a clue.

For two months, Goodloe Banks and I—separately—tried every scheme we could think of to track the runaways. We used our friendship and influence with the ticket agent, with livery-stable men, railroad conductors, and our one lone, lorn constable, but without results.

Then we became better friends and worse enemies than ever. We foregathered in the back room of Snyder's saloon every afternoon after work, and played dominoes, and laid conversational traps to find out from each other if anything had been discovered. That is the way of rivals.

Now, Goodloe Banks had a sarcastic way of displaying his own learning and putting me in the class that was reading "Poor Jane Ray, her bird is dead, she cannot play." Well, I rather liked Goodloe, and I had a contempt for his college learning, and I was always regarded as good-natured, so I kept my temper. And I was trying to find out if he knew anything about May Martha, so I endured his society.

In talking things over one afternoon he said to me: "Suppose you do find her, Ed, whereby would you profit? Miss Mangum has a mind. Perhaps it is yet uncultured, but she is destined for higher things than you could give her. I have talked with no one who seemed to appreciate more the enchantment of the ancient poets and writers and the modern cults that have assimilated and expended their philosophy of life. Don't you think you are wasting your time looking for her?"

"My idea," said I, "of a happy home is an eight-room house in a grove of live oaks by the side of a *charco* on a Texas prairie. A piano," I went on, "with an automatic player in the sitting room, three thousand head of cattle under fence for a starter, a buckboard and ponies always hitched at a post for 'the missus'—and May Martha Mangum to spend the profits of the ranch as she pleases, and to abide with me, and put my slippers and pipe away every day in places where they cannot be found of evenings. That," said I, "is what is to be—and a fig, a dried, Smyrna, dago-stand fig for your curriculums, cults, and philosophy."

"She is meant for higher things," repeated Goodloe Banks.

"Whatever she is meant for," I answered, "just now she is out of pocket. And I shall find her as soon as I can without aid of the colleges."

"The game is blocked," said Goodloe, putting down a domino; and we had the beer.

Shortly after that a young farmer whom I knew came into town and brought me a folded blue paper. He said his grandfather had just died. I concealed a tear; and he went on to say that the old man had jealously guarded this paper for twenty years. He left it to his family as part of his estate, the rest of which consisted of two mules and a hypotenuse of nonarable land.

The sheet of paper was of the old, blue kind used during the rebellion of the abolitionists against the secessionists. It was dated June 14, 1863; and it described the hiding place of ten burro-loads of gold and silver coin valued at three hundred thousand dollars. Old Rundle—grandfather of his grandson, Sam—was given the information by a Spanish priest who was in on the treasure burying, and who died many years before—no, afterward—in old Rundle's house. Old Rundle wrote it down from dictation.

"Why didn't your father look this up?" I asked young Rundle.

"He went blind before he could do so," he replied.

"Why didn't you hunt for it yourself?" I asked.

"Well," said he, "I've only know about the paper for ten years. First there was the spring plowin' to do, and then choppin' the weeds out of the corn; and then come takin' fodder; and mighty soon winter was on us. It seemed to run along that way year after year."

That sounded perfectly reasonable to me, so I took it up with young Lee Rundle at once.

The directions on the paper were simple. The whole burro cavalcade laden with the treasure started from an old Spanish mission in Dolores County. They traveled due south by the compass until they reached the Alamito River. They forded this, and buried the treasure on the top of a little mountain shaped like a packsaddle standing in a row between two higher ones. A heap of stones marked the place of the buried treasure. All the party except the Spanish priest were killed by Indians a few days later. The secret was a monopoly. It looked good to me.

Lee Rundle suggested that we rig out a camping outfit, hire a surveyor to run out the line from the Spanish mission, and then spend the three hundred thousand dollars seeing the sights in Fort Worth. But, without being highly educated, I knew a way to save time and expense.

We went to the State land office and had a practical, what they call a "working," sketch made of all the surveys of land from the old mission to the Alamito River. On this map I drew a line due southward to the river. The length of lines of each survey and section of land was accurately given on the sketch. By these we found the point on the river and had a "connection" with it, and an important, well-identified corner of the Los Animos five-league survey—a grant made by King Philip of Spain.

By doing this we did not need to have the line run out by a surveyor. It was a great saving of expense and time.

So Lee Rundle and I fitted out a two-horse wagon team with all the accessories, and drove a hundred and forty-nine miles to Chico, the nearest town to the point we wished to reach. There we picked up a deputy county surveyor. He found the corner of the Los Animos survey for us, ran out the five thousand seven hundred and twenty varas west that our sketch called for, laid a stone on the spot, had coffee and bacon, and caught the mail stage back to Chico.

I was pretty sure we would get that three hundred thousand dollars. Lee Rundle's was to be only one-third, because I was paying all the expenses. With that two hundred thousand dollars I knew I could find May Martha Mangum if she was on earth. And with it I could flutter the butterflies in old man Mangum's dovecote, too. If I could find that treasure!

But Lee and I established camp. Across the river were a dozen little mountains densely covered by cedar brakes, but not one shaped like a packsaddle. That did not deter us. Appearances are deceptive. A packsaddle, like beauty, may exist only in the eye of the beholder.

I and the grandson of the treasure examined those cedar-covered hills with the care of a lady hunting for the wicked flea. We explored every side, top, circumference, mean elevation, angle, slope and concavity of every one for two miles up and down the river. We spent four days doing so. Then we hitched up the roan and the dun, and hauled the remains of the coffee and bacon the one hundred and forty-nine miles back to Concho City.

Lee Rundle chewed much tobacco on the return trip. I was busy driving because I was in a hurry.

As shortly as could be after our empty return Goodloe Banks and

I foregathered in the back room of Snyder's saloon to play dominoes and fish for information. I told Goodloe about my expedition after the buried treasure.

"If I could have found that three hundred thousand dollars," I said to him, "I could have scoured and sifted the surface of the earth to find May Martha Mangum."

"She is meant for higher things," said Goodloe. "I shall find her myself. But, tell me how you went about discovering the spot where this unearthed increment was imprudently buried."

I told him in the smallest detail. I showed him the draftsman's sketch with the distances marked plainly upon it.

After glancing over it in a masterly way, he leaned back in his chair and bestowed upon me an explosion of sardonic, superior, collegiate laughter.

"Well, you *are* a fool, Jim," said he, when he could speak.

"It's your play," said I patiently, fingering my double-six.

"Twenty," said Goodloe, making two crosses on the table with his chalk.

"Why am I a fool?" I asked. "Buried treasure has been found before in many places."

"Because," said he, "in calculating the point on the river where your line would strike you neglected to allow for the variation. The variation there would be nine degrees west. Let me have your pencil."

Goodloe Banks figured rapidly on the back of an envelope.

"The distance, from north to south, of the line run from the Spanish mission," said he, "is exactly twenty-two miles. It was run by a pocket-compass, according to your story. Allowing for the variation, the point on the Alamito River where you should have searched for your treasure is exactly six miles and nine hundred and forty-five varas farther west than the place you hit upon. Oh, what a fool you are, Jim!"

"What is this variation that you speak of?" I asked. "I thought figures never lied."

"The variation of the magnetic compass," said Goodloe, "from the true meridian."

He smiled in his superior way; and then I saw come out in his face the singular, eager, consuming cupidity of the seeker after buried treasure.

"Sometimes," he said, with the air of the oracle, "these old traditions of hidden money are not without foundation. Suppose you let me look over that paper describing the location. Perhaps together we might——"

The result was that Goodloe Banks and I, rivals in love, became companions in adventure. We went to Chico by stage from Huntersburg, the nearest railroad town. In Chico we hired a team drawing a covered spring wagon and camping paraphernalia. We had the same surveyor run out our distance, as revised by Goodloe and his variations, and then dismissed him and set him on his homeward road.

It was night when we arrived. I fed the horses and made a fire near the bank of the river and cooked supper. Goodloe would have helped; but his education had not fitted him for practical things.

But while I worked he cheered me with the expression of great thoughts handed down from the dead ones of old. He quoted some translations from the Greek at much length.

"Anacreon," he explained. "That was a favorite passage with Miss Mangum—as I recited it."

"She is meant for higher things," said I, repeating his phrase.

"Can there be anything higher," asked Goodloe, "than to dwell in the society of the classics, to live in the atmosphere of learning and culture? You have often decried education. What of your wasted efforts through your ignorance of simple mathematics? How soon would you have found your treasure if my knowledge had not shown you your error?"

"We'll take a look at those hills across the river first," said I, "and see what we find. I am still doubtful about variations. I have been brought up to believe that the needle is true to the pole."

The next morning was a bright June one. We were up early and had breakfast. Goodloe was charmed. He recited—Keats, I think it was, and Kelly or Shelley, while I broiled the bacon. We were getting ready to cross the river, which was little more than a shallow creek there, and explore the many sharp-peaked, cedar-covered hills on the other side.

"My good Ulysses," said Goodloe, slapping me on the shoulder while I was washing the tin breakfast plates, "let me see the enchanted document once more. I believe it gives directions for climbing the hill shaped like a packsaddle. I never saw a packsaddle. What is it like, Jim?"

"Score one against culture," said I. "I'll know it when I see it."

Goodloe was looking at old Rundle's document when he ripped out a most uncollegiate swearword.

"Come here," he said, holding the paper up against the sunlight. "Look at that," he said, laying his finger against it.

On the blue paper—a thing I had never noticed before—I saw stand out in white letters the word and figures: "Malvern, 1898."

"What about it?" I asked.

"It's the watermark," said Goodloe. "The paper was manufactured in 1898. The writing on the paper is dated 1863. This is a palpable fraud."

"Oh, I don't know," said I. "The Rundles are pretty reliable, plain, uneducated country people. Maybe the paper manufacturers tried to perpetrate a swindle."

And then Goodloe Banks went as wild as his education permitted. He dropped the glasses off his nose and glared at me.

"I've often told you you were a fool," he said. "You have let yourself be imposed upon by a clodhopper. And you have imposed upon me."

"How," I asked, "have I imposed upon you?"

"By your ignorance," said he. "Twice I have discovered serious flaws in your plans that a common-school education should have enabled you to avoid. And," he continued, "I have been put to expense that I could ill afford in pursuing this swindling quest. I am done with it."

I rose and pointed a large pewter spoon at him, fresh from the dishwater.

"Goodloe Banks," I said, "I care not one parboiled navy bean for your education. I always barely tolerated it in anyone, and I despised it in you. What has your learning done for you? It is a curse to yourself and a bore to your friends. Away," I said, "away with your watermarks and variations! They are nothing to me. They shall not deflect me from the quest."

I pointed with my spoon across the river to a small mountain shaped like a packsaddle.

"I am going to search that mountain," I went on, "for the treasure. Decide now whether you are in it or not. If you wish to let a watermark or a variation shake your soul, you are no true adventurer. Decide."

A white cloud of dust began to rise far down the river road. It was the mail wagon from Hesperus to Chico. Goodloe flagged it.

"I am done with the swindle," said he sourly. "No one but a fool would pay any attention to that paper now. Well, you always were a fool, Jim. I leave you to your fate."

He gathered his personal traps, climbed into the mail wagon, adjusted his glasses nervously, and flew away in a cloud of dust.

After I had washed the dishes and staked the horses on new grass, I crossed the shallow river and made my way slowly through the cedar brakes up to the top of the hill shaped like a packsaddle.

It was a wonderful June day. Never in my life had I seen so many birds, so many butterflies, dragonflies, grasshoppers, and such winged and stinged beasts of the air and fields.

I investigated the hill shaped like a packsaddle from base to summit. I found an absolute absence of signs relating to buried treasure. There was no pile of stones, no ancient blazes on the trees, none of the evidences of the three hundred thousand dollars, as set forth in the document of old man Rundle.

I came down the hill in the cool of the afternoon. Suddenly, out of the cedar brake I stepped into a beautiful green valley where a tributary small stream ran into the Alamito River.

And there I was startled to see what I took to be a wild man, with unkempt beard and ragged hair, pursuing a giant butterfly with brilliant wings.

"Perhaps he is an escaped madman," I thought; and wondered how he had strayed so far from seats of education and learning.

And then I took a few more steps and saw a vine-covered cottage near the small stream. And, in a little grassy glade, I saw May Martha Mangum plucking wildflowers.

She straightened up and looked at me. For the first time since I knew her I saw her face—which was the color of the white keys of a new piano—turn pink. I walked toward her without a word. She let the gathered flowers trickle slowly from her hand to the grass.

"I knew you would come, Jim," she said clearly. "Father wouldn't let me write, but I knew you would come."

What followed you may guess—there was my wagon and team just across the river.

I'VE OFTEN WONDERED what good too much education is to a man if he can't use it for himself. If all the benefits of it are to go to others where does it come in?

For, May Martha Mangum abides with me. There is an eight-room house in a live-oak grove, and a piano with an automatic player, and a good start toward the three thousand head of cattle is under fence.

And when I ride home at night my pipe and slippers are put away in places where they cannot be found.

But, who cares for that—who cares—who cares?

Ulysses and the Dogman

Do you know the time of the dogmen?

When the forefinger of twilight begins to smudge the clear-drawn lines of the Big City there is inaugurated an hour devoted to one of the most melancholy sights of urban life.

Out from the towering flat crags and apartment peaks of the cliff dwellers of New York steals an army of beings that were once men. Even yet they go upright upon two limbs and retain human form and speech; but you will observe that they are behind animals in progress. Each of these beings follows a dog, to which he is fastened by an artificial ligament.

These men are all victims to Circe. Not willingly do they become flunkys to Fido, bell boys to bull terriers, and toddlers after Towzer. Modern Circe, instead of turning them into animals, has kindly left the difference of a six-foot leash between them. Every one of those dogmen has been either cajoled, bribed, or commanded by his own particular Circe to take the dear Household pet out for an airing.

By their faces and manner you can tell that the dogmen are bound in a hopeless enchantment. Never will there come even a dog-catcher Ulysses to remove the spell.

The faces of some are stonily set. They are past the commiseration, the curiosity, or the jeers of their fellow-beings. Years of matrimony, of continuous compulsory canine constitutionals, have made them callous. They unwind their beasts from lampposts, or the ensnared legs of profane pedestrians, with the stolidity of mandarins manipulating the strings of their kites.

Others, more recently reduced to the ranks of Rover's retinue, take their medicine sulkily and fiercely. They play the dog on the end of their line with the pleasure felt by the girl out fishing when she catches a sea robin on her hook. They glare at you threateningly if you look at them, as if it would be their delight to let slip the dogs of war. These are half-mutinous dogmen, not quite Circe-ized, and you will do well not to kick their charges, should they sniff around your ankles.

Others of the tribe do not seem to feel so keenly. They are mostly unfresh youths, with gold caps and drooping cigarettes, who do not harmonize with their dogs. The animals they attend wear satin bows in their collars; and the young men steer them so assiduously that you are tempted to the theory that some personal advantage, contingent upon satisfactory service, waits upon the execution of their duties.

The dogs thus personally conducted are of many varieties; but they are one in fatness, in pampered, diseased vileness of temper, in insolent, snarling capriciousness of behavior. They tug at the leash fractiously, they make leisurely nasal inventory of every doorstep, railing, and post. They sit down to rest when they choose; they wheeze like the winner of a Third Avenue beefsteak-eating contest; they blunder clumsily into open cellars and coal holes; they lead the dogmen a merry dance.

These unfortunate dry nurses of dogdom, the cur cuddlers, mongrel managers, Spitz stalkers, poodle pullers, Skye scrapers, dachshund dandlers, terrier trailers, and Pomeranian pushers of the cliff-dwelling Circes follow their charges meekly. The doggies neither fear nor respect them. Masters of the house these men whom they hold in leash may be, but they are not masters of them. From cozy corner to fire escape, from divan to dumbwaiter, doggy's snarl easily drives this two-legged being who is commissioned to walk at the other end of his string during his outing.

One twilight the dogmen came forth as usual at their Circes' pleading, guerdon, or crack of the whip. One among them was a strong man, apparently of too solid virtues for this airy vocation. His expression was melancholic, his manner depressed. He was leashed to a vile white dog, loathsomely fat, fiendishly ill-natured, gloatingly intractable toward his despised conductor.

At a corner nearest to his apartment house the dogman turned down a side street, hoping for fewer witnesses to his ignominy. The surfeited beast waddled before him, panting with spleen and the labor of motion.

Suddenly the dog stopped. A tall, brown, long-coated, wide-brimmed man stood like a Colossus blocking the sidewalk and declaring, "Well, I'm a son of a gun!"

"Jim Berry!" breathed the dogman, with exclamation points in his voice.

"Sam Telfair," cried Wide-Brim again, "you ding-basted old willy walloo, give us your hoof!"

Their hands clasped in the brief, tight greeting of the West that is death to the handshake microbe.

"You old fat rascal!" continued Wide-Brim with a wrinkled brown smile; "it's been five years since I seen you, I been in this town a week, but you can't find nobody in such a place. Well, you dinged old married man, how are they coming?"

Something mushy and heavily soft like raised dough leaned against Jim's leg and chewed his trousers with a yeasty growl.

"Get to work," said Jim, "and explain this yard-wide hydrophobia yearling you've throwed your lasso over. Are you the pound-master of this burg? Do you call that a dog or what?"

"I need a drink," said the dogman, dejected at the reminder of his old dog of the sea. "Come on."

Hard by was a café. 'Tis ever so in the big city.

They sat at a table, and the bloated monster yelped and scrambled at the end of his leash to get at the café cat.

"Whiskey," said Jim to the waiter.

"Make it two," said the dogman.

"You're fatter," said Jim, "and you look subjugated. I don't know about East agreeing with you. All the boys asked me to hunt you up when I started. Sandy King, he went to the Klondike. Watson Burrel, he married the oldest Peters girl. I made some money buying beeves, and I bought a lot of wild land up on the Little Powder. Going to fence next fall. Bill Rawlins, he's gone to farming. You remember Bill, of course—he was courting Marcella—excuse me, Sam—I mean the lady you married, while she was teaching school at Prairie View. But you was the lucky man. How is Missis Telfair?"

"S-h-h-h!" said the dogman, signaling the waiter; "give it a name."

"Whiskey," said Jim.

"Make it two," said the dogman.

"She's well," he continued, after his chaser. "She refused to live anywhere but in New York, where she came from. We live in a flat. Every evening at six I take that dog out for a walk. It's Marcella's pet.

There never were two animals on earth, Jim, that hated one another like me and that dog does. His name's Lovekins. Marcella dresses for dinner while we're out. We eat tabble dote. Ever try one of them, Jim?"

"No, I never," said Jim. "I seen the signs, but I thought they said 'table de hole.' I thought it was French for pool tables. How does it taste?"

"If you're going to be in the city for awhile we will——"

"No, sir-ee. I'm starting for home this evening on the seven twenty-five. Like to stay longer, but I can't."

"I'll walk down to the ferry with you," said the dogman.

The dog had bound a leg each of Jim and the chair together, and had sunk into a comatose slumber. Jim stumbled, and the leash was slightly wrenched. The shrieks of the awakened beast rang for a block around.

"If that's your dog," said Jim, when they were on the street again, "what's to hinder you from running that habeas corpus you've got around his neck over a limb and walking off and forgetting him?"

"I'd never dare to," said the dogman, awed at the bold proposition. "He sleeps in the bed. I sleep on a lounge. He runs howling to Marcella if I look at him. Some night, Jim, I'm going to get even with that dog. I've made up my mind to do it. I'm going to creep over with a knife and cut a hole in his mosquito bar so they can get in to him. See if I don't do it!"

"You ain't yourself, Sam Telfair. You ain't what you was once. I don't know about these cities and flats over here. With my own eyes I seen you stand off both the Tillotson boys in Prairie View with the brass faucet out of a molasses barrel. And I seen you rope and tie the wildest steer on Little Powder in thirty-nine and a half."

"I did, didn't I?" said the other with a temporary gleam in his eye. "But that was before I was dogmatized."

"Does Missis Telfair——" began Jim.

"Hush!" said the dogman. "Here's another café."

They lined up at the bar. The dog fell asleep at their feet.

"Whiskey," said Jim.

"Make it two," said the dogman.

"I thought about you," said Jim, "when I bought that wild land. I wished you was out there to help me with the stock."

"Last Tuesday," said the dogman, "he bit me on the ankle be-cause I asked for cream in my coffee. He always gets the cream."

"You'd like Prairie View now," said Jim. "The boys from the roundups for fifty miles around ride in there. One corner of my pasture is in sixteen miles of the town. There's a straight forty miles of wire on one side of it."

"You pass through the kitchen to get to the bedroom," said the dogman, "and you pass through the parlor to get to the bathroom, and you back out through the dining room to get into the bedroom so you can turn around and leave by the kitchen. And he snores and barks in his sleep, and I have to smoke in the park on account of his asthma."

"Don't Missis Telfair——" began Jim.

"Oh, shut up!" said the dogman. "What is it this time?"

"Whiskey," said Jim.

"Make it two," said the dogman.

"Well, I'll be racking along down toward the ferry," said the other.

"Come on, there, you mangy, turtle-backed, snaked-headed, bench-legged ton-and-a-half of soap grease!" shouted the dogman with a new note in his voice and a new hand on the leash. The dog scrambled after them with an angry whine at such unusual language from his guardian.

At the foot of Twenty-third Street the dogman led the way through swinging doors.

"Last chance," said he. "Speak up."

"Whiskey," said Jim.

"Make it two," said the dogman.

"I don't know," said the ranchman, "where I'll find the man I want to take charge of the Little Powder outfit. I want somebody I know something about. Finest stretch of prairie and timber you ever squinted your eye over, Sam. Now if you was——"

"Speaking of hydrophobia," said the dogman, "the other night he chewed a piece out of my leg because I knocked a fly off of Marcella's arm. 'It ought to be cauterized,' says Marcella, and I was thinking so myself. I telephones for the doctor, and when he comes Marcella says to me: 'Help me hold the poor dear while the doctor fixes his mouth. Oh, I hope he got no virus on any of his toofies when he bit you.' Now what do you think of that?"

"Does Missis Telfair——" began Jim.

"Oh, drop it," said the dogman. "Come again!"

"Whiskey," said Jim.

"Make it two," said the dogman.

They walked on to the ferry. The ranchman stepped to the ticket window.

Suddenly the swift landing of three or four heavy kicks was heard, the air was rent by piercing canine shrieks, and a pained, outraged, lubberly, bow-legged pudding of a dog ran frenziedly up the street alone.

"Ticket to Denver," said Jim.

"Make it two," shouted the ex-dogman, reaching for his inside pocket.

A Ghost of a Chance

"Actually, a hod!" repeated Mrs. Kinsolving pathetically.

Mrs. Bellamy Bellmore arched a sympathetic eyebrow. Thus she expressed condolence and a generous amount of apparent surprise.

"Fancy her telling, everywhere," recapitulated Mrs. Kinsolving, "that she saw a ghost in the apartment she occupied here—our choicest guest room—a ghost, carrying a hod on its shoulder—the ghost of an old man in overalls, smoking a pipe and carrying a hod! The very absurdity of the thing shows her malicious intent. There never was a Kinsolving that carried a hod. Everyone knows that Mr. Kinsolving's father accumulated his money by large building contracts, but he never worked a day with his own hands. He had this house built from his own plans; but—oh, a hod! Why need she have been so cruel and malicious?"

"It is really too bad," murmured Mrs. Bellmore with an approving glance of her fine eyes about the vast chamber done in lilac and old gold. "And it was in this room she saw it! Oh, no, I'm not afraid of ghosts. Don't have the least fear on my account. I'm glad you put me in here. I think family ghosts so interesting! But, really, the story does sound a little inconsistent. I should have expected something better from Mrs. Fischer-Suympkins. Don't they carry bricks in hods? Why should a ghost bring bricks into a villa built of marble and stone? I'm so sorry, but it makes me think that age is beginning to tell upon Mrs. Fischer-Suympkins."

"This house," continued Mrs. Kinsolving, "was built upon the site of an old one used by the family during the Revolution. There wouldn't be anything strange in its having a ghost. And there was a Captain Kinsolving who fought in General Greene's army, though we've never been able to secure any papers to vouch for it. If there is to be a family ghost, why couldn't it have been his, instead of a bricklayer's?"

"The ghost of a Revolutionary ancestor wouldn't be a bad idea," agreed Mrs. Bellmore; "but you know how arbitrary and inconsiderate ghosts can be. Maybe, like love, they are 'engendered in the eye.' One advantage of those who see ghosts is that their stories can't be disproved. By a spiteful eye, a Revolutionary knapsack might easily be construed to be a hod. Dear Mrs. Kinsolving, think no more of it. I am sure it was a knapsack."

"But she told everybody!" mourned Mrs. Kinsolving, inconsolable. "She insisted upon the details. There is the pipe. And how are you going to get out of the overalls?"

"Sha'n't get into them," said Mrs. Bellmore with a prettily suppressed yawn; "too stiff and wrinkly. Is that you, Felice? Prepare my bath, please. Do you dine at seven at Clifftop, Mrs. Kinsolving? So kind of you to run in for a chat before dinner! I love those little touches of informality with a guest. They give such a home flavor to a visit. So sorry; I must be dressing. I am so indolent I always postpone it until the last moment."

Mrs. Fischer-Suympkins had been the first large plum that the Kinsolvings had drawn from the social pie. For a long time, the pie itself had been out of reach on a top shelf. But the purse and the pursuit had at last lowered it. Mrs. Fischer-Suympkins was the heliograph of the smart society parading corps. The glitter of her wit and actions passed along the line, transmitting whatever was latest and most daring in the game of peepshow. Formerly, her fame and leadership had been secure enough not to need the support of such artifices as handing around live frogs for favors at a cotillion. But, now, these things were necessary to the holding of her throne. Besides, middle-age had come to preside, incongruous, at her capers. The sensational papers had cut her space from a page to two columns. Her wit developed a sting; her manners became more rough and inconsiderate, as if she felt the royal necessity of establishing her autocracy by scorning the conventionalities that bound lesser potentates.

To some pressure at the command of the Kinsolvings, she had yielded so far as to honor their house by her presence, for an evening and night. She had her revenge upon her hostess by relating, with grim enjoyment and sarcastic humor, her story of the vision carrying the hod. To that lady, in raptures at having penetrated thus far toward the coveted inner circle, the result came as a crushing disappointment. Everybody either sympathized or laughed, and there was little to choose between the two modes of expression.

But, later on, Mrs. Kinsolving's hopes and spirits were revived by the capture of a second and greater prize.

Mrs. Bellamy Bellmore had accepted an invitation to visit at Clifftop, and would remain for three days. Mrs. Bellmore was one of the younger matrons, whose beauty, descent and wealth gave her a reserved seat in the holy of holies that required no strenuous bolstering. She was generous enough thus to give Mrs. Kinsolving the accolade that was so poignantly desired; and, at the same time, she thought how much it would please Terence. Perhaps it would end by solving him.

Terence was Mrs. Kinsolving's son, aged twenty-nine, quite good-looking enough, and with two or three attractive and mysterious traits. For one, he was very devoted to his mother, and that was sufficiently odd to deserve notice. For others, he talked so little that it was irritating, and he seemed either very shy or very deep. Terence interested Mrs. Bellmore, because she was not sure which it was. She intended to study him a little longer, unless she forgot the matter. If he was only shy, she would abandon him, for shyness is a bore. If he was deep, she would also abandon him, for depth is precarious.

On the afternoon of the third day of her visit, Terence hunted up Mrs. Bellmore, and found her in a nook actually looking at an album.

"It's so good of you," said he, "to come down here and retrieve the day for us. I suppose you have heard that Mrs. Fischer-Suympkins scuttled the ship before she left. She knocked a whole plank out of the bottom with a hod. My mother is grieving herself ill about it. Can't you manage to see a ghost for us while you are here, Mrs. Bellmore—a bang-up, swell ghost, with a coronet on his head and a checkbook under his arm?"

"That was a naughty old lady, Terence," said Mrs. Bellmore, "to tell such stories. Perhaps you gave her too much supper. Your mother doesn't really take it seriously, does she?"

"I think she does," answered Terence. "One would think every brick in the hod had dropped on her. It's a good mammy, and I don't like to see her worried. It's to be hoped that the ghost belongs to the hod-carriers' union, and will go out on a strike. If he doesn't, there will be no peace in this family."

"I'm sleeping in the ghost chamber," said Mrs. Bellmore pensively. "But it's so nice I wouldn't change it, even if I were afraid, which I'm not. It wouldn't do for me to submit a counter story of a desirable, aristocratic shade, would it? I would do so, with pleasure, but it seems to me it would be too obviously an antidote for the other narrative to be effective."

"True," said Terence, running two fingers thoughtfully into his crisp, brown hair. "That would never do. How would it work to see the same ghost again, minus the overalls, and have gold bricks in the hod? That would elevate the specter from degrading toil to a financial plane. Don't you think that would be respectable enough?"

"There was an ancestor who fought against the Britishers, wasn't there? Your mother said something to that effect."

"I believe so; one of those old chaps in raglan vests and golf trousers. I don't care a continental for a continental, myself. But the mother has set her heart on pomp and heraldry and pyrotechnics, and I want her to be happy."

"You are a good boy, Terence," said Mrs. Bellmore, sweeping her silks close to one side of her, "not to beat your mother. Sit here by me, and let's look at the album, just as people used to do twenty years ago. Now, tell me about every one of them. Who is this tall, dignified gentleman leaning against the horizon, with one arm on the Corinthian column?"

"That old chap with the big feet?" inquired Terence, craning his neck. "That's great-uncle O'Brannigan. He used to keep a rathskeller on the Bowery."

"I asked you to sit down, Terence. If you are not going to amuse, or obey, me, I shall report in the morning that I saw a ghost wearing an apron and carrying schooners of beer. Now, that is better. To be shy, at your age, Terence, is a thing that you should blush to acknowledge."

At breakfast on the last morning of her visit, Mrs. Bellmore startled and entranced everyone present by announcing positively that she had seen the ghost.

"Did it have a—a—a—?" Mrs. Kinsolving, in her suspense and agitation, could not bring out the word.

"No, indeed—far from it."

There was a chorus of questions from others at the table. "Weren't you frightened?" "What did it do?" "How did it look?" "How was it dressed?" "Did it say anything?" "Didn't you scream?"

"I'll try to answer everything at once," said Mrs. Bellmore heroically, "although I'm frightfully hungry. Something awakened me—I'm not sure whether it was a noise or a touch—and there stood the phantom. I never burn a light at night, so the room was quite dark, but I saw it plainly. I wasn't dreaming. It was a tall man, all misty white from head to foot. It wore the full dress of the old, colonial days—powdered hair, baggy coat skirts, lace ruffles and a sword. It looked intangible and luminous in the dark, and moved without a sound. Yes, I was a little frightened at first—or startled, I should say. It was the first ghost I had ever seen. No, it didn't say anything. I didn't scream. I raised up on my elbow, and then it glided silently away, and disappeared when it reached the door."

Mrs. Kinsolving was in the seventh heaven. "The description is that of Captain Kinsolving, of General Greene's army, one of our ancestors," she said in a voice that trembled with pride and relief. "I really think I must apologize for our ghostly relative, Mrs. Bellmore. I am afraid he must have badly disturbed your rest."

Terence sent a smile of pleased congratulation toward his mother. Attainment was Mrs. Kinsolving's, at last, and he loved to see her happy.

"I suppose I ought to be ashamed to confess," said Mrs. Bellmore, who was now enjoying her breakfast, "that I wasn't very much disturbed. I presume it would have been the customary thing to scream and faint, and have all of you running about in picturesque costumes. But, after the first alarm was over, I really couldn't work myself up to a panic. The ghost retired from the stage quietly and peacefully, after doing its little turn, and I went to sleep again."

Nearly all who listened, politely accepted Mrs. Bellmore's story as a made-up affair, charitably offered as an offset to the unkind vision seen by Mrs. Fischer-Suympkins. But one or two present perceived that her assertions bore the genuine stamp of her own convictions. Truth and candor seemed to attend upon every word. Even a scoffer at ghosts—if he were very observant—would have been forced to admit that she had, at least in a very vivid dream, been honestly aware of the weird visitor.

Soon, Mrs. Bellmore's maid was packing. In two hours, the auto would come to convey her to the station. As Terence was strolling upon the east piazza, Mrs. Bellmore came up to him, with a confidential sparkle in her eye.

"I didn't wish to tell the others all of it," she said, "but I will tell you. In a way, I think you should be held responsible. Can you guess in what manner that ghost awakened me last night?"

"Rattled chains," suggested Terence after some thought, "or groaned? They usually do one or the other."

"Do you happen to know," continued Mrs. Bellmore with sudden irrelevancy, "if I resemble any one of the female relatives of your restless ancestor, Captain Kinsolving?"

"Don't think so," said Terence with an extremely puzzled air. "Never heard of any of them being noted beauties."

"Then, why," said Mrs. Bellmore, looking the young man gravely in the eye, "should that ghost have kissed me, as I'm sure it did?"

"Heavens!" exclaimed Terence, in wide-eyed amazement. "You don't mean that, Mrs. Bellmore! Did he actually kiss you?"

"I said *it,*" corrected Mrs. Bellmore. "I hope the impersonal pronoun is correctly used."

"But why did you say I was responsible?"

"Because you are the only living male relative of the ghost."

"I see. 'Unto the third and fourth generation.' But, seriously, did he—did it—how do you——?"

"Know? How does anyone know? I was asleep, and that is what awakened me, I'm almost certain."

"Almost?"

"Well, I awoke just as—oh, can't you understand what I mean? When anything arouses you suddenly, you are not positive whether you dreamed, or—and yet you know that— Dear me, Terence, must I dissect the most elementary sensations in order to accommodate your extremely practical intelligence?"

"But, about kissing ghosts, you know," said Terence, humbly, "I require the most primary instruction. I never kissed a ghost. Is it—is it——?"

"The sensation," said Mrs. Bellmore, with deliberate, but slightly smiling, emphasis, "since you are seeking instruction, is a mingling of the material and the spiritual."

"Of course," said Terence, suddenly growing serious, "it was a dream or some kind of a hallucination. Nobody believes in spirits, these days. If you told the tale out of kindness of heart, Mrs. Bellmore, I can't express how grateful I am to you. It has made my mother supremely happy. That Revolutionary ancestor was a stunning idea."

Mrs. Bellmore sighed. "The usual fate of ghost-seers is mine," she said resignedly. "My privileged encounter with a spirit is attributed to lobster salad or mendacity. Well, I have, at least, one memory left from the wreck—a kiss from the unseen world. Was Captain Kinsolving a very brave man, do you know, Terence?"

"He was licked at Yorktown, I believe," said Terence, reflecting. "They say he skedaddled with his company, after the first battle there."

"I thought he must have been timid," said Mrs. Bellmore absently. "He might have had another."

"Another battle?" asked Terence dully.

"What else could I mean? I must go and get ready now; the auto will be here in an hour. I've enjoyed Clifftop immensely. Such a lovely morning, isn't it, Terence?"

On her way to the station, Mrs. Bellmore took from her bag a silk handkerchief, and looked at it with a little, peculiar smile. Then she tied it in several very hard knots, and threw it, at a convenient moment, over the edge of the cliff along which the road ran.

In his room, Terence was giving some directions to his man, Brooks. "Have this stuff done up in a parcel," he said, "and ship it to the address on that card."

The card was that of a New York costumer. The "stuff" was a gentleman's costume of the days of '76, made of white satin, with silver buckles, white silk stockings and white kid shoes. A powdered wig and a sword completed the dress.

"And look about, Brooks," added Terence a little anxiously, "for a silk handkerchief with my initials in one corner. I must have dropped it somewhere."

It was a month later when Mrs. Bellmore and one or two others of the smart crowd were making up a list of names for a coaching trip through the Catskills. Mrs. Bellmore looked over the list for a final censoring. The name of Terence Kinsolving was there. Mrs. Bellmore ran her prohibitive pencil lightly through the name.

"Too shy!" she murmured sweetly, in explanation.

WITCHES' LOAVES

⁓ MISS MARTHA MEACHAM kept the little bakery on the corner (the one where you go up three steps, and the bell tinkles when you open the door).

Miss Martha was forty, her bankbook showed a credit of two thousand dollars, and she possessed two false teeth and a sympathetic heart. Many people have married whose chances to do so were much inferior to Miss Martha's.

Two or three times a week a customer came in, in whom she began to take an interest. He was a middle-aged man, wearing spectacles and a brown beard trimmed to a careful point.

He spoke English with a strong German accent. His clothes were worn and darned in places, and wrinkled and baggy in others. But he looked neat, and had very good manners.

He always bought two loaves of stale bread. Fresh bread was five cents a loaf. Stale ones were two for five. Never did he call for anything but stale bread.

Once Miss Martha saw a red and brown stain on his fingers. She was sure then that he was an artist and very poor. No doubt he lived in a garret, where he painted pictures and ate stale bread and thought of the good things to eat in Miss Martha's bakery.

Often when Miss Martha sat down to her chops and light rolls and jam and tea she would sigh, and wish that the gentle-mannered artist might share her tasty meal instead of eating his dry crust in that draughty attic. Miss Martha's heart, as you have been told, was a sympathetic one.

In order to test her theory as to his occupation, she brought from her room one day a painting that she had bought at a sale, and set it against the shelves behind the bread counter.

It was a Venetian scene. A splendid marble palazzo (so it said on the picture) stood in the foreground—or rather forewater. For the rest there were gondolas (with the lady trailing her hand in the water), clouds, sky, and chiaroscuro in plenty. No artist could fail to notice it.

Two days afterward the customer came in.

"Two loafs of stale bread, if you blease.

"You haf here a fine bicture, madame," he said while she was wrapping up the bread.

"Yes?" says Miss Martha, reveling in her own cunning. "I do so admire art and" (no, it would not do to say "artists" thus early) "and paintings," she substituted. "You think it is a good picture?"

"Der balace," said the customer, "is not in good drawing. Der bairspective of it is not true. Goot morning, madame."

He took his bread, bowed, and hurried out.

Yes, he must be an artist. Miss Martha took the picture back to her room.

How gentle and kindly his eyes shone behind his spectacles! What a broad brow he had! To be able to judge perspective at a glance—and to live on stale bread! But genius often has to struggle before it is recognized.

What a thing it would be for art and perspective if genius were backed by two thousand dollars in bank, a bakery, and a sympathetic heart to—— But these were daydreams, Miss Martha.

Often now when he came he would chat for a while across the showcase. He seemed to crave Miss Martha's cheerful words.

He kept on buying stale bread. Never a cake, never a pie, never one of her delicious Sally Lunns.

She thought he began to look thinner and discouraged. Her heart ached to add something good to eat to his meager purchase, but her courage failed at the act. She did not dare affront him. She knew the pride of artists.

Miss Martha took to wearing her blue-dotted silk waist behind the counter. In the back room she cooked a mysterious compound of quince seeds and borax. Ever so many people use it for the complexion.

One day the customer came in as usual, laid his nickel on the showcase, and called for his stale loaves. While Miss Martha was reaching for them there was a great tooting and clanging, and a fire engine came lumbering past.

The customer hurried to the door to look, as anyone will. Suddenly inspired, Miss Martha seized the opportunity.

On the bottom shelf behind the counter was a pound of fresh butter that the dairyman had left ten minutes before. With bread knife Miss Martha made a deep slash in each of the stale loaves, inserted a generous quantity of butter, and pressed the loaves tight again.

When the customer turned once more she was tying the paper around them.

When he had gone, after an unusually pleasant little chat, Miss Martha smiled to herself, but not without a slight fluttering of the heart.

Had she been too bold? Would he take offense? But surely not. There was no language of edibles. Butter was no emblem of unmaidenly forwardness.

For a long time that day her mind dwelt on the subject. She imagined the scene when he should discover her little deception.

He would lay down his brushes and palette. There would stand his easel with the picture he was painting in which the perspective was beyond criticism.

He would prepare for his luncheon of dry bread and water. He would slice into a loaf—ah!

Miss Martha blushed. Would he think of the hand that placed it there as he ate? Would he——

The front doorbell jangled viciously. Somebody was coming in, making a great deal of noise.

Miss Martha hurried to the front. Two men were there. One was a young man smoking a pipe—a man she had never seen before. The other was her artist.

His face was very red, his hat was on the back of his head, his hair was widely rumpled. He clinched his two fists and shook them ferociously at Miss Martha. *At Miss Martha.*

"Dummkopf!" he shouted with extreme loudness; and then *"Tausendonfer!"* or something like it in German.

The young man tried to draw him away.

"I vill not go," he said angrily, "else I shall told her."

He made a bass drum of Miss Martha's counter.

"You haf shpoilt me," he cried, his blue eyes blazing behind his spectacles. "I vill tell you. You vas von *meddlingsome old cat!"*

Miss Martha leaned weakly against the shelves and laid one hand on her blue-dotted silk waist. The young man took the other by the collar.

"Come on," he said, "you've said enough." He dragged the angry one out at the door to the sidewalk, and then came back.

"Guess you ought to be told, ma'am," he said, "what the row is about. That's Blumberger. He's an architectural draftsman. I work in the same office with him.

"He's been working hard for three months drawing a plan for a new city hall. It was a prize competition. He finished inking the lines yesterday. You know, a draftsman always makes his drawings in pencil first. When it's done he rubs out the pencil lines with handfuls of stale bread crumbs. That's better than India rubber.

"Blumberger's been buying the bread here. Well, today—well, you know, ma'am, that butter isn't—well, Blumberger's plan isn't good for anything now except to cut up into railroad sandwiches."

Miss Martha went into the back room. She took off the blue-dotted silk waist and put on the old brown serge she used to wear. Then she poured the quince seed and borax mixture out of the window into the ashcan.

The Church with an
Overshot Wheel

LAKELANDS IS NOT to be found in the catalogs of fashionable summer resorts. It lies on a low spur of the Cumberland range of mountains on a little tributary of the Clinch river. Lakelands proper is a contented village of two dozen houses situated on a forlorn, narrow-gauge railroad line. You wonder whether the railroad lost itself in the pinewoods and ran into Lakelands from fright and loneliness, or whether Lakelands got lost and huddled itself along the railroad to wait for the cars to carry it home. You wonder again why it was named Lakelands. There are no lakes, and the lands about it are too poor to be worth mentioning.

Half a mile from the village stands the Eagle House, a big, roomy old mansion run by Mr. Josiah Rankin for the accommodation of visitors who desire the mountain air at inexpensive rates. The Eagle House is delightfully mismanaged. It is full of ancient instead of modern improvements, and it is altogether as comfortably neglected and pleasingly disarranged as your own home. But you are furnished with clean rooms and good and abundant fare; yourself and the piny woods must do the rest. Nature has provided a mineral spring, grapevine swings, and croquet—even the wickets are wooden. You have Art to thank only for the fiddle-and-guitar music twice a week at the hop in the rustic pavilion.

The patrons of the Eagle House are those who seek recreation as a necessity as well as pleasure. They are busy people who may be likened to clocks that need a fortnight's winding to ensure a year's running of their wheels. You will find students there from the lower towns, now and then an artist, or a geologist absorbed in construing the ancient strata of the hills. A few quiet families spend the summers there; and often one or two tired members of that patient sisterhood known to Lakelands as "schoolmarms."

A quarter of a mile from the Eagle House was what would have been described to its guests as "an object of interest" in the catalog, had the Eagle House issued a catalog. This was an old, old mill that was no longer a mill. In the words of Mr. Josiah Rankin, it was "the only church in the United States, sah, with an overshot wheel; and the only mill in the world, sah, with pews and a pipe organ." The guests of the Eagle House attended the old mill church each Sabbath, and heard the preacher liken the purified Christian to bolted flour, ground to usefulness between the millstones of experience and suffering.

Every year about the beginning of autumn there came to the Eagle House one Mr. Abram Strong, who remained for a time an honored and beloved guest. In Lakelands he was called "Father Abram," because his hair was so white, his face so strong and kind and florid, his laugh so merry, and his black clothes and broad hat so priestly in appearance. Even new guests after three or four days' acquaintance gave him this familiar title.

Father Abram came a long way to Lakelands. He lived in a big, roaring town in the northwest where he owned mills—not little mills with pews and an organ in them, but great, ugly, mountain-like mills that the freight trains crawled around all day like ants around an antheap. And now you must be told about Father Abram and the mill that was a church, for their stories run together.

In the days when the church was a mill, Mr. Strong was the miller. There was no jollier, dustier, busier, happier miller in all the land than he. He lived in a little cottage across the road from the mill. His hand was heavy but his toll was light, and the mountaineers brought their grain to him across many weary miles of rocky roads.

The delight of the miller's life was his little daughter, Aglaia. That was a brave name, truly, for a flaxen-haired toddler; but the mountaineers love sonorous and stately names. The mother had encountered it somewhere in a book, and the deed was done. In her babyhood Aglaia herself repudiated the name as far as common use went, and persisted in calling herself "Dums." The miller and his wife often tried to coax from Aglaia the source of this mysterious name, but without results. At last they arrived at a theory. In the little garden behind the cottage was a bed of rhododendrons in which the child took a peculiar delight and interest. It may have been that she perceived in "Dums" a kinship to the formidable name of her favorite flowers.

When Aglaia was four years old she and her father used to go through a little performance in the mill every afternoon, that never failed to come off, the weather permitting. When supper was ready her mother would brush her hair and put on a clean apron and send her across to the mill to bring her father home. When the miller saw her coming in the mill door he would come forward, all white with the flour dust, and wave his hand and sing an old miller's song that was familiar in those parts and ran something like this:

> "The wheel goes round,
> The grist is ground,
>   The dusty miller's merry.
> He sings all day,
> His work is play,
>   While thinking of his dearie."

Then Aglaia would run to him laughing, and call: "Da-da, come take Dums home"; and the miller would swing her to his shoulder and march over to supper, singing the miller's song. Every evening this would take place.

One day, only a week after her fourth birthday, Aglaia disappeared. When last seen she was plucking wildflowers by the side of the road in front of the cottage. A little while later her mother went out to see that she did not stray too far away, and she was already gone.

Of course every effort was made to find her. The neighbors gathered, and searched the woods and the mountains for miles around. They dragged every foot of the mill race and the creek for a long distance below the dam. Never a trace of her did they find. A night or two before there had been a family of wanderers camped in a grove nearby. It was conjectured that they might have stolen the child; but when their wagon was overtaken and searched she could not be found.

The miller remained at the mill for nearly two years; and then his hope of finding her died out. He and his wife moved to the northwest. In a few years he was the owner of a modern mill in one of the important milling cities in that region. Mrs. Strong never recovered from the shock caused by the loss of Aglaia, and two years after they moved away the miller was left to bear his sorrow alone.

When Abram Strong became prosperous he paid a visit to Lakelands and the old mill. The scene was a sad one for him, but he was a strong man, and always appeared cheery and kindly. It was then that he was inspired to convert the old mill into a church. Lakelands was too poor to build one; and the still poorer mountaineers could not assist. There was no place of worship nearer than twenty miles.

The miller altered the appearance of the mill as little as possible. The big overshot wheel was left in its place. The young people who came to the church used to cut their initials in its soft and slowly decaying wood. The dam was partly destroyed, and the clear mountain stream rippled unchecked down its rocky bed. Inside the mill the changes were greater. The shafts and millstones and belts and pulleys were, of course, all removed. There were two rows of benches with aisles between, and a little raised platform and pulpit at one end. On three sides overhead was a gallery containing seats, and reached by a stairway inside. There was also an organ—a real pipe organ—in the gallery, that was the pride of the congregation of the Old Mill church. Miss Phoebe Summers was the organist. The Lakelands boys proudly took turns at pumping it for her at each Sunday's service. The Rev. Mr. Banbridge was the preacher, and rode down from Squirrel Gap on his old white horse without ever missing a service. And Abram Strong paid for everything. He paid the preacher $500 a year; and Miss Phoebe $200.

Thus, in memory of Aglaia, the old mill was converted into a blessing for the community in which she had once lived. It seemed that the brief life of the child had brought about more good than the three-score years and ten of many. But Abram Strong set up yet another monument to her memory.

Out from his mills in the northwest came the "Aglaia" flour, made from the hardest and finest wheat that could be raised. The country soon found out that the "Aglaia" flour had two prices. One was the highest market price, and the other was—nothing.

Wherever there happened a calamity that left people destitute—a fire, a flood, a tornado, a strike or a famine—there would go hurrying a generous consignment of the "Aglaia" at its "nothing" price. It was given away cautiously and judiciously, but it was freely given, and not a penny could the hungry ones pay for it. There got to be a saying that whenever there was a disastrous fire in the poor districts of a city the fire chief's buggy reached the scene first, and next the "Aglaia" flour wagon, and then the fire engines.

So this was Abram Strong's other monument to Aglaia. Perhaps to a poet the theme may seem too utilitarian for beauty; but to some the fancy will seem sweet and fine that the pure, white, virgin flour flying on its mission of love and charity might be likened to the spirit of the lost child whose memory it signalized.

There came a year that brought hard times to the Cumberlands. Grain crops everywhere were light; and there were no local crops at all. Mountain floods had done much damage to property. Even game in the woods was so scarce that the hunters brought hardly enough home to keep their folk alive. Especially about Lakelands was the rigor felt.

As soon as Abram Strong heard of this his messages flew; and the little narrow-gauge cars began to unload "Aglaia" flour there. The miller's orders were to store the flour in the gallery of the Old Mill church; and that everyone who attended the church was to carry home a sack of it.

Two weeks after that Abram Strong came for his yearly visit to the Eagle House, and became "Father Abram" again.

That season the Eagle House had fewer guests than usual. Among them was Rose Chester. Miss Chester came to Lakelands from Atlanta where she worked in a department store. This was the first vacation outing of her life. The wife of the store manager had once spent a summer at the Eagle House. She had taken a fancy to Rose, and had persuaded her to go there for her three-weeks' holiday. The manager's wife gave her a letter to Mrs. Rankin, who gladly received her in her own charge and care.

Miss Chester was not very strong. She was about twenty, and pale and delicate from an indoor life. But one week of Lakelands gave her a brightness and spirit that changed her wonderfully. The time was early September, when the Cumberlands are at their greatest beauty. The mountain foliage was growing brilliant with autumnal colors, one breathed aerial champagne, the nights were deliciously cool, causing one to snuggle cosily under the warm blankets of the Eagle House.

Father Abram and Miss Chester became great friends. The old miller learned her story from Mrs. Rankin, and his interest went out quickly to the slender, lonely girl who was making her own way in the world.

The mountain country was new to Miss Chester. She had lived many years in the warm, flat town of Atlanta; and the grandeur and variety of the Cumberlands delighted her. She was determined to enjoy every moment of her stay. Her little hoard of savings had been estimated so carefully in connection with her expenses that she knew almost to a penny what her very small surplus would be when she returned to work.

Miss Chester was fortunate in gaining Father Abram for a friend and companion. He knew every road and peak and slope of the mountains near Lakelands. Through him she became acquainted with the solemn delight of the shadowy, tilted aisles of the pine forests, the dignity of the bare crags, the crystal, tonic mornings, the dreamy, golden afternoons full of mysterious sadness. So her health improved, and her spirits grew light. She had a laugh as genial and hearty in its feminine way as the famous laugh of Father Abram. Both of them were natural optimists; and both knew how to present a serene and cheerful face to the world.

One day Miss Chester learned from one of the guests the history of Father Abram's lost child. Quickly she hurried away and found the miller seated on his favorite rustic bench near the chalybeate spring. He was surprised when his little friend slipped her hand into his, and looked at him with tears in her eyes.

"Oh, Father Abram," she said, "I'm so sorry! I didn't know until today about your little daughter. You will find her yet some day—oh, I hope you will."

The miller looked down at her with his strong, ready smile.

"Thank you, Miss Rose," he said in his usual cheery tones. "But I do not expect to find Aglaia. For a few years I hoped that she had been stolen by vagrants, and that she still lived, but I have lost that hope. I believe that she was drowned."

"I can understand," said Miss Chester, "how the doubt must have made it so hard to bear. And yet you are so cheerful and so ready to make other people's burdens light. Good Father Abram!"

"Good Miss Rose!" mimicked the miller, smiling. "Who thinks of others more than you do?"

A whimsical mood seemed to strike Miss Chester.

"Oh, Father Abram," she cried, "wouldn't it be grand if I should prove to be your daughter? Wouldn't it be romantic? And wouldn't you like to have me for a daughter?"

"Indeed I would," said the miller heartily. "If Aglaia had lived I could wish for nothing better than for her to have grown up to be just such a little woman as you are. Maybe you are Aglaia," he continued, falling in with her playful mood; "can't you remember when we lived at the mill?"

Miss Chester fell swiftly into serious meditation. Her large eyes were fixed vaguely upon something in the distance. Father Abram was amused at her quick return to seriousness. She sat thus for a long time before she spoke.

"No," she said at length, with a long sigh, "I can't remember anything at all about a mill. I don't think that I ever saw a flour mill in my life until I saw your funny little church. And if I were your little girl I would remember it, wouldn't I? I'm so sorry, Father Abram."

"So am I," said Father Abram, humoring her. "But if you cannot remember that you are my little girl, Miss Rose, surely you can recollect being someone else's. You remember your own parents, of course."

"Oh, yes; I remember them very well—especially my father. He wasn't a bit like you, Father Abram. Oh, I was only making believe. Come, now, you've rested long enough. You promised to show me the pool where you can see the trout playing, this afternoon. I never saw a trout."

Late one afternoon Father Abram set out for the old mill alone. He often went there to sit and think of the old days when he lived in the cottage across the road. Time had smoothed away the sharpness of his grief until he no longer found the memory of those times painful. But whenever Abram Strong sat in the melancholy September afternoons on the spot where "Dums" used to run in every day with her yellow curls flying, the smile that Lakelands always saw upon his face was not there.

The miller made his way slowly up the winding, steep road. The trees crowded so close to the edge of it that he walked in their shade, with his hat in his hand. Squirrels ran playfully upon the old rail fence at his right. Quails were calling to their young broods in the wheat stubble. The low sun sent a torrent of pale gold up the ravine that opened to the west. Early September!—it was within a few days only of the anniversary of Aglaia's disappearance.

The old overshot wheel, half covered with mountain ivy, caught patches of the warm sunlight filtering through the trees. The cottage across the road was still standing, but it would doubtless go down before the next winter's mountain blasts. It was overrun with morning glory and wild gourd vines; and the door hung by one hinge.

Father Abram pushed open the mill door, and entered softly.

And then he stood still, wondering. He heard the sound of someone within, weeping inconsolably. He looked, and saw Miss Chester sitting in a dim pew, with her head bowed upon an open letter that her hands held.

Father Abram went to her, and laid one of his strong hands firmly upon her. She looked up, breathed his name, and tried to speak further.

"Not yet, Miss Rose," said the miller kindly. "Don't try to talk yet. There's nothing as good for you as a nice, quiet little cry when you are feeling blue."

It seemed that the old miller, who had known so much sorrow himself, was a magician in driving it away from others. Miss Chester's sobs grew easier. Presently she took her little plain-bordered handkerchief and wiped away a drop or two that had fallen from her eyes upon Father Abram's big hand. Then she looked up and smiled through her tears. Miss Chester could always smile before her tears had dried, just as Father Abram could smile through his own grief. In that way the two were very much alike.

The miller asked her no questions; but by and by Miss Chester began to tell him.

It was the old story that always seems so big and important to the young, and that brings reminiscent smiles to their elders. Love was the theme, as may be supposed. There was a young man in Atlanta, full of all goodness and the graces, who had discovered that Miss Chester also possessed these qualities above all other people in Atlanta or anywhere else from Greenland to Patagonia. She showed Father Abram the letter over which she had been weeping. It was a manly, tender letter, a little superlative and urgent, after the style of love letters written by young men full of goodness and the graces. He proposed for Miss Chester's hand in marriage at once. Life, he said, since her departure for a three-weeks' visit, was not to be endured. He begged for an immediate answer; and if it were favorable he promised to fly—ignoring the narrow-gauge railroad—at once to Lakelands.

"And now where does the trouble come in?" asked the miller when he had read the letter.

"I can not marry him," said Miss Chester.

"Do you want to marry him?" asked Father Abram.

"Oh, I love him," she answered, "but—." Down went her head and she sobbed again.

"Come, Miss Rose," said the miller; "you can give me your confidence. I do not question you, but I think you can trust me."

"I do trust you," said the girl. "I will tell you why I must refuse Ralph. I am nobody—I haven't even a name—the name I call myself is a lie. Ralph is a noble man. I love him with all my heart, but I can never be his."

"What talk is this?" said Father Abram. "You said that you remember your parents. Why do you say you have no name? I do not understand."

"I do remember them," said Miss Chester. "I remember them too well. My first recollections are of our life somewhere in the far South. We moved many times to different towns and states. I have picked cotton, and worked in factories, and have often gone without enough food and clothes. My mother was sometimes good to me; my father was always cruel, and beat me. I think they were both idle and unsettled.

"One night when we were living in a little town on a river near Atlanta they had a great quarrel. It was while they were abusing and taunting each other that I learned—oh, Father Abram, I learned that I didn't even have the right to be—don't you understand?—I had no right even to a name—I was nobody.

"I ran away that night. I walked to Atlanta and found work. I gave myself the name of Rose Chester, and have earned my own living ever since. Now you know why I cannot marry Ralph—and oh, I can never tell him why."

Better than any sympathy, more helpful than pity was Father Abram's depreciation of her woes.

"Why, dear, dear! Is that all?" he said. "Fie, fie! I thought something was in the way. If this perfect young man is a man at all he will not care a pinch of bran for your family tree. Dear Miss Rose, take my word for it, it is yourself he cares for. Tell him frankly, just as you have told me, and I'll warrant that he will laugh at your story, and think all the more of you for it."

"I shall never tell him," said Miss Chester sadly. "And I shall never marry him or anyone else. I have not the right."

But they saw a long shadow come bobbing up the sunlit road. And then came a shorter one bobbing by its side; and presently two strange figures approached the church. The long shadow was made by Miss Phoebe Summers, the organist, come to practice. Tommy Teague, aged twelve, was responsible for the shorter shadow. It was Tommy's day to pump the organ for Miss Phoebe, and his bare toes proudly spurned the dust of the road.

Miss Phoebe, in her lilac spray chintz dress, with her accurate little curls hanging over each ear, curtsied low to Father Abram and shook her curls ceremoniously at Miss Chester. Then she and her assistant climbed the steep stairway to the organ loft.

In the gathering shadows below, Father Abram and Miss Chester lingered. They were silent; and it is likely that they were busy with their memories. Miss Chester sat, leaning her head on her hand, with her eyes fixed far away. Father Abram stood in the next pew, looking thoughtfully out of the door at the road and the ruined cottage.

Suddenly the scene was transformed for him back almost a score of years into the past. For, as Tommy pumped away, Miss Phoebe struck a low bass note on the organ and held it to test the volume of air that it contained. The church ceased to exist, so far as Father Abram was concerned. The deep, booming vibration that shook the little frame building was no note from an organ, but the humming of the mill machinery. He felt sure that the old overshot wheel was turning; that he was back again, a dusty, merry miller in the old mountain mill. And now evening was come, and soon would come Aglaia with flying curls, toddling across the road to take him home to supper. Father Abram's eyes were fixed upon the broken door of the cottage.

And then came another wonder. In the gallery overhead the sacks of flour were stacked in long rows. Perhaps a mouse had been at one of them; anyway the jar of the deep organ note shook down between the cracks of the gallery floor a stream of flour, covering Father Abram from head to foot with the white dust. And then the old miller stepped into the aisle, and waved his arms and began to sing the miller's song:

> "The wheel goes round,
> The grist is ground,
> The dusty miller's merry—"

And then the rest of the miracle happened. Miss Chester was leaning forward from her pew, as pale as the flour itself, her wide-open eyes staring at Father Abram like one in a waking dream. When he began the song she stretched out her arms to him; her lips moved; she called to him in dreamy tones: "Da-da, come take Dums home!"

Miss Phoebe released the low key of the organ. But her work had been well done. The note that she struck had beaten down the doors of a closed memory; and Father Abram held his lost Aglaia close in his arms.

When you visit Lakelands they will tell you more of this story. They will tell you how the lines of it were afterward traced, and the history of the miller's daughter revealed after the gypsy wanderers had stolen her on that September day, attracted by her childish beauty. But you should wait until you sit comfortably on the shaded porch of the Eagle House, and then you can have the story at your ease. It seems best that our part of it should close while Miss Phoebe's deep bass note was yet reverberating softly.

And yet, to my mind, the finest thing of it all happened while Father Abram and his daughter were walking back to the Eagle House in the long twilight, almost too glad to speak.

"Father," she said, somewhat timidly and doubtfully, "have you a great deal of money?"

"A great deal?" said the miller. "Well, that depends. There is plenty unless you want to buy the moon or something equally expensive."

"Would it cost very, very much," asked Aglaia, who had always counted her dimes so carefully, "to send a telegram to Atlanta?"

"Ah," said Father Abram with a little sigh. "I see. You want to ask Ralph to come."

Aglaia looked up at him with a tender smile.

"I want to ask him to wait," she said. "I have just found my father, and I want it to be just we two for a while. I want to tell him he will have to wait."

The Enchanted Profile

THERE ARE FEW Caliphesses. Women are Scheherezades by birth, predilection, instinct, and arrangement of the vocal chords. The thousand and one stories are being told every day by hundreds of thousands of viziers' daughters to their respective sultans. But the bowstring will get some of 'em yet if they don't watch out.

I heard a story, though, of one lady Caliph. It isn't precisely an *Arabian Nights* story, because it brings in Cinderella, who flourished her dishrag in another epoch and country. So, if you don't mind the mixed dates (which seem to give it an Eastern flavor, after all), we'll get along.

In New York there is an old, old hotel. You have seen the woodcuts of it in the magazines. It was built—let's see—at a time when there was nothing above Fourteenth Street except the old Indian trail to Boston and Hammerstein's office. Soon the old hostelry will be torn down. And as the stout walls are riven apart and the bricks go roaring down the chutes, crowds of citizens will gather at the nearest corners and weep over the destruction of a dear old landmark. Civic pride is strong in New Bagdad; and the wettest weeper and the loudest howler against the iconoclasts will be the man (originally from Terre Haute) whose fond memories of the old hotel are limited to his having been kicked out from its free-lunch counter in 1873.

At this hotel always stopped Mrs. Maggie Brown. Mrs. Brown was a bony woman of sixty, dressed in the rustiest black, and carrying a handbag made, apparently, from the skin of the original animal that Adam decided to call an alligator. She always occupied a small parlor and bedroom at the top of the hotel at a rental of two dollars per day.

And always, while she was there, each day came hurrying to see her many men, sharp-faced, anxious-looking, with only seconds to spare. For Maggie Brown was said to be the third richest woman in the world; and these solicitous gentlemen were only the city's wealthiest brokers and businessmen seeking trifling loans of half a dozen millions or so from the dingy old lady with the prehistoric handbag.

The stenographer and typewriter of the Acropolis Hotel (there! I've let the name of it out) was Miss Ida Bates. She was a holdover from the Greek classics. There wasn't a flaw in her looks. Some old-timer in paying his regards to a lady said: "To have loved her was a liberal education." Well, even to have looked over the back hair and neat white shirtwaist of Miss Bates was equal to a full course in any correspondence school in the country. She sometimes did a little typewriting for me and, as she refused to take the money in advance, she came to look upon me as something of a friend and protégé. She had unfailing kindliness and good nature; and not even a white-lead drummer or a fur importer had ever dared to cross the dead line of good behavior in her presence. The entire force of the Acropolis, from the owner, who lived in Vienna, down to the head porter, who had been bedridden for sixteen years, would have sprung to her defense in a moment.

One day I walked past Miss Bates's little sanctum Remingtorium (or whatever make of machine advertises in these pages), and saw in her place a black-haired unit—unmistakably a person—pounding with each of her forefingers upon the keys. Musing on the mutability of temporal affairs, I passed on. The next day I went on a two weeks' vacation. Returning, I strolled through the lobby of the Acropolis, and saw, with a little warm glow of auld lang syne, Miss Bates, as Grecian and kind and flawless as ever, just putting the cover on her Smith-Prem. (advertising department please correct), or whatever machine it was. The hour for closing had come; but she asked me in to sit for a few minutes in the dictation chair. Miss Bates explained her absence from and return to the Acropolis Hotel in words identical with or similar to these following.

"Well, Man, how are the stories coming?"

"Pretty regularly," said I. "About equal to their going."

"I'm sorry," said she. "Good typewriting is the main thing in a story. You've missed me, haven't you?"

"No one," said I, "whom I have ever known knows as well as you do how to place properly belt buckles, semicolons, hotel guests, and hairpins. But you've been away, too. I saw a package of pepper-mint-pepsin in your place the other day."

"I was going to tell you about it," said Miss Bates, "if you hadn't interrupted me.

"Of course you know about Maggie Brown who stops here. Well, she's worth forty million dollars. She lives in Jersey in a ten-dollar flat. She's always got more cash on hand than half a dozen business candidates for vice president. I don't know whether she carries it in her stocking or not, but I know she's mighty popular down in the part of the town where they worship the golden calf.

"Well, about two weeks ago Mrs. Brown stops at the door and rubbers at me for ten minutes. I'm sitting with my side to her, striking off some manifold copies of a coppermine proposition for a nice old man from Tonopah. But I always see everything all around me. When I'm hard at work I can see things through my side combs; and I can leave one button unbuttoned in the back of my shirtwaist and see who's behind me. I didn't look around, because I make from eighteen to twenty dollars a week, and I didn't have to.

"That evening at knocking-off time she sends for me to come up to her apartment. I expected to have to typewrite about two thousand words of notes-of-hands, liens, and contracts, with a ten-cent tip in sight; but I went. Well, Man, I was certainly surprised. Old Maggie Brown had turned human.

" 'Child,' says she, 'you're the most beautiful creature I ever saw in my life. I want you to quit your work and come and live with me. I've no kith or kin,' says she, 'except a husband and a son or two, and I hold no communication with any of 'em. They're extravagant burdens on a hardworking woman. I want you to be a daughter to me. They say I'm stingy and mean, and the papers print lies about my doing my own cooking and washing. It's a lie,' she goes on. 'I put my washing out, except the handkerchiefs and stockings and petticoats and collars, and light stuff like that. I've got forty million dollars in cash and stocks and bonds that are as negotiable as Standard Oil, preferred, at a church fair. I'm a lonely old woman and I need companionship. You're the most beautiful human being I ever saw,' says she. 'Will you come and live with me? I'll show 'em whether I can spend money or not,' she says.

"Well, Man, what would you have done? Of course I fell to it. And, to tell you the truth, I began to like old Maggie. It wasn't all on account of the forty millions and what she could do for me. I was kind of lonesome in the world, too. Everybody's got to have somebody they can explain to about the pain in their left shoulder and how fast patent-leather shoes wear out when they begin to crack. And you can't talk about such things to men you meet in hotels—they're looking for just such openings.

"So I gave up my job in the hotel and went with Mrs. Brown. I certainly seemed to have a mash on her. She'd look at me for half an hour at a time when I was sitting, reading, or looking at the magazines.

"One time I says to her: 'Do I remind you of some deceased relative or friend of your childhood, Mrs. Brown? I've noticed you give me a pretty good optical inspection from time to time.'

" 'You have a face,' she says, 'exactly like a dear friend of mine— the best friend I ever had. But I like you for yourself, child, too,' she says.

"And say, Man, what do you suppose she did? Loosened up like a Marcel wave in the surf at Coney. She took me to a swell dressmaker and gave her *à la carte* to fit me out—money no object. They were rush orders, and madame locked the front door and put the whole force to work.

"Then we moved to—where do you think?—no; guess again— that's right—the Hotel Bonton. We had a six-room apartment; and it cost one hundred dollars a day. I saw the bill. I began to love that old lady.

"And then, Man, when my dresses began to come in—oh, I won't tell you about 'em! You couldn't understand. And I began to call her Aunt Maggie. You've read about Cinderella, of course. Well, what Cinderella said when the prince fitted that three-and-a-half-A on her foot was a hard-luck story compared to the things I told myself.

"Then Aunt Maggie says she is going to give me a coming-out banquet in the Bonton that'll make moving Vans of all the old Dutch families on Fifth Avenue.

" 'I've been out before, Aunt Maggie,' says I. 'But I'll come out again. But you know,' says I, 'that this is one of the swellest hotels in the city. And you know—pardon me—that it's hard to get a bunch of notables together unless you've trained for it.'

" 'Don't fret about that, child,' says Aunt Maggie. 'I don't send out invitations—I issue orders. I'll have fifty guests here that couldn't be brought together again at any reception unless it were given by King Edward or William Travers Jerome. They are men, of course, and all of 'em either owe me money or intend to. Some of their wives won't come, but a good many will.'

"Well, I wish you could have been at that banquet. The dinner service was all gold and cut glass. There were about forty men and eight ladies present besides Aunt Maggie and I. You'd never have known the third richest woman in the world. She had on a new black silk dress with so much passementerie on it that it sounded exactly like a hailstorm I heard once when I was staying all night with a girl that lived in a top-floor studio.

"And my dress!—say, Man, I can't waste the words on you. It was all handmade lace—where there was any of it at all—and it cost three hundred dollars. I saw the bill. The men were all bald-headed or white-side-whiskered, and they kept up a running fire of light repartee about 3-percents, and Bryan, and the cotton crop.

"On the left of me was something that talked like a banker, and on my right was a young fellow who said he was a newspaper artist. He was the only—well, I was going to tell you.

"After the dinner was over Mrs. Brown and I went up to the apartment. We had to squeeze our way through a mob of reporters all the way through the halls. That's one of the things money does for you. Say, do you happen to know a newspaper artist named Lathrop— a tall man with nice eyes and an easy way of talking? No, I don't remember what paper he works on. Well, all right.

"When we got upstairs Mrs. Brown telephones for the bill right away. It came, and it was six hundred dollars. I saw the bill. Aunt Maggie fainted. I got her on a lounge and opened the beadwork.

" 'Child,' says she, when she got back to the world, 'what was it? A raise of rent or an income tax?'

" 'Just a little dinner,' says I. 'Nothing to worry about—hardly a drop in the bucket shop. Sit up and take notice—a dispossess notice if there's no other kind.'

"But say, Man, do you know what Aunt Maggie did? She got cold feet. She hustled me out of that Hotel Bonton at nine the next morning. We went to a rooming house on the lower West Side. She rented one room that had water on the floor below and light on the floor above. After we got moved all you could see in the room was about fifteen hundred dollars' worth of new swell dresses and a one-burner gas stove.

"Aunt Maggie had a sudden attack of the hedges. I guess everybody has got to go on a spree once in their life. A man spends his on highballs, and a woman gets woozy on clothes. But with forty million dollars—say! I'd like to have a picture of—but, speaking of pictures, did you ever run across a newspaper artist named Lathrop—a tall— oh, I asked you that before, didn't I? He was mighty nice to me at the dinner. His voice just suited me. I guess he must have thought I was to inherit some of Aunt Maggie's money.

"Well, Mr. Man, three days of that light housekeeping was plenty for me. Aunt Maggie was as affectionate as ever. She'd hardly let me get out of her sight. But let me tell you. She was a hedger from Hedgersville, Hedger County. Seventy-five cents a day was the limit she set. We cooked our own meals in the room. There I was, with a thousand dollars' worth of the latest things in clothes, doing stunts over a one-burner gas stove.

"As I say, on the third day I flew the coop. I couldn't stand for throwing together a fifteen-cent kidney stew while wearing, at the same time, a hundred-and-fifty-dollar housedress, with Valenciennes lace insertion. So I goes into the closet and puts on the cheapest dress Mrs. Brown had bought for me—it's the one I've got on now—not so bad for seventy-five dollars, is it? I'd left all my own clothes in my sister's flat in Brooklyn.

" 'Mrs. Brown, formerly "Aunt Maggie," ' says I to her, 'I am going to extend my feet alternately, one after the other, in such a manner and direction that this tenement will recede from me in the quickest possible time. I am no worshiper of money,' says I, 'but there are some things I can't stand: I can stand the fabulous monster that I've read about that blows hot birds and cold bottles with the same breath. But I can't stand a quitter,' says I. 'They say you've got forty million dollars—well, you'll never have any less. And I was beginning to like you, too,' says I.

"Well, the late Aunt Maggie kicks till the tears flow. She offers to move into a swell room with a two-burner stove and running water.

" 'I've spent an awful lot of money, child,' says she. 'We'll have to economize for a while. You're the most beautiful creature I ever laid eyes on,' she says, 'and I don't want you to leave me.'

"Well, you see me, don't you? I walked straight to the Acropolis and asked for my job back, and I got it. How did you say your writings were getting along? I know you've lost out some by not having me to typewrite 'em. Do you ever have 'em illustrated? And, by the way, did you ever happen to know a newspaper artist—oh, shut up! I know I asked you before. I wonder what paper he works on. It's funny, but I couldn't help thinking that he wasn't thinking about the money he might have been thinking I was thinking I'd get from old Maggie Brown. If I only knew some of the newspaper editors I'd—"

The sound of an easy footstep came from the doorway. Ida Bates saw who it was with her back hair comb. I saw her turn pink, perfect statue that she was—a miracle that I share with Pygmalion only.

"Am I excusable?" she said to me—adorable petitioner that she was. "It's—it's Mr. Lathrop. I wonder if it really wasn't the money—I wonder if, after, all, he—"

Of course I was invited to the wedding. After the ceremony I dragged Lathrop aside.

"You an artist," said I, "and haven't figured out why Maggie Brown conceived such a strong liking for Miss Bates—that was? Let me show you."

The bride wore a simple white dress as beautifully draped as the costumes of the ancient Greeks. I took some leaves from one of the decorative wreaths in the little parlor, and made a chaplet of them, and placed them on née Bates's shining chestnut hair, and made her turn her profile to her husband.

"By jingo!" said he. "Isn't Ida's a dead ringer for the lady's head on the silver dollar?"

THE CALIPH AND THE CAD

SURELY THERE IS no pastime more diverting than that of mingling, incognito, with persons of wealth and station. Where else but in those circles can one see life in its primitive, crude state unhampered by the conventions that bind the dwellers in a lower sphere?

There was a certain Caliph of Bagdad who was accustomed to go down among the poor and lowly for the solace obtained from the relation of their tales and histories. Is it not strange that the humble and poverty-stricken have not availed themselves of the pleasure they might glean by donning diamonds and silks and playing Caliph among the haunts of the upper world?

There was one who saw the possibilities of thus turning the tables on Haroun al Raschid. His name was Corny Brannigan, and he was a truck driver for a Canal Street importing firm. And if you read further you will learn how he turned upper Broadway into Bagdad, and learned something about himself that he did not know before.

Many people would have called Corny a snob—preferably by means of a telephone. His chief interest in life, his chosen amusement and his sole diversion after working hours was to place himself in juxtaposition—since he could not hope to mingle—with people of fashion and means.

Every evening after Corny had put up his team and dined at a lunch counter that made immediateness a specialty, he would clothe himself in evening raiment as correct as any you will see in the palm rooms. Then he would betake himself to that ravishing, radiant roadway devoted to Thespis, Thais, and Bacchus.

For a time he would stroll about the lobbies of the best hotels, his soul steeped in blissful content. Beautiful women, cooing like doves, but feathered like birds of Paradise, flicked him with their robes as they passed. Courtly gentlemen attended them, gallant and assiduous. And Corny's heart within him swelled like Sir Lancelot's, for the mirror spoke to him as he passed and said: "Corny, lad, there's not a guy among 'em that looks a bit the sweller than yerself. And you drivin' of a truck and them swearin' off their taxes and playin' the red in art galleries with the best in the land!"

And the mirrors spake the truth. Mr. Corny Brannigan had acquired the outward polish, if nothing more. Long and keen observation of polite society had gained for him its manner, its genteel air, and —most difficult of acquirement—its repose and ease.

Now and then in the hotels Corny had managed conversation and temporary acquaintance with substantial, if not distinguished, guests. With many of these he had exchanged cards, and the ones he received he carefully treasured for his own use later.

Leaving the hotel lobbies, Corny would stroll leisurely about, lingering at the theater entrances, dropping into the fashionable restaurants as if seeking some friend. He rarely patronized any of these places; he was no bee come to suck honey, but a butterfly flashing his wings among the flowers whose calyces held no sweets for him. His wages were not large enough to furnish him with more than the outside garb of the gentleman. To have been one of the beings he so cunningly imitated, Corny Brannigan would have given his right hand.

One night Corny had an adventure. After absorbing the delights of an hour's lounging in the principal hotels along Broadway, he passed up into the stronghold of Thespis. Cab drivers hailed him as a likely fare, to his prideful content. Languishing eyes were turned upon his as a hopeful source of lobsters and the delectable, ascendant globules of effervesence. These overtures and unconscious compliments Corny swallowed as manna, and hoped Bill, the off horse, would be less lame in the left forefoot in the morning.

Beneath a cluster of milky globes of electric light Corny paused to admire the sheen of his low-cut patent leather shoes. The building occupying the angle was a pretentious café. Out of this came a couple, a lady in a white, cobwebby evening gown with a lace wrap like a wreath of mist thrown over it, and a man, tall, faultless, assured—too assured. They moved to the edge of the sidewalk and halted. Corny's eye, ever alert for "pointers" in "swell" behavior, took them in with a sidelong glance.

"The carriage is not here," said the lady. "You ordered it to wait?"

"I ordered it for 9:30," said the man. "It should be here now."

A familiar note in the lady's voice drew a more especial attention from Corny. It was pitched in a key well known to him. The soft electric shone upon her face. Sisters of sorrow have no quarters fixed for them. In the index to the book of breaking hearts you will find that Broadway follows very soon after the Bowery. This lady's face was sad, and her voice was attuned with it. They waited, as if for the carriage. Corny waited too, for it was out-of-doors, and he was never tired of accumulating and profiting by knowledge of gentlemanly conduct.

"Jack," said the lady, "don't be angry. I've done everything I could to please you this evening. Why do you act so?"

"Oh, you're an angel," said the man. "Depend upon a woman to throw the blame upon a man."

"I'm not blaming you. I'm only trying to make you happy."

"You go about it in a very peculiar way."

"You have been cross with me all the evening without any cause."

"Oh, there isn't any cause except—you make me tired."

Corny took out his card case and looked over his collection. He selected one that read: "Mr. R. Lionel Whyte-Melville, Bloomsbury Square, London." This card he had inveigled from a tourist at the King Edward Hotel. Corny stepped up to the man and presented it with a correctly formal air.

"May I ask why I am selected for the honor?" asked the lady's escort.

Now, Mr. Corny Brannigan had a very wise habit of saying little during his imitations of the Caliph of Bagdad. The advice of Lord Chesterfield: "Wear a black coat and hold your tongue," he believed in without having heard. But now speech was demanded and required of him.

"No gent," said Corny, "would talk to a lady like you done. Fie upon you, Willie! Even if she happens to be your wife you ought to have more respect for your clothes than to chin her back that way. Maybe it ain't my butt-in, but it goes, anyhow—you strike me as bein' a whole lot to the wrong."

The lady's escort indulged in more elegantly expressed but fetching repartee. Corny, eschewing his truck driver's vocabulary, retorted as nearly as he could in polite phrases. Then diplomatic relations were severed; there was a brief but lively set-to with other than oral weapons, from which Corny came forth easily victor.

A carriage dashed up, driven by a tardy and solicitous coachman.

"Will you kindly open the door for me?" asked the lady. Corny assisted her to enter, and took off his hat. The escort was beginning to scramble up from the sidewalk.

"I beg your pardon, ma'am," said Corny, "if he's your man."

"He's no man of mine," said the lady. "Perhaps he—but there's no chance of his being now. Drive home, Michael. If you care to take this—with my thanks."

Three red roses were thrust out through the carriage window into Corny's hand. He took them, and the hand for an instant; and then the carriage sped away.

Corny gathered his foe's hat and began to brush the dust from his clothes.

"Come along," said Corny, taking the other man by the arm.

His late opponent was yet a little dazed by the hard knocks he had received. Corny led him carefully into a saloon three doors away.

"The drinks for us," said Corny—"me and my friend."

"You're-a-queer feller," said the late lady's escort—"lick a man and then want to set 'em up."

"You're my best friend," said Corny exultantly. "You don't understand? Well, listen. You just put me wise to somethin'. I been playin' gent a long time, thinkin' it was just the glad rags I had and nothin' else. Say—you're a swell, ain't you? Well, you trot in that class, I guess. I don't; but I found out one thing—I'm a gentleman, by——and I know it now. What'll you have to drink?"

THE SPARROWS IN MADISON SQUARE

THE YOUNG MAN in straitened circumstances who comes to New York City to enter literature has but one thing to do, provided he has studied carefully his field in advance. He must go straight to Madison Square, write an article about the sparrows there, and sell it to the *Sun* for $15.

I cannot recall either a novel or a story dealing with the popular theme of the young writer from the provinces who comes to the metropolis to win fame and fortune with his pen in which the hero does not get his start that way. It does seem strange that some author, in casting about for startlingly original plots, has not hit upon the idea of having his hero write about the bluebirds in Union Square and sell it to the *Herald*. But a search through the files of metropolitan fiction counts up overwhelmingly for the sparrows and the old Garden Square, and the *Sun* always writes the check.

Of course it is easy to understand why this first city venture of the budding author is always successful. He is primed by necessity to a superlative effort; mid the iron and stone and marble of the roaring city he has found this spot of singing birds and green grass and trees; every tender sentiment in his nature is battling with the sweet pain of homesickness; his genius is aroused as it never may be again; the birds chirp, the tree branches sway, the noise of wheels is forgotten; he writes with his soul in his pen—and he sells it to the *Sun* for $15.

I had read of this custom during many years before I came to New York. When my friends were using their strongest arguments to dissuade me from coming, I only smiled serenely. They did not know of that sparrow graft I had up my sleeve.

When I arrived in New York, and the car took me straight from the ferry up Twenty-third Street to Madison Square, I could hear that $15 check rustling in my inside pocket.

I obtained lodging at an unhyphenated hostelry, and the next morning I was on a bench in Madison Square almost by the time the sparrows were awake. Their melodious chirping, the benignant spring foliage of the noble trees and the clean, fragrant grass reminded me so potently of the old farm I had left that tears almost came into my eyes.

Then, all in a moment, I felt my inspiration. The brave, piercing notes of those cheerful small birds formed a keynote to a wonderful, light, fanciful song of hope and joy and altruism. Like myself, they were creatures with hearts pitched to the tune of woods and fields; as I was, so were they captives by circumstance in the discordant, dull city —yet with how much grace and glee they bore the restraint!

And then the early morning people began to pass through the square to their work—sullen people, with sidelong glances and glum faces, hurrying, hurrying, hurrying. And I got my theme cut out clear from the bird notes, and wrought it into a lesson, and a poem, and a carnival dance, and a lullaby; and then translated it all into prose and began to write.

For two hours my pencil traveled over my pad with scarcely a rest. Then I went to the little room I had rented for two days, and there I cut it to half, and then mailed it, white-hot, to the *Sun*.

The next morning I was up by daylight and spent two cents of my capital for a paper. If the word "sparrow" was in it I was unable to find it.

I took it up to my room and spread it out on the bed and went over it, column by column. Something was wrong.

Three hours afterward the postman brought me a large envelope containing my MS. and a piece of inexpensive paper, about three inches by four—I suppose some of you have seen them—upon which was written in violet ink, "With the *Sun*'s thanks."

I went over to the square and sat upon a bench. No; I did not think it necessary to eat any breakfast that morning. The confounded pests of sparrows were making the square hideous with their idiotic "cheep, cheep." I never saw birds so persistently noisy, impudent, and disagreeable in all my life.

By this time, according to all traditions, I should have been standing in the office of the editor of the *Sun*. That personage—a tall, grave, white-haired man—would strike a silver bell as he grasped my hand and wiped a suspicious moisture from his glasses.

"Mr. McChesney," he would be saying when a subordinate appeared, "this is Mr. Henry, the young man who sent in that exquisite gem about the sparrows in Madison Square. You may give him a desk at once. Your salary, sir, will be eighty dollars a week, to begin with."

This was what I had been led to expect by all writers who have evolved romances of literary New York.

Something was decidedly wrong with tradition. I could not assume the blame; so I fixed it upon the sparrows. I began to hate them with intensity and heat.

At that moment an individual wearing an excess of whiskers, two hats, and a pestilential air slid into the seat beside me.

"Say, Willie," he muttered cajolingly, "could you cough up a dime out of your coffers for a cup of coffee this morning?"

"I'm lung-weary, my friend," said I. "The best I can do is three cents."

"And you look like a gentleman, too," said he. "What brung you down—booze?"

"Birds," I said fiercely. "The brown-throated songsters caroling songs of hope and cheer to weary man toiling amid the city's dust and din. The little feathered couriers from the meadows and woods chirping sweetly to us of blue skies and flowering fields. The confounded little squint-eyed nuisances yawping like a flock of steam pianos, and stuffing themselves like aldermen with grass seeds, and bugs, while a man sits on a bench and goes without his breakfast. Yes, sir, birds! Look at them!"

As I spoke I picked up a dead tree branch that lay by the bench, and hurled it with all my force into a close congregation of the sparrows on the grass. The flock flew to the trees with a babel of shrill cries; but two of them remained prostrate upon the turf.

In a moment my unsavory friend had leaped over the row of benches and secured the fluttering victims, which he thrust hurriedly into his pockets. Then he beckoned me with a dirty forefinger.

"Come on, cully," he said hoarsely. "You're in on the feed."

Weakly I followed my dingy acquaintance. He led me away from the park down a side street and through a crack in a fence into a vacant lot where some excavating had been going on. Behind a pile of old stones and lumber he paused, and took out his birds.

"I got matches," said he. "You got any paper to start a fire with?"

I drew forth my manuscript story of the sparrows, and offered it for burnt sacrifice. There were old planks, splinters, and chips for our fire. My frowsy friend produced from some interior of his frayed clothing half a loaf of bread, pepper, and salt.

In ten minutes each of us was holding a sparrow spitted upon a stick over the leaping flames.

"Say," said my fellow bivouacker, "this ain't so bad when a fellow's hungry. It reminds me of when I struck New York first—about fifteen years ago. I come in from the West to see if I could get a job on a newspaper. I hit the Madison Square Park the first mornin' after, and was sitting around on the benches. I noticed the sparrows chirpin', and the grass and trees so nice and green that I thought I was back in the country again. Then I got some papers out of my pocket and——"

"I know," I interrupted. "You sent it to the *Sun* and got fifteen dollars."

"Say," said my friend, suspiciously, "you seem to know a good deal. Where was you? I went to sleep on the bench there, in the sun, and somebody touched me for every cent I had—fifteen dollars."

"The Guilty Party"

An East Side Tragedy

A RED-HAIRED, UNSHAVEN, untidy man sat in a rocking chair by a window. He had just lighted a pipe and was puffing blue clouds with great satisfaction. He had removed his shoes and donned a pair of blue, faded carpet-slippers. With the morbid thirst of the confirmed daily news drinker, he awkwardly folded back the pages of an evening paper, eagerly gulping down the strong, black headlines, to be followed as a chaser by the milder details of the smaller type.

In an adjoining room a woman was cooking supper. Odors from strong bacon and boiling coffee contended against the cut-plug fumes from the vespertine pipe.

Outside was one of those crowded streets of the east side, in which, as twilight falls, Satan sets up his recruiting office. A mighty host of children danced and ran and played in the street. Some in rags, some in clean white and beribboned, some wild and restless as young hawks, some gentle-faced and shrinking, some shrieking rude and sinful words, some listening, awed, but soon, grown familiar, to embrace —here were the children playing in the corridors of the House of Sin. Above the playground forever hovered a great bird. The bird was known to humorists as the stork. But the people of Chrystie Street were better ornithologists. They called it a vulture.

A little girl of twelve came up timidly to the man reading and resting by the window, and said: "Papa, won't you play a game of checkers with me if you aren't too tired?"

The red-haired, unshaven, untidy man sitting shoeless by the window answered, with a frown. "Checkers. No, I won't. Can't a man who works hard all day have a little rest when he comes home? Why don't you go out and play with the other kids on the sidewalk?"

The woman who was cooking came to the door.

"John," she said. "I don't like for Lizzie to play in the street. They learn too much there that ain't good for 'em. She's been in the house all day long. It seems that you might give up a little of your time to amuse her when you come home."

"Let her go out and play like the rest of 'em if she wants to be amused," said the red-haired, unshaven, untidy man, "and don't bother me."

∾

"You're on," said Kid Mullaly. "Fifty dollars to twenty-five I take Annie to the dance. Put up."

The Kid's black eyes were snapping with the fire of the baited and challenged. He drew out his "roll" and slapped five tens upon the bar. The three or four young fellows who were thus "taken" more slowly produced their stake. The bartender, ex-officio stakeholder, took the money, laboriously wrapped it, recorded the bet with an inch-long pencil and stuffed the whole into a corner of the cash register.

"And, oh, what'll be done to you'll be a plenty," said a bettor with anticipatory glee.

"That's my lookout," said the Kid sternly. "Fill 'em up all around, Mike."

After the round, Burke, the Kid's sponge, sponge-holder, pal, mentor, and Grand Vizier, drew him out to the bootblack stand at the saloon corner where all the official and important matters of the Small Hours Social Club were settled. As Tony polished the light tan shoes of the club's President and Secretary for the fifth time that day, Burke spake words of wisdom to his chief.

"Cut that blonde out, Kid," was his advice, "or there'll be trouble. What do you want to throw down that girl of yours for? You'll never find one that'll freeze to you like Liz has. She's worth a hallfull of Annies."

"I'm no Annie admirer!" said the Kid, dropping a cigarette ash on his polished toe and wiping it off on Tony's shoulder. "But I want to teach Liz a lesson. She thinks I belong to her. She's been bragging that I daren't speak to another girl. Liz is all right—in some ways.

She's drinking a little too much lately. And she uses language that a lady oughtn't."

"You're engaged, ain't you?" asked Burke.

"Sure. We'll get married next year, maybe."

"I saw you make her drink her first glass of beer," said Burke. "That was two years ago, when she used to come down to the corner of Chrystie bareheaded to meet you after supper. She was a quiet sort of a kid then, and couldn't speak without blushing."

"She's a little spitfire, sometimes, now," said the Kid. "I hate jealousy. That's why I'm going to the dance with Annie. It'll teach her some sense."

"Well, you better look a little out" were Burke's last words. "If Liz was my girl and I was to sneak out to a dance coupled up with an Annie, I'd want a suit of chain armor on under my gladsome rags, all right."

Through the land of the stork-vulture wandered Liz. Her black eyes searched the passing crowds fierily but vaguely. Now and then she hummed bars of foolish little songs. Between times she set her small, white teeth together, and spake crisp words that the east side has added to language.

Liz's skirt was green silk. Her waist was a large brown-and-pink plaid, well-fitting and not without style. She wore a cluster ring of huge imitation rubies, and a locket that banged her knees at the bottom of a silver chain. Her shoes were rundown over twisted high heels, and were strangers to polish. Her hat would scarcely have passed into a flour barrel.

The "Family Entrance" of the Blue Jay Café received her. At a table she sat, and punched the button with the air of milady ringing for her carriage. The waiter came with his large chinned, low-voiced manner of respectful familiarity. Liz smoothed her silken skirt with a satisfied wriggle. She made the most of it. Here she could order and be waited upon. It was all that her world offered her of the prerogative of woman.

"Whiskey, Tommy," she said as her sisters further uptown murmur, "Champagne, James."

"Sure, Miss Lizzie. What'll the chaser be?"

"Seltzer. And say, Tommy, has the Kid been around today?"

"Why, no, Miss Lizzie, I haven't saw him today."

Fluently came the "Miss Lizzie," for the Kid was known to be one who required rigid upholdment of the dignity of his fiancee.

"I'm lookin' for 'm," said Liz, after the chaser had sputtered under her nose. "It's got to me that he says he'll take Annie Karlson to the dance. Let him. The pink-eyed white rat! I'm lookin' for 'm. You know me, Tommy. Two years me and the Kid's been engaged. Look at that ring. Five hundred, he said it cost. Let him take her to the dance. What'll I do? I'll cut his heart out. Another whiskey, Tommy."

"I wouldn't listen to no such reports, Miss Lizzie," said the waiter smoothly, from the narrow opening above his chin. "Kid Mullaly's not the guy to throw a lady like you down. Seltzer on the side?"

"Two years," repeated Liz, softening a little to sentiment under the magic of the distiller's art. "I always used to play out on the street of evenin's 'cause there was nothin' doin' for me at home. For a long time I just sat on doorsteps and looked at the lights and the people goin' by. And then the Kid came along one evenin' and sized me up, and I was mashed on the spot for fair. The first drink he made me take, I cried all night at home, and got a lickin' for makin' a noise. And now—say, Tommy, you ever see this Annie Karlson? If it wasn't for peroxide the chloroform limit would have put her out long ago. Oh, I'm lookin' for 'm. You tell the Kid if he comes in. Me? I'll cut his heart out. Leave it to me. Another whiskey, Tommy."

A little unsteadily, but with watchful and brilliant eyes, Liz walked up the avenue. On the doorstep of a brick tenement a curly-haired child sat, puzzling over the convolutions of a tangled string. Liz flopped down beside her, with a crooked, shifting smile on her flushed face. But her eyes had grown clear and artless of a sudden.

"Let me show you how to make a cat's cradle, kid," she said, tucking her green silk skirt under her rusty shoes.

And while they sat there the lights were being turned on for the dance in the hall of the Small Hours Social Club. It was a bimonthly dance, a dress affair in which the members took great pride and be-stirred themselves huskily to further and adorn.

At 9 o'clock the President, Kid Mullaly, paced upon the floor with a lady on his arm. As the Loreley's was her hair golden. Her "yes" was softened to a "yah," but its quality of assent was patent to the most Milesian ears. She stepped upon her own train and blushed, and—she smiled into the eyes of Kid Mullaly.

And then, as the two stood in the middle of the waxed floor, the thing happened to prevent which many lamps are burning nightly in many studies and libraries.

Out from the circle of spectators in the hall leaped Fate in a green silk skirt, under the *nom de guerre* of "Liz." Her eyes were hard and blacker than jet. She did not scream or waver. Most unwomanly, she cried out one oath—the Kid's own favorite oath—and in his own deep voice; and then while the Small Hours Social Club went frantically to pieces, she made good her boast to Tommy, the waiter—made good as far as the length of her knife blade and the strength of her arm permitted.

And next came the primal instinct of self-preservation—or was it self-annihilation, the instinct that society has grafted on the natural branch?

Liz ran out and down the street swift and true as a woodcock flying through a grove of saplings at dusk.

And then followed the big city's biggest shame, its most ancient and rotten surviving canker, its pollution and disgrace, its blight and perversion, its forever infamy and guilt, fostered, unreproved and cherished, handed down from a long-ago century of the basest barbarity—the Hue and Cry. Nowhere but in the big cities does it survive, and here most of all, where the ultimate perfection of culture, citizenship, and alleged superiority joins, bawling, in the chase.

They pursued—a shrieking mob of fathers, mothers, lovers, and maidens—howling, yelling, calling, whistling, crying for blood. Well may the wolf in the big city stand outside the door. Well may his heart, the gentler, falter at the siege. Knowing her way, and hungry for her surcease, she darted down the familiar ways until at last her feet struck the dull solidity of the rotting pier. And then it was but a few more panting steps—and good mother East River took Liz to her bosom, smoothed her muddily but quickly, and settled in five minutes the problem that keeps lights burning o' nights in thousands of pastorates and colleges.

IT'S MIGHTY FUNNY what kind of dreams one has sometimes. Poets call them visions, but a vision is only a dream in blank verse. I dreamed the rest of this story.

I thought I was in the next world. I don't know how I got there; I suppose I had been riding on the Ninth Avenue elevated or taking patent medicine or trying to pull Jim Jeffries's nose, or doing some such little injudicious stunt. But, anyhow, there I was, and there was a great crowd of us outside the courtroom where the judgments were going on. And every now and then a very beautiful and imposing court-officer angel would come outside the door and call another case.

While I was considering my own worldly sins and wondering whether there would be any use of my trying to prove an alibi by claiming that I lived in New Jersey, the bailiff angel came to the door and sang out, "Case No. 99,852,743."

Up stepped a plainclothes man—there were lots of 'em there, dressed exactly like preachers and hustling us spirits around just like cops do on earth—and by the arm he dragged—whom, do you think? Why, Liz!

The court officer took her inside and closed the door. I went up to Mr. Fly-Cop and inquired about the case.

"A very sad one," says he, laying the points of his manicured fingers together. "An utterly incorrigible girl. I am Special Terrestrial Officer the Reverend Jones. The case was assigned to me. The girl murdered her fiancé and committed suicide. She had no defense. My report to the court relates the facts in detail, all of which are substantiated by reliable witnesses. The wages of sin is death. Praise the Lord."

The court officer opened the door and stepped out.

"Poor girl," said Special Terrestrial Officer the Reverend Jones, with a tear in his eye. "It was one of the saddest cases that I ever met with. Of course she was——"

"Discharged," said the court officer. "Come here, Jonesy. First thing you know you'll be switched to the pot-pie squad. How would you like to be on the missionary force in the South Sea Islands—hey? Now, you quit making these false arrests, or you'll be transferred— see? The guilty party you've got to look for in this case is a red-haired, unshaven, untidy man, sitting by the window reading, in his stocking feet, while his children play in the streets. Get a move on you."

Now, wasn't that a silly dream?

BRICKDUST ROW

BLINKER WAS DISPLEASED. A man of less culture and poise and wealth would have sworn. But Blinker always remembered that he was a gentleman—a thing that no gentleman should do. So he merely looked bored and sardonic while he rode in a hansom to the center of disturbance, which was the Broadway office of Lawyer Oldport, who was agent for the Blinker estate.

"I don't see," said Blinker, "why I should be always signing confounded papers. I am packed, and was to have left for the North Woods this morning. Now I must wait until tomorrow morning. I hate night trains. My best razors are, of course, at the bottom of some unidentifiable trunk. It is a plot to drive me to bay rum and a monologueing, thumb-handed barber. Give me a pen that doesn't scratch. I hate pens that scratch."

"Sit down," said double-chinned, gray Lawyer Oldport. "The worst has not been told you. Oh, the hardships of the rich! The papers are not yet ready to sign. They will be laid before you tomorrow at eleven. You will miss another day. Twice shall the barber tweak the helpless nose of a Blinker. Be thankful that your sorrows do not embrace a haircut."

"If," said Blinker, rising, "the act did not involve more signing of papers I would take my business out of your hands at once. Give me a cigar, please."

"If," said Lawyer Oldport, "I had cared to see an old friend's son gulped down at one mouthful by sharks I would have ordered you to take it away long ago. Now, let's quit fooling, Alexander. Besides the grinding task of signing your name some thirty times tomorrow, I must impose upon you the consideration of a matter of business—of business, and I may say humanity or right. I spoke to you about this five years ago, but you would not listen—you were in a hurry for a coaching trip, I think. The subject has come up again. The property——"

"Oh, property!" interrupted Blinker. "Dear Mr. Oldport, I think you mentioned tomorrow. Let's have it all at one dose tomorrow—signatures and property and snappy rubber bands and that smelly sealing wax and all. Have luncheon with me? Well, I'll try to remember to drop in at eleven tomorrow. Morning."

The Blinker wealth was in lands, tenements, and hereditaments, as the legal phrase goes. Lawyer Oldport had once taken Alexander in his little pulmonary gasoline runabout to see the many buildings and rows of buildings that he owned in the city. For Alexander was sole heir. They had amused Blinker very much. The houses looked so incapable of producing the big sums of money that Lawyer Oldport kept piling up in banks for him to spend.

In the evening Blinker went to one of his clubs, intending to dine. Nobody was there except some old fogies playing whist who spoke to him with grave politeness and glared at him with savage contempt. Everybody was out of town. But here he was kept in like a schoolboy to write his name over and over on pieces of paper. His wounds were deep.

Blinker turned his back on the fogies, and said to the club steward who had come forward with some nonsense about cold fresh salmon roe: "Symons, I'm going to Coney Island." He said it as one might say: "All's off, I'm going to jump into the river."

The joke pleased Symons. He laughed within a sixteenth of a note of the audibility permitted by the laws governing employees.

"Certainly, sir," he tittered. "Of course, sir, I think I can see you at Coney, Mr. Blinker."

Blinker got a paper and looked up the movements of Sunday steamboats. Then he found a cab at the first corner and drove to a North River pier. He stood in line, as democratic as you or I, and bought a ticket, and was trampled upon and shoved forward until, at last, he found himself on the upper deck of the boat staring brazenly at a girl who sat alone upon a camp stool. But Blinker did not intend to be brazen; the girl was so wonderfully good looking that he forgot for one minute that he was the prince incog, and behaved just as he did in society.

She was looking at him, too, and not severely. A puff of wind threatened Blinker's straw hat. He caught it warily and settled it again. The movement gave the effect of a bow. The girl nodded and smiled, and in another instant he was seated at her side. She was dressed all in white, she was paler than Blinker imagined milkmaids and girls of humble stations to be, but she was as tidy as a cherry blossom, and her steady, supremely frank gray eyes looked out from the intrepid depths of an unshadowed and untroubled soul.

"How dare you raise your hat to me?" she asked with a smile-redeemed severity.

"I didn't," Blinker said, but he quickly covered the mistake by extending it to "I didn't know how to keep from it after I saw you."

"I do not allow gentlemen to sit by me to whom I have not been introduced," she said with a sudden haughtiness that deceived him. He rose reluctantly, but her clear, teasing laugh brought him down to his chair again.

"I guess you weren't going far," she declared with beauty's magnificent self-confidence.

"Are you going to Coney Island?" asked Blinker.

"Me?" She turned upon him wide-open eyes full of bantering surprise. "Why, what a question! Can't you see that I'm riding a bicycle in the park?" Her drollery took the form of impertinence.

"And I am laying bricks on a tall factory chimney," said Blinker. "Mayn't we see Coney together? I'm all alone and I've never been there before."

"It depends," said the girl, "on how nicely you behave. I'll consider your application until we get there."

Blinker took pains to provide against the rejection of his application. He strove to please. To adopt the metaphor of his nonsensical phrase, he laid brick upon brick on the tall chimney of his devoirs until, at length, the structure was stable and complete. The manners of the best society come around finally to simplicity; and as the girl's way was that naturally, they were on a mutual plane of communication from the beginning.

He learned that she was twenty, and her name was Florence; that she trimmed hats in a millinery shop; that she lived in a furnished room with her best chum Ella, who was cashier in a shoe store; and that a glass of milk from the bottle on the windowsill and an egg that boils itself while you twist up your hair makes a breakfast good enough for anyone. Florence laughed when she heard "Blinker."

"Well," she said. "It certainly shows that you have imagination. It gives the 'Smiths' a chance for a little rest, anyhow."

They landed at Coney, and were dashed on the crest of a great human wave of mad pleasure-seekers into the walks and avenues of Fairyland gone into vaudeville.

With a curious eye, a critical mind, and a fairly withheld judgment Blinker considered the temples, pagodas and kiosks of popularized delights. Hoi polloi trampled, hustled, and crowded him. Basket parties bumped him; sticky children tumbled, howling, under his feet, candying his clothes. Insolent youths strolling among the booths with hard-won canes under one arm and easily won girls on the other, blew defiant smoke from cheap cigars into his face. The publicity gentlemen with megaphones, each before his own stupendous attraction, roared like Niagara in his ears. Music of all kinds that could be tortured from brass, reed, hide, or string, fought in the air to gain space for its vibrations against its competitors. But what held Blinker in awful fascination was the mob, the multitude, the proletariat shrieking, struggling, hurrying, panting, hurling itself in incontinent frenzy, with unabashed abandon, into the ridiculous sham palaces of trumpery and tinsel pleasures. The vulgarity of it, its brutal overriding of all the tenets of repression and taste that were held by his caste, repelled him strongly.

In the midst of his disgust he turned and looked down at Florence by his side. She was ready with her quick smile and upturned, happy eyes, as bright and clear as the water in trout pools. The eyes were saying that they had the right to be shining and happy, for was their owner not with her (for the present) Man, her Gentleman Friend and holder of the keys to the enchanted city of fun.

Blinker did not read her look accurately, but by some miracle he suddenly saw Coney aright.

He no longer saw a mass of vulgarians seeking gross joys. He now looked clearly upon a hundred thousand true idealists. Their offenses were wiped out. Counterfeit and false though the garish joys of these spangled temples were, he perceived that deep under the gilt surface they offered saving and apposite balm and satisfaction to the restless human heart. Here, at least, was the husk of Romance, the empty but shining casque of Chivalry, the breath-catching though safe-guarded dip and flight of Adventure, the magic carpet that transports you to the realms of fairyland, though its journey be through but a few poor yards of space. He no longer saw a rabble, but his brothers seeking the ideal. There was no magic of poesy here or of art; but the glamour of their imagination turned yellow calico into cloth of gold and the megaphone into the silver trumpets of joy's heralds.

Almost humbled, Blinker rolled up the shirt sleeves of his mind and joined the idealists.

"You are the lady doctor," he said to Florence. "How shall we go about doing this jolly conglomeration of fairy tales, incorporated?"

"We will begin there," said the Princess, pointing to a fun pagoda on the edge of the sea, "and we will take everything in, one by one."

They caught the eight o'clock returning boat and sat, filled with pleasant fatigue, against the rail in the bow, listening to the Italians' fiddle and harp. Blinker had thrown off all care. The North Woods seemed to him an uninhabitable wilderness. What a fuss he had made over signing his name—pooh! he could sign it a hundred times. And her name was as pretty as she was—"Florence," he said it to himself a great many times.

As the boat was nearing its pier in the North River a two-fun-neled, drab, foreign-looking seagoing steamer was dropping down toward the bay. The boat turned its nose in toward its slip. The steamer veered as if to seek midstream, and then yawned, seemed to increase its speed and struck the Coney boat on the side near the stern, cutting into it with a terrifying shock and crash.

While the six hundred passengers on the boat were mostly tum bling about the decks in a shrieking panic the captain was shouting at the steamer that it should not back off and leave the rent exposed for the water to enter. But the steamer tore its way out like a savage sawfish and cleaved its heartless way, full speed ahead.

The boat began to sink at its stern, but moved slowly toward the slip. The passengers were a frantic mob, unpleasant to behold.

Blinker held Florence tightly until the boat had righted itself. She made no sound or sign of fear. He stood on a camp stool, ripped off the slats above his head and pulled down a number of the life preserv-ers. He began to buckle one around Florence. The rotten canvas split and the fraudulent granulated cork came pouring out in a stream. Florence caught a handful of it and laughed gleefully.

"It looks like breakfast food," she said. "Take it off. They're no good."

She unbuckled it and threw it on the deck. She made Blinker sit down and sat by his side and put her hand in his. "What'll you bet we don't reach the pier all right?" she said, and began to hum a song.

And now the captain moved among the passengers and compelled order. The boat would undoubtedly make her slip, he said, and ordered the women and children to the bow, where they could land first. The boat, very low in the water at the stern, tried gallantly to make his promise good.

"Florence," said Blinker, as she held him close by an arm and hand, "I love you."

"That's what they all say," she replied, lightly.

"I am not one of 'they all,' " he persisted. "I never knew anyone I could love before. I could pass my life with you and be happy every day. I am rich. I can make things all right for you."

"That's what they all say," said the girl again, weaving the words into her little, reckless song.

"Don't say that again," said Blinker in a tone that made her look at him in frank surprise.

"Why shouldn't I say it?" she asked calmly. "They all do."

"Who are 'they'?" he asked, jealous for the first time in his existence.

"Why, the fellows I know."

"Do you know so many?"

"Oh, well, I'm not a wallflower," she answered with modest complacency.

"Where do you see these—these men? At your home?"

"Of course not. I meet them just as I did you. Sometimes on the boat, sometimes in the park, sometimes on the street. I'm a pretty good judge of a man. I can tell in a minute if a fellow is one who is likely to get fresh."

"What do you mean by 'fresh'?"

"Who, try to kiss you—me, I mean."

"Do any of them try that?" asked Blinker, clenching his teeth.

"Sure. All men do. You know that."

"Do you allow them?"

"Some. Not many. They won't take you out anywhere unless you do."

She turned her head and looked searchingly at Blinker. Her eyes were as innocent as a child's. There was a puzzled look in them, as though she did not understand him.

"What's wrong about my meeting fellows?" she asked wonderingly.

"Everything," he answered, almost savagely. "Why don't you entertain your company in the house where you live? Is it necessary to pick up Tom, Dick, and Harry on the streets?"

She kept her absolutely ingenuous eyes upon his.

"If you could see the place where I live you wouldn't ask that. I live in Brickdust Row. They call it that because there's red dust from the bricks crumbling over everything. I've lived there for more than four years. There's no place to receive company. You can't have anybody come to your room. What else is there to do? A girl has got to meet the men, hasn't she?"

"Yes," he said, hoarsely. "A girl has got to meet a—has got to meet the men."

"The first time one spoke to me on the street," she continued, "I ran home and cried all night. But you get used to it. I meet a good many nice fellows at church. I go on rainy days and stand in the vestibule until one comes up with an umbrella. I wish there was a parlor, so I could ask you to call, Mr. Blinker—are you really sure it isn't 'Smith,' now?"

The boat landed safely. Blinker had a confused impression of walking with the girl through quiet crosstown streets until she stopped at a corner and held out her hand.

"I live just one more block over," she said. "Thank you for a very pleasant afternoon."

Blinker muttered something and plunged northward till he found a cab. A big, gray church loomed slowly at his right. Blinker shook his fist at it through the window.

"I gave you a thousand dollars last week," he cried under his breath, "and she meets them in your very doors. There is something wrong; there is something wrong."

At eleven the next day Blinker signed his name thirty times with a new pen provided by Lawyer Oldport.

"Now let me get to the woods," he said surlily.

"You are not looking well," said Lawyer Oldport. "The trip will do you good. But listen, if you will, to that little matter of business of which I spoke to you yesterday, and also five years ago. There are some buildings, fifteen in number, of which there are new five-year leases to be signed. Your father contemplated a change in the lease provisions, but never made it. He intended that the parlors of these houses should not be sublet, but that the tenants should be allowed to use them for reception rooms. These houses are in the shopping districts, and are mainly tenanted by young working girls. As it is they are forced to seek companionship outside. This row of red brick——"

Blinker interrupted him with a loud, discordant laugh.

"Brickdust Row for an even hundred," he cried. "And I own it. Have I guessed right?"

"The tenants have some such name for it," said Lawyer Oldport.

Blinker arose and jammed his hat down to his eyes.

"Do what you please with it," he said harshly. "Remodel it, burn it, raze it to the ground. But, man, it's too late, I tell you. It's too late, It's too late. It's too late."

New York by Campfire Light

Away out in the Creek Nation we learned things about New York.

We were on a hunting trip, and were camped one night on the bank of a little stream. Bud Kingsbury was our skilled hunter and guide, and it was from his lips that we had explanations of Manhattan and the queer folks that inhabit it. Bud had once spent a month in the metropolis, and a week or two at other times, and he was pleased to discourse to us of what he had seen.

Fifty yards away from our camp was pitched the teepee of a wandering family of Indians that had come up and settled there for the night. An old, old Indian woman was trying to build a fire under an iron pot hung upon three sticks.

Bud went over to her assistance, and soon had her fire going. When he came back we complimented him playfully upon his gallantry.

"Oh," said Bud, "don't mention it. It's a way I have. Whenever I see a lady trying to cook things in a pot and having trouble I always go to the rescue. I done the same thing once in a high-toned house in New York City. Heap big society teepee on Fifth Avenue. That Injun lady kind of recalled it to my mind. Yes, I endeavors to be polite and help the ladies out."

The camp demanded the particulars.

"I was manager of the Triangle-B Ranch in the Panhandle," said Bud. "It was owned at that time by old man Sterling, of New York. He wanted to sell out, and he wrote for me to come on to New York and explain the ranch to the syndicate that wanted to buy. So I sends to

Fort Worth and has a forty-dollar suit of clothes made, and hits the trail for the big village.

"Well, when I got there, old man Sterling and his outfit certainly laid themselves out to be agreeable. We had business and pleasure so mixed up that you couldn't tell whether it was a treat or a trade half the time. We had trolley rides, and cigars, and theater roundups, and rubber parties."

"Rubber parties?" said a listener, inquiringly.

"Sure," said Bud. "Didn't you never attend 'em? You walk around and try to look at the tops of the skyscrapers. Well, we sold the ranch, and old man Sterling asks me 'round to his house to take grub on the night before I started back. It wasn't any high-collared affair— just me and the old man and his wife and daughter. But they was a fine-haired outfit all right, and the lilies of the field wasn't in it. They made my Fort Worth clothes carpenter look like a dealer in horse blankets and gee strings. And then the table was all pompous with flowers, and there was a whole kit of tools laid out beside everybody's plate. You'd have thought you was fixed out to burglarize a restaurant before you could get your grub. But I'd been in New York over a week then, and I was getting on to stylish ways. I kind of trailed behind and watched others use the hardware supplies, and then I tackled the chuck with the same weapons. It ain't much trouble to travel with the high-flyers after you find out their gait. I got along fine. I was feeling cool and agreeable, and pretty soon I was talking away fluent as you please, all about the ranch and the West, and telling 'em how the Indians eat grasshopper stew and snakes, and you never saw people so interested.

"But the real joy of that feast was that Miss Sterling. Just a little trick she was, not bigger than two bits' worth of chewing plug; but she had a way about her that seemed to say she was the people, and you believed it. And yet, she never put on any airs, and she smiled at me the same as if I was a millionaire while I was telling about a Creek dog feast and listened like it was news from home.

"By and by, after we had eat oysters and some watery soup and truck that never was in my repertory, a Methodist preacher brings in a kind of camp stove arrangement, all silver, on long legs, with a lamp under it.

"Miss Sterling lights up and begins to do some cooking right on the supper table. I wondered why old man Sterling didn't hire a cook with all the money he had. Pretty soon she dished some cheesy tasting truck that she said was rabbit, but I swear there had never been a Molly cotton tail in a mile of it.

"The last thing on the program was lemonade. It was brought around in little flat glass bowls and set by your plate. I was pretty thirsty, and I picked up mine and took a big swig of it. Right there was where the little lady had made a mistake. She had put in the lemon all right, but she'd forgot the sugar. The best housekeepers slip up some-time. I thought maybe Miss Sterling was just learning to keep house and cook—that rabbit would surely make you think so—and I says to myself, 'Little lady, sugar or no sugar I'll stand by you,' and I raises up my bowl again and drinks the last drop of the lemonade. And then all the balance of 'em picks up their bowls and does the same. And then I gives Miss Sterling the laugh proper, just to carry it off like a joke, so she wouldn't feel bad about the mistake.

"After we all went into the sitting room she sat down and talked to me quite a while.

" 'It was so kind of you, Mr. Kingsbury,' says she, 'to bring my blunder off so nicely. It was so stupid of me to forget the sugar.'

" 'Never you mind,' says I, 'some lucky man will throw his rope over a mighty elegant little housekeeper some day, not far from here.'

" 'If you mean me, Mr. Kingsbury,' says she laughing out loud, 'I hope he will be as lenient with my poor housekeeping as you have been.'

" 'Don't mention it,' says I. 'Anything to oblige the ladies.' "

Bud ceased his reminiscences. And then someone asked him what he considered the most striking and prominent trait of New Yorkers.

"The most visible and peculiar trait of New York folks," answered Bud, "is New York. Most of 'em has New York on the brain. They have heard of other places, such as Waco, and Paris, and Hot Springs, and London; but they don't believe in 'em. They think that town is all Merino. Now to show you how much they care for their village I'll tell you about one of 'em that strayed out as far as the Triangle-B while I was working there.

"This New Yorker come out there looking for a job on the ranch. He said he was a good horseback rider, and there were pieces of tanbark hanging on his clothes yet from his riding school.

"Well, for a while they put him to keeping books in the ranch store, for he was a devil at figures. But he got tired of that, and asked for something more in the line of activity. The boys on the ranch liked him all right, but he made us tired shouting New York all the time. Every night he'd tell us about East River and J. P. Morgan and the Eden Musee and Hetty Green and Central Park till we used to throw tin plates and branding irons at him.

"One day this chap gets on a pitching pony, and the pony kind of sidled up his back and went to eating grass while the New Yorker was coming down.

"He come down on his head on a chunk of mesquite wood, and he didn't show any designs toward getting up again. We laid him out in a tent, and he begun to look pretty dead. So Gideon Pease saddles up and burns the wind for old Doc Sleeper's residence in Dogtown, thirty miles away.

"The doctor comes over and investigates the patient.

" 'Boys,' says he, 'you might as well go to playing seven-up for his saddle and clothes, for his head's fractured and if he lives ten minutes it will be a remarkable case of longevity.'

"Of course we didn't gamble for the poor rooster's saddle—that was one of Doc's jokes. But we stood around feeling solemn, and all of us forgive him for having talked us to death about New York.

"I never saw anybody about to hand in his checks act more peaceful than this fellow. His eyes were fixed 'way up in the air, and he was using rambling words to himself all about sweet music and beautiful streets and white-robed forms, and he was smiling like dying was a pleasure.

" 'He's about gone now,' said Doc. 'Whenever they begin to think they see heaven it's all off.'

"Blamed if that New York man didn't sit right up when he heard the Doc say that.

" 'Say,' says he, kind of disappointed, 'was that heaven? Confound it all, I thought it was Broadway. Some of you fellows get my clothes. I'm going to get up.'

"And I'll be blamed," concluded Bud, "if he wasn't on the train with a ticket for New York in his pocket four days afterward!"